SCIENCE FICTION

This is a volume in the
Arno Press collection

SCIENCE FICTION

ADVISORY EDITORS

R. Reginald

Douglas Menville

See last pages of this volume
for a complete list of titles

HIS WISDOM THE DEFENDER

𝔄 𝔖𝔱𝔬𝔯𝔶

SIMON NEWCOMB

ARNO PRESS
A New York Times Company
New York — 1975

Reprint Edition 1974 by Arno Press Inc.

Reprinted from a copy in The Library
of the University of California, Riverside

SCIENCE FICTION
ISBN for complete set: 0-405-06270-2
See last pages of this volume for titles.

Manufactured in the United States of America

Library of Congress Cataloging in Publication Data

Newcomb, Simon, 1835-1909.
   His wisdom, the defender.

   (Science fiction)
   Reprint of the 1900 ed. published by Harper, New York.
   I. Title. II. Series.
PZ3.N435Hi6 [PS2459.N3485]   813'.4   74-16513
ISBN 0-405-06308-3

HIS WISDOM THE DEFENDER

A Story

By SIMON NEWCOMB

HARPER & BROTHERS
New York and London
M - D - C - C - C - C

Copyright, 1900, by HARPER & BROTHERS.

All rights reserved.

Contents

		PAGE
	Prologue	vii
I.	An Uncanny Workshop	1
II.	The City of the Potomac	16
III.	An Italian Romance	32
IV.	The Angelic Order of Seraphim	44
V.	The First Motes	66
VI.	Mystery on Mystery	74
VII.	And Another for the Duke	92
VIII.	The Great Unveiling	102
IX.	A Voyage Through Space	120
X.	How the World Received the News	144
XI.	The Red-Headed Man Scores the Greatest "Beat" in the History of Journalism	165
XII.	Our Hero Makes a Clean Breast	187
XIII.	The Mysterious Expedition	206
XIV.	The Attack on the German Armies	221
XV.	A Captive Emperor	241
XVI.	The Naval Attack on Elba	257
XVII.	The French Attempt on the *Cynthia*	276
XVIII.	Austria Threatens Checkmate	293
XIX.	The Dawn	304
XX.	The Proclamation	314
XXI.	Rah! Rah! Rah! the Defender	326

"THE *HESPERUS* THEN ROSE SLOWLY AND MAJESTICALLY IN THE AIR"

Prologue

WE who live in this Golden Age never tire of comparing our happy lot with the backward condition of our forefathers. We need not go further back than the beginning of the century now closing to see the striking contrast between our powers over nature and theirs. Did we not have historical evidence of the fact, it would be scarcely credible to the rising generation that nearly half of this century had elapsed before such a thing as a mote was known or even imagined; before the words etherine and therm were found in any dictionary. We can hardly imagine what a dull life even the greatest and most powerful men must have lived. President Reed never took a spin round the world. He never saw the Antarctic glacier, or even knew of its existence. He never set foot upon the North Pole. He never looked down on the clouds from the window of a himote. Had any one told him that before he had been dead thirty years it would be an everyday occurrence for a merchant to talk with a furrier in Siberia and a leather dealer in Australia on

Prologue

the same day, he would have looked upon the speaker as Washington would have looked upon a prophet of the ocean cable and what men would do with it. The idea of utilizing the action of ether on matter, simple though it seems to us, never entered the mind of any nineteenth-century philosopher.

As all our readers are aware, the history of the steps by which the Golden Age was inaugurated, and the evils which afflicted humanity removed, has been enveloped in great mystery. We well know that the revolution was brought about by the first Defender, whose work, for reasons which he deemed imperative, was carried on in profound secrecy. But recently his successor has permitted the publication of a great mass of historical documents bearing on the subject. These are, however, too voluminous to be read by a busy man. We have, therefore, by their aid, and by a diary which has been placed at our disposal, prepared a brief history of such part of the first Defender's life and work as has hitherto been unknown to the public.

His Wisdom the Defender

I

An Uncanny Workshop

AMONG the historic monuments so carefully preserved in the university town of Cambridge, in the State of Massachusetts, the one which attracts most visitors is, in its aspect, the least attractive of all. It is nothing more than a long, unsightly old house, whose sixty feet of front are unbroken by a single ornament. Its material is the rough red brick of the early years of the century. The joints between the bricks have never been smoothed except by the trowel that originally fashioned them. The window-sills and caps are of wood, painted white. Not even a branch of ivy variegates the walls which, at the top of their three stories, are surmounted by an old-fashioned tile roof, sloping to the front and back. The only visible doorway is but the breadth of an ordinary room from the east end. If a visitor unacquainted with the history of

His Wisdom the Defender

the place, as we assume the reader to be, should wonder why so ugly and seemingly useless an old trap had not long ago given way to the two or three modern houses that could have found room on its site, an answer would at once have been suggested by its situation. It fronts on a narrow lane leading out from the little-frequented Church Street, where no one would ever look for a residence unless he wanted to be forgotten by the world.

As our visitor went through the house he would find nothing to explain the mystery. Passing through a narrow vestibule, he would see before him an entrance hall, with a door on each side and a stairway in the rear. If he opened either of the doors he would see nothing but bare plastered walls and old oak furniture, of which the uniformity is not relieved by a trace of ornament. But few stop for this, and we in imagination may follow the crowd. The attractive part of the house is in the third story, and thither we mount with the others. But even when we get there our curiosity would be whetted rather than gratified. We should see nothing but what might be collected from a few sufficiently old and dilapidated blacksmith and carpenter shops. What can people see here to interest them?

To answer this question we must ask the reader to go back with us two generations while we describe the place as it would then have been seen. There was one particular evening when the scene within would have raised our curiosity to the highest pitch.

An Uncanny Workshop

This was Thursday, May 15, 1941. The hour is of great importance; let us make our visit at nine o'clock. Mounting to the third story, we see a door on each side of the hall, as in the stories below. That on the right has nailed to it a printed card:

Professor Campbell.

The opposite door bears the forbidding sign

No Admittance.

Having taken the liberty of choosing our time, we take the further liberty of paying no attention to this warning. Entering the forbidden door, we should have found ourselves in a study, rather narrow, but extending along the whole breadth of the building. Seeing nothing but a lounge, tables, chairs, and four walls covered with books, we should have wondered why visitors should be excluded. But looking around we should have noticed a door facing the one by which we entered, with the same sign painted on it in large capitals. Of course, after going thus far the mandate would not have stopped us. Opening the second door, we should have found ourselves in a room of ample size. The walls on one side were without windows, while on the other side they were pierced for two, which, however, were closed by solid wooden shutters. There was no ceiling; the roof of the building was that of the room. It was pierced with four skylights on each slope, sufficient to give ample light during the day. At

His Wisdom the Defender

the hour of which we speak, the place was brilliant with electric lights.

Looking around him, the visitor would have been unable to decide whether he was in a physical laboratory, a workshop, or a garret for the deposit of old junk. Two turning-lathes, a small forge, chemical and electrical apparatus, a carpenter's bench, countless old bottles, half of them filled with chemicals, balls of cord, bundles of rope, and every kind of tool used by carpenters or blacksmiths would have suggested to us the laboratory of some twentieth-century Faust.

At the hour in question the room had three occupants, two of whom were preparing to leave for the night. From their garb they were evidently workmen. They laid aside their tools, put on their coats, and departed. The third, who seemed to be their employer, followed them through the study, carefully locked and tried the door after them, then, returning, locked the inner door with equal care. Thus left alone he would have riveted our attention both by his appearance and his movements.

In build he was a man of medium height, but slender and wiry. His ample supply of dark-brown hair and his full though thin beard betokened one disposed to avoid the barber's chair. His dark, quick-moving eyes had an anxious look. Two characters seemed to be combined in his person—the business man and the philosopher. It would have been difficult to decide which element was the dominant one.

An Uncanny Workshop

His photograph would have suggested nothing but a keen, active man of business. But no sooner had his workmen gone than he fell into the brown study appropriate to a mathematical professor.

Whatever his calling, he evidently wished to be enveloped in mystery. When he felt himself alone he glanced furtively around on all sides, even scanning the skylights with the greatest solicitude, as if to make sure that no indiscreet eye was prying into his doings. Every now and then, sometimes when walking across the room, he stood still for a moment, evidently buried deep in thought; then as suddenly darted forward.

On one side of the room, set in the wall, was a high but shallow safe. Near it the wall was penetrated by a key-hole, so minute that no one would have noticed it except on careful examination. The man took a key from his vest-pocket, put it into this hole and opened a small and almost invisible door. Here was nothing but a closet with one shelf, on the inner corner of which lay another key. He took the latter, and with it opened the safe. From the safe he took what looked like a polished metal rod, four feet long and about an inch in diameter, rounded off at each end. He carried it carefully to the middle of the room and stood it up. Left to itself, it behaved as rod never did before; it stood alone. Worse still, it refused to fall down, even when the little man pressed against it. He could only make the bottom slide along the floor as fast as the upper part was moved. Placing his foot against the bottom to keep it from sliding, he seized the top and swung himself around to get the rod out of its perpendicular position, but in vain.

Determined, it would seem, to enforce the law of gravitation, he continued the experiment by screwing firmly to the floor a small block of wood with a hole in the centre. He stood the rod in this hole. Near him was a cord and several heavy weights. The cord passed around a pulley and had suspended to its lower end a scale-pan, in which the weights could be put. The cord was then attached to the upper part of the rod as if to force it out of the perpendicular position if possible. But the heaviest weight that the cord could bear did not appear to budge the rod. The little man made a record of the weight, and with some sort of a small optical instrument was evidently measuring the minute amount, invisible to our unpractised eyes, by which the rod could be made to diverge.

The trial of the rod completed, he carried it back to the safe, it retaining its vertical position all the while, and stood it carefully up in its original place. He then took from the shelf of the safe something which, at first sight, looked like a tall half-gallon mug. But it had no bottom, being nothing but a hollow cylinder, perhaps a foot high and three inches in diameter, with a handle. It was of a black substance, which shone with a metallic lustre, though the color was not that of any metal. It was

An Uncanny Workshop

surrounded at top and bottom by thin metallic rings, in which were set clamps for holding wires. On a stand near the chimney-piece was an electric battery. He set the implement upon the hearth and connected the wires of the battery with it. He then took from the work-bench a roll of copper wire, cut off a piece about a yard in length, and returned to the hearth. He took the mug in his left hand, and with the other held the wire so that it passed vertically through the centre of the cylinder. In a few seconds the portion of the wire within the mug was white-hot, then it began to melt and run to the hearth in drops; and yet all the while the implement was so cool that he held it in his hand.

Then he held a pipe-stem in the centre in place of the wire. Soon white frost began to collect on the outside of the mug, while the pipe became red-hot. But nothing else occurred. With a look of disappointment he took a hollow spirit-lamp, shaped like the lamp of a light-house, lit it, and placed the mug within the flame. Then, placing the pipe-stem in the centre, it grew red-hot, white-hot, and at length melted down and fell on the hearth in metallic drops.

Going back to the safe, he next took from it an article of clothing. It was a close-fitting leather coat, fastened to the outside of which were a number of tubes of the size and shape of small organ-pipes. When the little man arrayed himself in this coat he stood in the centre of the circle of pipes and looked

His Wisdom the Defender

as if an organist might have played a tune on him. The coat was a very close fit. He buttoned it as tightly as if he feared it would be torn off. He then walked to the carpenter's bench, on which lay an instrument looking like a pair of wooden pincers about four feet long. Near them lay two or three little round metal handles, rather more than a hand's-breadth long. Simple though these things looked, he seemed afraid to touch or even approach them. He carefully took hold of the long pincers, and, reaching out his arm, took the handles one by one and laid them on the floor. Near where he put them a solid staple had been driven firmly into the floor. He then took a piece of cord some twenty feet long, tied one end to his foot and fastened the other end to the staple, as if he were a cow allowed to graze, but secured from running away. As soon as the knots were tied he tested each of them by a pull this way and that with all his strength, as if resolved to make escape impossible. Then he stooped cautiously to where the handles were lying and took one in each hand, being careful at first to hold both at arm's-length. He gradually brought them closer to his body, holding them in a vertical position.

As they approached the organ-pipes, the reason for his caution became evident. The little man began to rise from the floor as the spiritual mediums were said to do a hundred years ago, and was very soon nearly up to the roof, being prevented from striking it and perhaps passing through it only by

An Uncanny Workshop

the rope with which his leg was tied. As he moved the handles slightly from him he began to descend. He then proceeded to amuse himself by alternately swinging up and down in the way described. He could apparently move in any direction he might choose through the air, by a very slight inclination of the handles. Holding them in one way, he swung round and round a circle having for its radius the length of the rope; holding them another way, he swung in the reverse direction. And, all the while, he kept peering round as if fearful that he might be seen.

Having completed this exercise to his satisfaction, he returned slowly to the floor, untied the rope from his leg, and deposited the handles in the little closet where the key of the safe was kept. He removed his organ-pipe coat, replaced it carefully in the safe, and took from the latter what seemed like a smooth wooden log, drew it to the middle of the room, and carefully fastened it at the end of the same rope with which he had been tied, evidently to keep it from running away. He then sat astride of the log, looking like a man riding an alligator. The careful observer would have noticed two holes on opposite sides of the log near the forward end. From each of these projected a little lever. The would-be rider seized these levers in his fingers and gave them a slight turn. Immediately the log, with him on it, rose in the air until it was at the full height of the rope. He then rode around, evidently to his great

His Wisdom the Defender

amusement, with motions much the same as those he had made with the organ-pipe coat. Looking round to be sure he could not be heard, he laughed heartily to himself, so much did he enjoy the sport. When he had satisfied himself he descended to the ground by simply taking hold of the levers, guided the log alligator back to the safe as if it had been a tame animal, and returned it to its place. The secrecy which he threw around his operations was clearly justified, unless he wished to make the looker-on doubt the evidence of his senses or lose confidence in the law of gravitation.

Again a fit of abstraction came over him, which lasted several minutes. Then he took a large folio blank-book, very strongly bound, from the safe, placed it on the work-bench, took a seat in front of it, and proceeded to write. It was evidently a diary. When he had finished his entry, which took some time, the book was returned to the safe, the latter locked, and the key itself again locked up in the closet with the greatest care, and the key of the closet returned to his vest-pocket. Looking carefully to see that all was secure, he extinguished the electric lights and left the room.

His experiments finished, he looked around in the adjoining study for something to read. The books with which the long walls were lined were of the most heterogeneous character. Scientific text-books, histories, old folios, with the writings of the Church fathers, law books, especially works on international

An Uncanny Workshop

law, old English state trials, and collections of all sorts were mixed up in the utmost confusion. Apparently quite at random, he took down a folio, Grotius's *De Lege belli et pacis,* in the original Latin, sat down and began to read. He could not have been much interested, for he soon began to nod. Probably he only used the book as a soporific after his exciting experiences, for he now arose and prepared to retire. He locked all the doors with the utmost care, tried each to make sure that there was no failure on the part of the keys to perform their function, put them in his pocket, went across to the rooms on the opposite side of the passage, which formed his reception and sleeping apartments, and retired to his bed.

The morning after these queer proceedings President Winthrop was sitting in his office. Professor Campbell was announced.

"Mr. President, I have called to apprise you of my resignation."

The president knew that Campbell generally used the English language to carry a point by assault rather than by regular approaches. But he fancied that his manner was even more abrupt than usual, as if he had come with an ultimatum to be immediately and unconditionally accepted.

"If you will allow me to be as abrupt as yourself, I reply that your resignation will not be accepted."

His Wisdom the Defender

"Not accepted! But if I stop work and leave, what is the corporation going to do about it? This is not a military organization."

"The corporation will do just this—it will give you leave of absence for a year. You have been entitled to your sabbatical year for some time, and now you shall have it. Scofield was here only ten minutes ago proposing that you should be forced to take it. We know that you have been overworked, and you must travel abroad and cease to think of your work here. This will be even better than accepting your resignation."

"But I do not propose to travel abroad. The fact is, I intend to completely change my occupation and go into business. If the university chooses to give me a year's leave of absence with that understanding, I have no objection."

"Of course, I have no right to inquire into the matter, but if you choose to tell me what business you expect to undertake, that information might be useful in enabling the corporation to decide upon a course."

"Well, I propose to go into a manufacturing business. First of all I shall start a brick-yard."

It took the president some moments to recover the power of speech.

"You do not expect me to take you seriously. The idea of the Professor of Molecular Physics in Harvard University resigning to make brick may do well in a comic paper, but can hardly be discussed before the corporation of the university."

An Uncanny Workshop

"I did not say I was going to do nothing but make brick; I said that was the first thing I should undertake. The fact is, there are cogent reasons, which I am not at liberty to set forth, which make me desire to proceed as quietly as possible in my enterprise, exciting neither remark nor surprise on the part of any one. I wish to disappear from the public gaze, with no notice whatever, if such a thing be possible, from my friends or the newspapers. The latter will be sure to find me out quicker than I want to be found out, but I shall postpone the evil day as long as I can."

"Are you not willing to solve for me, in the most private and confidential way if you wish, the mystery of your speech? You must see how enigmatical the situation is, as you present it."

"You know that I have very great confidence in your discretion; and yet I am not at liberty to unravel what may seem to you a mystery. I see as well as you do the reasonableness of your standpoint. But I will tell you one thing, if you will solemnly promise to keep it an absolute secret."

"As between knowing nothing and knowing a secret, I shall for the moment take the part of a woman and choose the secret. So you may rely on my confidence and talk freely."

"If the day ever comes when my enterprise succeeds and all my hopes are realized, that day will be the greatest in the history of the world."

The two men looked at each other for a moment in silence: the one to see the effect of his words; the other wondering if his companion was really sane.

"How you talk! Is that all you have to say?"

"That is all. I hope it is enough."

"Then I will bring the matter before the corporation, set forth the absolute necessity of giving you a year's relief from your work, and ask that you be allowed to take your sabbatical year without any questions as to where you shall go or what you shall do."

"Thank you. Please remember that I want the fact of my retirement kept secret as long as possible. I delivered my last lecture for the term yesterday, so there is no occasion that any one should notice my absence. I may at some future day have occasion to take you into my confidence. For the present, good-morning."

The president was deeply concerned. Either one of his favorite professors had gone completely daft or something incredible was going to occur. Were Campbell addicted to rhetorical exaggeration, some escape from the dilemma might have been possible. Knowing him to be the most exact of men in his talk, there was none. The president could not disguise from himself that the unfavorable horn of the dilemma was the more likely one. Two generations had passed without a scientific discovery that could be called epoch-making. Investigators had, to all appearance, found out everything of a radical nature that was to be learned, and were now quietly

An Uncanny Workshop

developing new phases of the known. How unlikely that one of them, without any premonitory announcement, would be able to make a revolution in human affairs. And, granting that a revolution was possible, how could it possibly begin with a brickyard?

II

The City of the Potomac

IF we had, at the time our history begins, searched the whole land east of the Mississippi to find some nook into which the forces of modern civilization had never been able to penetrate, we might well have hit upon a certain bend in the Potomac River less than a hundred miles south of Washington. In the peninsula thus formed no railway had ever been seen. What little produce was raised by the farmers found its way to market from occasional steamboat landings. No one had ever wanted to move into such a place, and so it happened that the land had remained in the families which held it for I know not how many generations. The ancestral houses in various stages of decay were scattered at great distances, and the only society which their inhabitants enjoyed was that afforded by an occasional frolic, coming off once a year, perhaps, when some farmer would invite all the inhabitants of the peninsula to a dance.

Great, therefore, was the surprise of Farmer Williams's household one fine morning when the children

The City of the Potomac

came running into the house in a condition of great excitement.

"Oh, Pop! there's somebody a-comin' in a buggy!"

"Boy, you're crazy! Who would ever come here in a buggy?"

"I don't know, but if you look out you'll see."

The father went to the door, and, sure enough, the boy was right. A person attired like a city gentleman was driving up in a more respectable-looking vehicle than was usual in those parts. A cigar in his mouth added greatly to the effect. It is very surprising how much more impressive a man driving a carriage looks when he has a cigar in his mouth. It gives him the appearance of knowing exactly what he is about—of being master of the situation, in fact.

The result of the city gentleman's visit to the region was that a few weeks later sundry deeds, conveying large areas of land to Archibald Campbell, were duly recorded in the land records of the county seat. The whole of Peter's Island was included, Campbell deeming the possession of an island necessary to the protection of some of his works from the curiosity of the public.

A few days later the new owner, accompanied by his attorney and a surveying-party, had engaged a river tug to make an inspection of his possessions. As the party were stepping into it, an unlooked-for interruption occurred.

"I was just going to engage a boat for a little

His Wisdom the Defender

excursion down the river. I see you gentlemen are on a similar errand. If it would be agreeable to you to join with me, I should be very glad to pay my share of the expense."

Campbell looked at the new-comer with amazement. He was a short and rather plump young man, of a decidedly florid complexion—round, unwrinkled face and bright-red hair and mustache. His prevailing tint had even entered his eyes. His rubicund visage was illuminated by what was intended to be a very pleasant smile. In the eyes of Campbell it was the most repulsive leer he had ever seen. The cool audacity of the proposal filled him with a surprise which must have been quite evident to its maker. But the latter was unaffected by the unpleasant impression he had made. As Campbell mutely surveyed him he surveyed back, and his manner, smile, and expression all seemed to say, " Now you need not put on any airs with me. I have got your measure exactly, and know who and what you are. It is for you to accept or decline my offer, as you may deem best. But no expressions of either courtesy or contempt will have the slightest effect upon me."

It took our friend several seconds to decide what to say.

" We are going on more than a mere excursion, and may not return for two or three days. Under any circumstances we do not desire additional company."

" All right; good-morning."

The City of the Potomac

As the two men boarded the tug, they saw the red-headed man engaging another at the next wharf below. It seemed a little puzzling that a lone man should hire a tug to make an excursion on his own account.

In a few minutes more steam was up and the party making its way down the river at a moderate speed. As they passed the next wharf the red-headed man gazed upon them, his smile undiminished, and his placidity undisturbed. They had not got half a mile down the river when the other tug had got up steam and was following them. Through his glass Campbell could see the red-headed man sitting in the bow, calmly smoking a cigar. The pursuer slowly gained upon them, and at Alexandria was not a hundred yards in the rear.

"I think," said Campbell, "we may as well let that fellow go past us. I have not brought along any materials for notes or sketches. So let us stop here a moment and buy pencils and paper. No doubt we shall find a stationery shop near the wharf."

So the tug fastened to a wharf, while he inquired the way to the nearest shop and made his purchase. Meanwhile the other tug passed and then slowed up. When he returned to his tug it was less than a mile below, and scarcely making headway. There was no time to lose, because it was desired to commence the inspection, if possible, before nightfall. Under a full head of steam the other tug was soon reached. The red-headed man was still placidly smoking his

His Wisdom the Defender

cigar, and bestowed only a glance upon the other party as it passed. But by this time his tug was making more rapid progress, and was soon again following them at a distance of a few hundred yards.

"That fellow is evidently out to watch us," said Campbell. "Do get away from him if possible. Here, Captain, put on all the steam your boilers will stand and get out of sight of the rascal."

But the other tug was nearly as fast as theirs. The black smoke from their own funnel was soon followed by black smoke from the other; her bows dashed up foam on both sides; the distance apart was only increased half a mile. Campbell turned to his companion.

"Has that fellow a right to follow us up this way? I am quite unacquainted with the law in such a case as this. Here we are, going down the river on our own private business, and the idle scamp turns out to follow us up. Can we do anything lawful to stop him?"

"I fear nothing can be done at the moment. He would claim that the river was free; and if there is any law for the case, we could only enforce it by returning at least to Alexandria to sue out an injunction. That would make our expedition public with a vengeance."

"Can you imagine what he is after?"

"I may have my suspicions, but they are not worth much. Let us wait and see."

They had only to wait till they could get a copy

The City of the Potomac

of the next day's New York *Herald*. As Campbell looked over it, a heading caught his eye. There was a despatch, a column long, "from our Washington correspondent." It began as follows:

A NEW LAND COMPANY.
Project for Improving the Lower Potomac.

A syndicate, having its headquarters in Boston, is about to establish a new watering-place on the lower Potomac. A well-known real-estate dealer in Baltimore and a distinguished Harvard Professor are the active promoters of the scheme. A site has already been selected near Nanjemoy. A large hotel will soon be erected, which, it is thought, will attract many Bostonians in search of a mild winter climate. . . .

The history of Campbelltown, the great manufacturing city of the Potomac, has been so often written that we need not repeat it. But the diary of the founder has recently come into our possession, and shed so new a light upon the beginning of his enterprise that we transcribe some passages:

"June 18, 1941.—I have murder in my heart. A *Herald* man has located my enterprise before I got it started. I must go on in the broad light of publicity. This is annoying, but, after all, my secret cannot be endangered. No one else has ever conceived of a substance whose vibrations could react on the ether of space in such a way as to fly through it as a bird flies through the air. If I should talk of etherine, as I call it, no one would know what I meant. And yet I am superstitious enough to feel troubled.

His Wisdom the Defender

"June 23, 1941.—Here I am, ready to begin work. What the end shall be I cannot foresee. It seems contrary to all human experience to suppose that one man should be able to revolutionize the world without letting his fellow-men know what he is about. I fear that when I have everything ready for the decisive move, my men will be unwilling to engage in what will seem a foolish and dangerous enterprise, not only without public support, but in the face of opposition by the whole world. I have been planning how to meet the difficulty. My army must have officers and men like any other. I have long thought of engaging Lieutenant Gheen, graduate of West Point, to command it. But will he be willing to brave such a risk? Will any one be willing?

"After much pondering I have concluded to choose the other officers from the athletes, especially the football players, of our leading colleges. These are the men who, having the greatest physical and mental vigor, will be most ready to engage in an exciting enterprise. If possible I must, before I begin active operations, arrange to have them isolated from all human society for several weeks, perhaps for several months. This, with the consciousness of their power, which will be evident to them, will induce that mental condition known as 'spoiling for a fight.' To add to their interest in the affair and their mutual confidence in each other, I propose to organize them into a secret society, to be

The City of the Potomac

called the *Angelic Order of Seraphim*. No one will at first see the significance of the name; but when actual operations are begun it will be apparent enough.

"In the case of the men, I will solve the problem by making up an army of Irishmen. The latter are loyal to employers who get into their good graces, and, like good soldiers, are always ready to obey orders without counting the cost. Once in a fight, they will go through it to the bitter end.

"July 8, 1941.—I have talked with Gheen and, to my pleasant surprise, found him quite ready to take the place of chief engineer of my works. Of course, I did not tell him what else I had in mind.

"July 11, 1941.—My counsel tells me I should have my business run under a company name, so I have decided to call myself the 'Anita Company.'

"September 8, 1941.—The first aluminium furnace is complete and the secret foundations and other underworks for five others are ready. I shall have the more delicate portions of these five completed before anybody suspects what I have in view. It is really amusing how I have mixed up the *Herald* man. He reports that the chimney is for the laundry of my proposed hotel! The wharf is nearly complete, and it is in perfect accord with his theory.

"September 25, 1941.—The aluminium furnace No. 1 is now in successful operation, and turning out a ton a day. So far only Gheen and two of his skilled workmen even know what we are making.

His Wisdom the Defender

The ingots are all purified and cast underground, and carried out after dark to be stored in a little brick building near the wharf, into which no outsider is allowed to penetrate.

"November 20, 1941.—To-day I shipped my first instalment of aluminium, about fifty tons, to Smithmeyer & Co., of New York, who will dispose of it according to their judgment, but will for the time being keep its origin secret.

"March 23, 1942.—The inevitable *dénouement* has come at last. The fact is discovered and published that I am turning out aluminium at the rate of six or eight tons a day by some process unknown to any one but myself. The first attempt to see the process was made only this morning, when three men, with a very suspicious combination of intelligent faces and dirty attire, sought employment. Of course, it would not do them a bit of good to see the whole process, because no one could carry it out without a furnace like mine, and no one can make such a furnace without a supply of etherine to begin with. This no one knows how to make; and if he did, it would take him years to do it, as it has taken me. But I do not want the world to suspect there is anything so very extraordinary in my proceedings or process, until the suspicion becomes inevitable, so I simply figure as the possessor of a secret process.

"April 1, 1942.—The newspapers are devoting more and more attention to me and my supposed eccentricities. Among the things that excite their

The City of the Potomac

curiosity is the name of my firm. It has been discovered that a young woman named Anita, the daughter of a Yale professor, died some ten years ago; and the theory is that I have held her in such affectionate remembrance as to take her name for my company. No one has ever heard of Tiana across the ocean. A friend indulged in a little pleasantry on the subject the other day. I reminded him with all seriousness that 'A.C.' were the initials both of the company and of myself, so that they could be applied to either, and refused to assign any other reason for the name.

"May 3, 1942.—Broke ground on Peter's Island for the foundation of the Coliseum. It will be, like its old Roman namesake, elliptical in form, but will greatly exceed it in size. I have decided, in order to have plenty of room, to build it a thousand feet in length and six hundred in breadth. How the public, guided by the red-headed man, will wonder when they see this monstrous structure rising! I am going, as long as possible, to let everybody examine its interior, on the same principle that a juggler asks the audience to examine his sleeves before he begins his work. So far I have not broached the subject of our ultimate object to Gheen, but must do so on the first occasion. I scarcely know how to begin.

"May 7, 1942.—Tried to sound Gheen on the ethical principles which should govern the relations of nations, especially the abstract rightfulness of

His Wisdom the Defender

war. The result was much as I expected. Practical man as he is, he looked upon war as inevitable in the present state of society. It was therefore useless to occupy ourselves with discussions of its rightfulness or wrongfulness. At length I broke out with the plain question: 'If you had the power to put an end to war, would you do it?'

"Of course he looked upon this as a pure abstraction and scarcely deemed the question worthy of a serious answer. How shall I make it clear to him that it is a really serious question on my part, and that, in spite of this, I am sane when I put it?

"June 15, 1942.—Strongly as I am impelled to the idea of having the great powers, with our own country as their leader, rule the world, two circumstances have happened within a week which make it clearer than ever to me that such a policy will be disastrous to the best interests of mankind.

"One is the brutal letter of the head of the German navy to the French ambassador, who had been accused, perhaps wrongfully, of seeking to purchase secrets respecting the German naval armament. Poor France is not in a condition to resent the insult, and must therefore put up with it. If this is the spirit which animates a great power, how must we expect such a power to behave towards Siam or Japan, or the Tartars, or any other of the weaker nations? Such tyranny as will be exercised and such humiliations as will be imposed seem to me so unendurable that, if I cannot make the arrange-

The City of the Potomac

ments for carrying through the enterprise myself, I feel like letting the secret die with me.

"Now comes the other event, showing how ready France is to do the same to a weaker power that Germany did to her. A party of sailors from a French ship of war in the harbor of Lisbon went ashore and got into a fight with a party of Portuguese. As might have been expected, the French were victorious. A formal complaint was made to their government by that of Portugal, which, after a careful investigation of the whole matter, claimed that the others were the aggressors. But a court of inquiry on board the French ship, after hearing the story as told by their side, reported that the Portuguese were the aggressors. In view of their difference of opinion, Portugal asked France to have the affair tried by an impartial joint commission, to be chosen by both governments. This France refused to do, replying that she could not go back of the findings of her own officers; that, according to these findings, the Portuguese were the aggressors, and that an indemnity must therefore be paid by Portugal without further question. The worst of it is that the attitude of their government is supported by the great body of the Paris press.

"June 20, 1942.—Every day I see more plainly that if I am to carry through my main enterprise all by myself, I shall need a great deal more than the seven million dollars of my former estimate. I have therefore decided not to rely on aluminium

His Wisdom the Defender

alone, and have perfected a form of bicycle which can be run with almost any speed, even forty miles an hour, with a thermic engine supplied with therm by a little petroleum lamp. I have an automobile carriage to run on the same system. To save people's eyes I shall also make an incandescent burner by which a white globe, surrounding a common gas-jet, shall glow with the soft light of day and fill a whole room with its radiance."

That every effort was made to penetrate Campbell's secret goes without saying. The two men described in his diary were simply the pioneers of a multitude. There was a singular frankness in his way of dealing with these curiosity seekers. When a suspicious visitor appeared, evidently bent on learning something of value, he was received either by the secretary of the company or a trusted subordinate with the greatest affability, and seemingly given every encouragement to make inquiries. He was informed that visitors were allowed to see the process of manufacture only on certain days, the reason being that their presence interfered with the workmen.

"But if you really wish to see the process, come next Wednesday morning and you may be allowed to do so."

"I supposed it was an impenetrable secret."

"In one sense it is and in another it is not. There may be something that Mr. Campbell is not yet pre-

The City of the Potomac

pared to reveal. But if you care to see what the process is, there is no objection."

At the appointed time the visitors, perhaps a dozen in number, were taken into the furnace-room. They found the base of the tall, large chimney surrounded by a furnace twenty feet in diameter and six feet high. The furnace was pierced through with eight round vertical openings, each about four feet in diameter, in each of which was a hollow cylinder of some hitherto unknown substance. The remaining space was filled with burning coal. Vertically above the surface, at a height of about ten feet, the chimney was surrounded by a circular platform having eight holes, each about six inches in diameter, one over the centre of each cylinder in the furnace below. Bars of baked clay, about two inches in diameter and eight or ten feet long, were suspended from this platform by machinery, so that their lower ends should pass through the heated cylinders. Here they were exposed to a temperature so high that the clay itself rapidly melted or dissolved in a shower of sparks. As fast as the lower portion was thus dissolved the bar was let down by machinery. The melted product ran down in a stream, which, being at the bottom of the cylinder, could not be seen by the visitor without endangering his eyes.

The substance of the cylinders possessed a physical property never before known to be possible, in virtue of which all the heat was radiated directly towards the centre. The result was that the heat was concen-

His Wisdom the Defender

trated as in the focus of an immense burning-glass. How such a result could be brought about, the visitor was left to conjecture.

"May we see what is going on below this furnace?"

"Oh, certainly; come down-stairs and we will show you."

Below, nothing was to be seen but a small stream of molten aluminium mixed with a large quantity of dross, which flowed into refining furnaces.

"There, gentlemen, you see the whole process. What more can we show you?"

The visitors had to admit that they had seen everything there was to see, and left as wise as they came. The injunction of secrecy was not a very difficult one to comply with.

No better off was the man who tried to see how the vital portion of the thermobike was made. All they could see were rows of workmen engaged in moulding, forging, boring, and performing every other process known in mechanics. Any one who chose could take the thermobike to pieces, analyze it, and see how it was made. A careful examination by scientific experts showed how the machine operated. The "bike," as it was familiarly called from the beginning, was driven by a petroleum lamp, the chimney of which was lined with aluminium bronze. Outside this lining was a layer, half an inch thick, of a substance which seemed to defy physical examination. It was unacted on by acids and had no

The City of the Potomac

chemical properties. Exposed to intense heat, it was resolved into a few commonplace substances, mostly silicon and carbon. It was a very poor conductor of electricity. Outside this again was a second metal cylinder. When the lamp was lit the interior and exterior cylinders at once became the poles of a powerful electric battery. The current from this battery was passed round the rim of a wheel, which again was coated with a substance having a peculiar relation to electricity. As the current passed in one direction, the wheel turned with great force and any required speed in the other. What was most singular was that scientific examination showed nearly all the energy set free by the petroleum to be turned into effective work in the turning of the wheel. The heat from a very small lamp sufficed to run a bike with any required speed.

The same principle was soon applied to the manufacture of the new kind of automobile carriage, or "mobie," as we now call it.

So the mysterious vehicles were rapidly coming into use without any one being able to penetrate the secret of their operation.

III

An Italian Romance

IT goes without saying that the interest in what was going on at Campbelltown, for such was the natural name of the new town, soon spread from America to Europe and thence over the world. Bikes and mobies were wanted everywhere. Manufacturers of bicycles, carriages, and machinery of every kind would have liked to supply this growing demand. As this was clearly impossible without Campbell's co-operation, the efforts which capitalists and manufacturers had already made in America were now seconded by those of Europe. By expending two or three million dollars in each European country in the necessary manufacturing plant, a prospect of reaping rich profits was opened. Steps were first taken by the Rothschilds. They organized a combination of well-known capitalists on both sides of the Atlantic, chose a committee of the ablest and most prominent men, including the best of those who had business relations with the Anita Company, and despatched it to headquarters to see what could be done.

Meantime Campbell had assumed an almost regal

An Italian Romance

inaccessibility to visitors. He took good care, however, to have a system by which no person having really serious and important business should be obliged to depart without having an interview either with him or with some one who could determine whether an interview was necessary. The Rothschild committee had no difficulty in securing an audience. It set forth its objects in a moderate way, laying great stress on the immense benefits which could be conferred on the people of Europe if Campbell would either place manufacturers in possession of his secret, or establish branch works in various countries of the same general character as those at Campbelltown.

"We venture to approach you with this proposition only because you have on various occasions stated that your first object is to promote the welfare of humanity in general, and that you are comparatively indifferent to accumulating wealth for your own use beyond such limit as you may find necessary to carry out your beneficent projects. We appear before you neither as rivals nor as seekers of your bounty, but as representative men, able and willing to aid in extending the benefits of your discoveries to men the world over who are impatient to share in them."

"I entirely sympathize with your objects," was the reply. "It has all along been my intention to enable mankind to share in the benefits to which you allude, as rapidly as possible. The only point of divergence between us is that perhaps you want to go ahead a little faster than seems to me conducive to ultimate success. If we reflect that the highest form of civilization existed for centuries without the thermic engine, may we not concede it possible for men to wait two or three years longer for its full development?

"I intend, as soon as possible, to found an establishment in Europe corresponding to this in America. Moreover, when this central branch is set up I shall proceed to the establishment of local branches in other countries. I shall be quite ready to see companies formed for the establishment and administration of these local branches. But the central branch I must establish as my own. As soon as that is in full operation, I shall, step by step, grant every facility for carrying on the manufactures in other European countries with all possible despatch."

"May we ask when and where your European branch will be set up?"

"I must ask to be excused from any statement on the subject at present, beyond the fact that I hope to decide the question within a few months."

The fact was that for a year past Campbell had been actively at work in Europe, in a way of which the world was quite ignorant. A young American lawyer had spent an entire summer in Spain, Portugal, and Italy, studying the laws of land tenure in these countries, and their applications to the islands owned by them. Maps of Madeira, the Bale-

An Italian Romance

aric Islands, Elba, and the shores of the Adriatic had been collected. A party of three or four men had personally visited all these islands, made the acquaintance of some of their leading inhabitants, and begun a general survey of their productions. It was due to the discretion with which they proceeded that they did not fall into the hands of the police as suspicious characters. Architects in Chicago were preparing plans of palaces, and artists of Paris were negotiating for the employment of Chinese carvers. Men were spying out the arsenals and factories of arms in every part of the Continent with the same secrecy, and reporting the results of their inquiries at Campbelltown, which was thus rapidly becoming a depot of information, the object of which no outsider could at the time have divined, even had he known of its collection.

Great was the public interest when it became known that the president of the Anita Company would establish a branch of his works in some European country. Every indication of his plan was eagerly watched. There was no way of gratifying public curiosity as to where the branch would be located, except by waiting to see, a necessity under which the newspapers chafed. They were soon electrified by the announcement that he had taken passage from New York to Genoa. But what it meant they could not imagine. His departure was not known until the very day on which the ship sailed, when his name was found among the list of

His Wisdom the Defender

passengers. On landing he was at once besieged by reporters who had been sent on in advance to interview him. But he refused to say anything except that he was in Italy on business of his own. He took rooms at a hotel, and secretly engaged a carriage to call for him at four o'clock in the morning. He got into it and drove off. Then for several days nothing certain was heard of him. At the end of a week it was learned that he was inspecting the island of Elba. It was soon announced from Rome that his European branch would be located on that island, and that its erection would be begun immediately. Before his return he paid a visit to the President of the Italian Republic, with whom he had a conference which lasted several hours. Then he returned to Genoa and sailed for home after a stay of less than two weeks.

This was all the reporters could find out about the movements of the man they were chasing. With the more ample sources of information at our disposal, we are able to fill the gaps in their history. To do so we must begin by narrating an almost forgotten incident near the city of Florence nearly twenty years before. Campbell, newly graduated from Harvard, was spending a year in Italy, and, at the time of which we speak, was studying in Florence. One morning, while walking near the hill of Arcetri, he saw a runaway landau, drawn by two horses and containing four people, coming towards him. As they approached him he stood squarely

An Italian Romance

in the middle of the road, until the horses were almost upon him. Then he ran forward a few steps to diminish the force of the shock, sprang upon the tongue of the coach between the two animals, and seized the bridles. He was thus enabled, with the aid of a few gentle words, to bring the team to a standstill, just before a turn in the road which might have been fatal was reached. But he suffered much in the encounter. The end of the tongue struck him in the face as he was jumping upon it, tearing and bruising the flesh and knocking out one of his teeth.

The occupants of the carriage were the Duke of Bernaletti, with his wife, son, and ten-year-old daughter. As they took their rescuer to their home, the most touching feature of the case was the intense concern of the little girl. She cried and lamented over his injury, and during the whole drive gave vent to the hope that he would not die. Although his injuries were severe, his recovery was rapid. In a couple of weeks he took leave of the family, and soon after returned home.

In the course of time the impression of the Duke and his château had nearly faded from the mind of the young man, who had soon become a professor. But there was one voice which never ceased to sound in his ears as clearly as if he had heard it but yesterday. It was that of the little child who forgot the danger she had run in her sympathy for him. "Are you much hurt, sir? Does it pain you? You will not die, will you, sir? Oh! papa, the surgeon will cure him, will he not?"

When he next visited Florence, seven years later, he found Tiana budding into womanhood. It seemed to him that the tenderness of feeling she had shown as a child had so permeated her nature that she was now the very embodiment of purity, sweetness, and love. Let us not blame him if, under such an influence, he lost no chance to make himself agreeable to the young lady, and perhaps strained the rigid etiquette of the country a little in his efforts to win her affection. Knowing how hopeless would be a suit prosecuted in the regular Italian way, his only excuse for the course he took was the hope that he might, by the scientific discoveries which he saw almost within his grasp, not only become the greatest benefactor of modern times, but win a position which the proudest ducal family in Europe would accept as the equivalent of princely birth.

It will not surprise our readers to learn that, in a few hours after the reporters lost track of him at Genoa, he was once more a guest at the Bernaletti palace.

"Will you not accompany me to Elba," said the guest at lunch, "and see what I am going to do? We shall drive over the island together while I fix upon a point for my establishment. Permit me to assure you that sympathy is, at the present moment, one of my greatest wants. Please give me the honor

An Italian Romance

and the pleasure of your company, if you possibly can."

"I shall think the matter over in the course of the afternoon," said the Duke. "If you will wait until morning, we shall see whether I can accompany you."

On rising from the table he sought a moment to whisper one word to the daughter.

"Do you remember," said he "my once telling you that I would try to be the best man in the world for your sake?"

"I—think—I—do; it was at the Villa Carlotta, was it not?"

"I am going to keep on trying, all for your sake."

"But there is no need of your doing it for my sake. You know I am going to be a sister in the convent."

"Do not say that. I cannot endure hearing you say it."

She hurried from the room, and he saw her no more until dinner-time. Next morning he had only a chance to say one word to her before leaving.

"Please never forget me, as I shall never forget you."

"A sister must sometimes forget what she would gladly remember," was the only reply.

The two men left for Elba. Campbell had chartered a steamer to carry them from point to point on the coast of the island. They first touched at Porto Ferrajo.

His Wisdom the Defender

"Here," said Campbell, "I intend to found a great city, which shall be for Europe what Campbelltown is for America."

Next morning they re-embarked, continued their journey westward, and landed at Brocchio. There a carriage was engaged, and they drove to the base of Mount Campanne, where they changed to a small mountain-cart drawn by two mules, and proceeded to make the ascent of the mountain.

The Duke noticed that his companion, who had shown a sparkling vivacity and fiery enthusiasm in unfolding his plans for the future, now became silent, abstracted, and even melancholy. Every now and then he closed his eyes as if in deep thought. He felt some concern at such a change under conditions that should have produced the opposite effect. At every turn of the narrow road there was a new and wider view both of the Mediterranean and of the island, which was to him a source of exhilaration, but seemed to the other a source of depression. He tried to interest him in the view.

"Is it not beautiful?" he said.

"It is, and I hope it will be still more so when we reach the top." Then, as if exhausted, he again relapsed into a fit of abstraction.

After two hours' drive in their rough vehicle, the summit was reached. Now a view was disclosed quite unlike any that either of the spectators had before seen. Below their feet, towards the east, the island stretched its length beyond the horizon.

An Italian Romance

The port from which they had started seemed almost beneath them. In every other direction the blue waters of the Mediterranean bounded the horizon. To the west and southwest the mountains of Corsica were as gray clouds resting on the water. The bright rays of the sun softened everything round them in a way that one sees only in Italy.

The elder of the two men wondered why his companion had brought him up. He seemed so meditative that he would have given many a penny for his thoughts. The fact is, he was dwelling on the plans which had for years centred round this place. Would they ever be realized? Was this to be the seat of future empire? Would the most splendid of palaces rear its dome upon the spot where they were standing? He at length ventured a word to his companion.

"What will our posterity see who shall look upon this place a hundred years from now? If I have my way, we shall see much before many years are over."

Seating himself on a rock, he took from his pocket a roll of tracing-paper, on which was copied the plan and front elevation of a building.

"Here is the site which I have chosen for my possible future residence. Here is the proposed plan; what think you of it?"

The old man scanned the drawing. "That will be the grandest and most beautiful palace I ever saw; but why erect it in so inaccessible a situation?

His Wisdom the Defender

How will you ever get even the materials to build it up here? And when your house is done you must either be a monk in a monastery or build a mountain railway."

"Or call it a convent," thought the other.

"The machinery which I command will transport the materials without difficulty; but this is a detail into which we need not go at present. I have brought you up here, first of all, to give you some idea of the future extent of my European establishment. I have also a favor to ask of you. On the first day of every month, after I begin to build, I shall have a photograph of my rising palace taken, showing its steady progress from foundation upward. I ask permission to have copies of these pictures sent you regularly for the use of your family."

"It seems to me that that is rather doing me a favor, and it is one which I shall accept with great pleasure."

"Perhaps you would like to know the name of the city I shall found here. I shall call it Uraniberg, the city of heaven."

Descending to the plain, Campbell spent another day in conference with his chief manager at the station, and then sailed for home.

It was fortunate that during the voyage home the daily papers could not reach his ship. Among all the eccentricities which had marked his conduct there was none to compare with that of choosing such a place for a great manufacturing establish-

An Italian Romance

ment. If he could have seen the comments on his doings, the questions raised as to his sanity, the discussions as to what might be done to bring him to his senses or to deprive him of control over his own works, and the torrents of abuse poured upon him on all sides, he would have been saved from discomfort only by forming a contemptuous opinion of human nature.

He had made arrangements for purchasing or leasing a considerable portion of the island. Within a few months a city began to take form, and an army of laborers was engaged in erecting machinery of the same sort as was in operation at Campbelltown. But there was no Coliseum. Much as the world wondered, no one anticipated that the little island in the Ligurian Sea was to be the centre from which the sun of the Golden Age should send its rays.

IV

The Angelic Order of Seraphim

PUBLIC attention was so concentrated upon the eccentric doings at Campbelltown that certain minor features of the situation were overlooked, even by the red-headed man. One was the number of college athletes that Campbell took into his service. It is hardly an exaggeration to say that every enthusiastic football player who graduated at any college in the land during the years 1942 – 44 received through some friend or travelling agent a glowing account of the advantages offered to young men of enterprise and ability by the great factory for bikes and mobies. If the young man had some profession in view, he was told that Campbell would need men of almost every profession, and would give every encouragement and facility in its study, even to supplying money should it be required. If he replied that Campbell could have no rational object in patronizing a young man he never saw or heard of, he was reminded that the ways of the owner of Campbelltown were past finding out; that the youth had better go and see him;

The Angelic Order of Seraphim

that free transportation was ready, and that when he arrived he might find that his reputation for scholarship and enterprise had preceded him.

Few could resist the temptation to see the famous establishment. Arriving at the gate of the factory, the doubting and diffident youth had only to state his errand to be immediately shown into the office of the manager, by whom he was received with the greatest urbanity.

"I am sorry that I cannot introduce you to the president of the company, as he is engaged at this moment; but if you will let me know your feelings on the subject of entering the service of the Anita Company, I shall gladly see what can be done."

"Well, really, sir, I have had no idea of asking employment here. A few days ago I met a friend who expressed a strong desire that I should come, and who, curiously enough, was supplied with a free ticket here, which he gave me to use. My intention always has been to study architecture at New York, and I do not feel like changing that plan. You may therefore consider that I am here out of pure curiosity."

"Your plan will meet our views exactly. The Anita Company has constant need of architects in extending the limits of its town and in putting up buildings elsewhere. This need will increase during the next few years rather than diminish. We shall be very glad to have you continue your studies in architecture under our auspices. If money will

His Wisdom the Defender

help, we are ready to advance it. The fact is, our president always takes the greatest interest in able young men studying a profession, and is ready to do all he can to promote them."

"That is very attractive, but I do not see the slightest reason why the Anita Company should bestow any such position on me. I do not deny that the help you propose would be very welcome, but, on the other hand, I have absolutely nothing to offer in return. I cannot, therefore, consent to receive it at this time."

"There is not the slightest occasion for any diffidence. Only two conditions are attached to our arrangements. One is that, during the course of your studies, you shall come down here once or twice a month to meet other young men like yourself and have a good time together. You can come down on Saturday and return on Sunday, so as not to interfere with your work in any way. The other condition is that, whenever the proper time comes, and you feel that you can do something on your own account, you will give us a chance of accepting your services. I forgot—there is a third condition. We do not desire you to say anything about this arrangement. It is to be regarded as a tribute from our company to a few of the best young men of the country; and we do not wish to be overwhelmed with applications from others."

In the large majority of cases so tempting an offer could not be declined. To some selected youths

The Angelic Order of Seraphim

who were willing to undertake it immediate employment was offered. It might be clerical or technical; it might be nothing more than overlooking the building of a house, the making of motors, or the running of machinery that the youth knew nothing about. If he objected on the score of ignorance, he was told that he only had to learn.

At the time of which we speak, the number of selected young men who were either in the employ of the company or studying under its auspices amounted to several hundred. All who were able to do so visited Campbelltown on the first and third Saturday of every month. Here they dined at a hospitable table, presided over by Gheen or the manager, and met their friends employed in the works. Naturally enough, the young men wondered much what possible object the Anita Company could have in all this. The only explanation that could be offered was that the president was a queer fellow, unlike other men in every point, conducting his business on principles utterly different from any on which business had ever been conducted before. Impenetrable as to his motives and invisible in his ways, the only certain facts were that he was piling up money by the million and was ready to expend some of it in this odd way. So the best policy was to accept what was offered and ask no questions.

One evening at a reunion a special invitation was extended to about a hundred of the company to

His Wisdom the Defender

call in a body on the president after dinner. The guests were first shown into a spacious anteroom. In one corner was a book containing a pledge of absolute secrecy as to the meeting about to be held. Each was asked to sign this pledge. As he did so a little ticket was handed to him by which he was to gain admittance to the assembly. The men were then shown into a spacious reception-room, at one end of which sat the president, the tickets being taken at the door. They passed him in single file, each being introduced by Gheen, and then sat in several circles around the room waiting for what was to come next. The president addressed them to the following effect:

"I believe, gentlemen, that you have all stood in a more or less intimate relation to the Anita Company. The end and objects of that relation may seem very mysterious. You must excuse me if I am not able at the present moment to unfold the mystery in its entirety. I may, however, do so in part. You see me here in sole possession of an enormous source of wealth and power. I have none of the ordinary motives for accumulating wealth. I have no family, no children; so far as I am aware, no near relatives. The whole human race is one to me, and my greatest object in life is to do what I can towards promoting its happiness. Of course I must have helpers. No helpers can be more effective than the best and most energetic of our college graduates. This is why I have called you together. We must

The Angelic Order of Seraphim

work together as a unit. The first condition of our success is absolute loyalty on the part of each member of our organization, both to myself, its patron, and the organization as a whole. What I therefore propose is the formation of a secret order pledged to fealty and obedience, and ready to act together whenever called upon.

" It may be that many among you do not feel disposed to form such an order, or to engage yourselves in the way I have suggested. All such are at perfect liberty to leave, if, after thinking the matter over during the next four weeks, they choose to do so. They have only to remember that the pledge of secrecy as to what I have here said has been taken, and remains absolute. All who feel like entering what I shall call the new order and subscribing to its pledges are invited to meet again four weeks from to-day. At that time as many of you as are willing to form the nucleus of the order are invited to be here. Until then, good-bye."

The question which burdened Campbell's mind during the next four weeks was whether it was possible that no one of that hundred young men would betray the secret. Every day the newspapers were searched to see if, in the numerous accounts of what was goiong on at Campbelltown, there was anything about this meeting. It was a real surprise to him to find that not even the red-headed man had found out anything on the subject.

Mystery has its attractions for youth. Our readers will not be surprised to learn that ninety of those present at the first meeting appeared at the second. On entering, each was asked whether he was prepared to sign the pledge of the new order. Replying in the affirmative, he was asked to read and sign the following, which was printed at the top of each page of a thin blank-book.

"We, the members of the proposed Angelic Order of Seraphim, pledge our sacred honor to keep all the secrets of said order; to be true and loyal under all circumstances both to each other and to the patron of the order, Archibald Campbell; to place ourselves at his service whenever required, and to obey all orders received from him."

Under the first of these printed pledges was written the following, of which all were invited to take notice:

"I, Archibald Campbell, president of the Anita Company and patron of the Angelic Order of Seraphim, hereby pledge myself to perform all my duties as patron of that order, and, to the best of my ability, to see that none of its members ever suffer want.—ARCHIBALD CAMPBELL."

When all was ready, the patron again briefly addressed them:

"Gentlemen, I have not much to add to what I said to you at our last meeting. The name of our order has been made known to you. Its appropriateness is not yet apparent—it will not be apparent until we have our initiation ceremonies, which may

The Angelic Order of Seraphim

not occur for several months, perhaps not for a year or more. They will be extremely interesting. It is not too much to say they will be as a new revelation to you. You will find yourselves possessed of powers never before given by God to man. Meanwhile let us pursue our usual vocations. I shall expect you to spend a good deal of your time in these precincts. It is desirable that the order be enlarged to about three hundred members. I must ask your assistance in doing this. If any of you know good and true young men who may be willing to come in, and whom you feel safe in trusting with your honor, consult them discreetly on the subject, give their names, and let their records be examined. I shall expect you to meet and talk together every month, and, during the interval, to engage in such exercises as will be prepared for you."

At the next Saturday's meeting of the Angelic Order the members were invited to accompany Gheen to the Coliseum and see what was there going on. Breathless was their curiosity as they approached the mysterious place. An odd scene met their eyes on entering. Near one end of the enclosure were erected two rows of massive iron towers about sixty feet apart and fifty feet in height. Stout ropes passed between the tops, like the wires of a suspension bridge. At each end they were connected with the towers by a spiral spring, so that if a heavy weight was hung to one of the ropes it would sink to a considerable distance. Suspended to each

His Wisdom the Defender

rope, near its mid-point, was an object of singular shape and aspect. Seen externally, it looked like a large hogshead, perhaps six feet in diameter and eight feet high. On top of the hogshead was what might be a little cask about a foot in diameter. This was pierced round its upper portion with little holes filled with glass, giving the appearance of as many eyes. On each side of the hogshead, two feet below the top, projected two jointed arms. Hanging below it, and reaching to within ten feet of the ground, were a pair of jointed legs. The whole looked like a grotesque caricature of the human form. The sight was greeted by the arriving party with a shout of " Daddy-Long-Legs," mixed with peals of laughter.

No other name had ever been invented for the machine, and this one was so appropriate that it stuck. Very soon, however, the last two syllables were dropped as unnecessary, and the machine was called the " daddie." This is the origin of our name for the useful implement used in lifting heavy weights, a term the derivation of which would have puzzled the most expert etymologists if its history had not been revealed.

If the spectators could have seen inside they would have found the interior structure to be very complex. Six vertical pipes, each a foot in diameter, were concealed within the hogshead, around its circumference. Levers without number were between them. In the centre of all a man was seated at his ease. His foot pressed one system of levers

The Angelic Order of Seraphim

and his hand had hold of another system. These levers were connected by a number of linked rods, which again connected with the arms and legs seen externally. I will so far reveal the secret in advance as to say that the arrangement was such that every motion that the man made with his arms or legs was communicated by means of etherine to the corresponding limb of the daddie with a force multiplied a hundredfold. Daddie might therefore be described as a being of enormous muscular force wielded by a human intellect.

The pairs of towers supporting the daddies were about one hundred feet apart. Across the line between the two central ones was stretched another rope with a netting suspended from it, and touching the ground as if a game of gigantic tennis was to be played. To make the resemblance complete, a huge wooden ball, two feet in diameter, bound round with three iron rings, lay on the ground beneath one of the daddies. It must have weighed several hundred pounds.

" Has a race of giants been playing tennis ?" asked the new-comers.

" Commence the game!" cried the leader.

The daddie beneath whose feet the ball lay immediately dipped towards the ground, tightening the rope and stretching the springs. He seized the ball between his feet as lightly and easily as a man would seize a tennis-ball, drew it back, and hurled it forward through the air at the other daddie. The

His Wisdom the Defender

latter stooped to catch it with his hands, but missed it at the first trial. It was caught by a third daddie and returned in tennis fashion to the thrower.

The game was played through with entire success. The daddie always threw the ball with his feet, but caught it sometimes with his hands and sometimes with his feet. To catch it with his hands he sometimes had to throw himself in an almost horizontal position. His dexterity in doing this seemed supernatural. At one moment he pulled and stretched the string by his weight; at another he sprang upward as lightly as a ballet-dancer.

"Now," said Gheen, "your first duty will be to learn this game and to play it well. Only expert players are eligible for initiation into the Angelic Order of Seraphim."

Those of the visitors who had read *Alice Behind the Looking-Glass* thought of the world there pictured. The temptation to betray the secret of the order was diminished rather than increased by the mystery of the proceedings. If they should have told all they had seen going on their hearers would have thought they were being made sport of.

During the following weeks the number of daddies was increased, so that one or more games were always going on, and the new men were gotten into practice as rapidly as possible. At first it was a clumsy proceeding, the exact connection between the movements of the player's limbs and the movements of the daddie in which he was seated was

The Angelic Order of Seraphim

difficult to bring about. Improvements were from time to time made in the machine so as to make the co-ordination more perfect.

Before a month had passed a new mystery was unveiled. The players with the daddie, entering the Coliseum one morning, saw at the other end of the enclosure a monstrous object, which certainly had not been there the night before. In shape it was a giant centipede. The body of the insect was a flat-bottomed boat, a hundred feet in length, thirty feet in breadth, and fifteen or twenty feet deep. It was suspended by a rope stretched between two pillars much like the daddies, and almost touched the ground.

Its numerous limbs were not unlike colossal human arms, fifteen feet in length. Each had a joint at the side of the mote to which it was fastened, an elbow near the middle, then a wrist-joint, and, instead of a hand, a sort of two-handed claw which could open out to the extent of eighteen inches, and close up when necessary. Inside the vessel, at each point where an arm was attached, was a piece of apparatus too complicated to be described in full without drawings. The visible part consisted of a breast-plate with two openings, through which a man could thrust his hands and seize a lever with each. There were ten arms on each side of the "centipede," as it came to be called, making twenty in all.

Campbell himself inaugurated the exercise with

His Wisdom the Defender

this machine. He took one of his neophytes with him into the centipede, showed him how to get hold of the levers attached to the arm, and then asked him to notice what could be done with them. On moving his own arms it was found that the arms of the centipede were mysteriously affected by a corresponding motion. Closing his hands together, the immense claws of the centipede closed up; then opened again when the hands were separated. Raising the lever, the shoulder and elbow joints of the centipede's arms rose in a corresponding way, and the claws were thrown high in the air.

"Now," said Campbell, "I want you to practise with this until you have all the motions, then we will see what we can do next."

The Seraph, having got himself into practice, so that he was able to move the arms in any way he chose, was now told to show his companions of the order how the machine worked. Two days were spent in getting about fifty men into practice. Then a number of large wooden logs, perhaps a foot in diameter and from six to twelve feet long, were placed on the ground near the centipede, and within reach of his arms. The men were then practised in taking hold of these logs with their giant claws, lifting them up and placing them on the deck above. Then a platform was erected above where the logs lay, and the logs were picked up and placed upon it.

Continued practice naturally suggested a num-

The Angelic Order of Seraphim

ber of improvements in the construction of the centipede's arms and of the levers which moved them. In time, however, the instrument was perfected, and then any number of them could be made on the same model.

We who look back at the whole proceeding can scarcely imagine how eccentric the scenes at the Coliseum appeared to all concerned in them. It seemed as if the "Little Professor," as he was familiarly called by all those nearest to him, must be the most singular compound of genius and insanity that the world had ever seen. So far as immediate results were concerned, all his plans had been made and executed with a success that evinced not only the greatness of his scientific powers, but the highest order of executive ability. How could a serious man of so much ability spend the time he was spending on so singular a proceeding as this now going on in the Coliseum? Why such secrecy? The answer seemed obvious. The chief actor knew how ridiculous his amusements would look to the world if they should ever be known. But this was only a part of the truth. Had the real object of all these doings been discovered, not a crowned head nor prime-minister in Europe would have slept that night.

The time had now come when an understanding whether Gheen was to be his active agent in carrying through his plans had to be reached.

One morning, when the daddie and the centipede were both perfected, Campbell invited Gheen to a

His Wisdom the Defender

conference. "I do not want you to do much today. I want to have a very important talk with you at four o'clock this afternoon; and I do not want you to have anything on your mind or to be fatigued by the day's work. So go where you please. If nothing suits you better, take a sail on the Potomac and be back here at the appointed hour."

At the appointed hour the two men sat in Campbell's private office. Gheen was all attention.

"A crisis in our arrangements is now approaching," said Campbell. "It must soon be decided whether you shall be as close to me in the future as you have been in the past, or whether you shall simply be the chief engineer of the works here, while some one else takes your place in confidential relations with me. My proceedings in the erection and running of these works have been marked by what the business world considers unaccountable eccentricities. The exercises in the Coliseum must have seemed to you and those engaged in them even more eccentric than my business management. Is not this the case?"

"I cannot deny that the management of your works, in which I have taken a prominent part from the beginning, has seemed to me very mysterious. They have been so mysterious that I am no longer surprised at anything, not even at what is going on in the Coliseum."

"Now I want to unravel to you the whole mys-

The Angelic Order of Seraphim

tery. But I want you in advance to make me a solemn and unconditional pledge of the most absolute secrecy. This pledge is to be equally binding whether you take part in my future plans or not. If you take the leading part in them which I wish you to, the secrecy will be necessary for your own interests. If you do not, you will be concerned only with the development of the works, and need not be concerned in what is going on in the Coliseum. To make the matter sure, I would like you to sign this pledge."

Gheen read over the paper which was handed to him and affixed his signature. Campbell proceeded:

" The world at large, which considers the making of money to be one of the chief ends of man, or at least the ultimate end of those engaged in business, cannot understand how I can have any other end in view than piling up wealth. If, as I have always maintained, my tastes lie in the scientific direction and not in that of money, why have I engaged in a wealth-producing enterprise? I will tell you. I am the possessor of a power which, if made public, would result in disaster to the human race, but which, if I wield it myself, so as to carry out my plans with entire success, will revolutionize the world, and make those who are instrumental in that revolution the greatest benefactors the world has ever seen. To speak plainly, I propose to put an end to war now and forever. May I have your co-operation in that work? Can you go into the work

His Wisdom the Defender

of putting an end to war with an approving conscience?"

"Abstractly, I agree with you that it would be an excellent thing to put an end to war. But I cannot help regarding it as impracticable. From what I know of human nature I do not see how it is possible to stop nations from engaging in war. What are armies for except to fight? How are you going to stop them from fighting?"

"That is the very secret I wish to unfold to you to-night. It is no use to tell you in advance. Let us meet at the private laboratory at the south end of the Coliseum at nine o'clock this evening. You shall enjoy the experience of your life."

The laboratory here referred to was a good-sized building, into which Campbell had carefully removed the entire contents of the uncanny workshop described in our first chapter. He had, during the past few months, spent much of his time in this workshop, improving and adding to the singular apparatus which it contained.

At the appointed hour the two men entered the Coliseum. The watchman in charge had been previously directed to make a thorough examination of the interior to see that every one left at the close of the day's work, and to allow no one to enter it during the evening except the owner and the man accompanying him. Curiously enough, Gheen himself had never been inside of this place. In fact, none of the employees had ever been allowed in it

The Angelic Order of Seraphim

except Campbell's three workmen, two of whom were the same men that we saw in Cambridge.

Campbell called Gheen's attention to two singular-looking chairs. In shape they were much like ordinary arm-chairs, only much larger. They were nicely cushioned, and each had a step at the bottom on which the sitter could rest his feet. The uprights were very large, consisting of tubes not less than three inches in diameter.

"Let us bring these chairs out," said Campbell.

Being mounted on rollers, they were pushed out without difficulty.

"Now I want to tie these chairs together," he continued. He got a piece of cord and thoroughly bound them side by side by the arms, backs, and spokes. Then, opening a case in the side of the room, he took out two standing rods, with one of which we are already familiar, and handed them to Gheen.

"Here, I want you to take these rods out and put them down through the two tubes which you see in the back of each chair; you will find an arrangement for fastening them in."

Gheen took the rods from Campbell's hands, and, as he went out, noticed their singular behavior. They remained in a vertical position, from which they could not be removed by any force he could exert. But as they could be picked up and moved about without any difficulty at all, they were put into the tubes as directed.

His Wisdom the Defender

"Now we need only one more piece of apparatus. We must attach these cranks to a little handle which you will see projecting from the arms of each chair."

The cranks were attached.

"Now let us take our seats. Plant your feet on the foot-rest and be careful not to move them. Now, I hope you are a man of nerve. Graduates of pieces which go across them. You are tightly fasttened, are you? Now put one foot on each lever, but be careful not to press it until you see me do so. The moment I say 'Press,' press the lever forward and I will do the same thing. Let us watch each other's hands, so that the pressure shall be simultaneous. Now, I hope you are a man of nerve. Graduates of West Point ought to be. I selected you with that supposition. If you have any doubt about your nerve, just say so, and we will give up the whole job. The fact is, if you go on you are now to be initiated as the head of the Angelic Order of Seraphim. Are you ready?"

"I am ready for anything, and burning all over with curiosity."

"Now press!"

Gheen's first impression on making the motion was that some kind of a noiseless bomb had burst under his chair. His second was that somebody had given it a push. His third and more correct impression was that the two chairs, with himself and Campbell in them, were flying through the air. Before he could collect his thoughts the Coliseum was

The Angelic Order of Seraphim

far below. A vertical wind was felt blowing downward because of the rapid flight.

"Where are we going?" exclaimed Gheen, as soon as he could get his breath.

"Wherever we please," was the reply. "Shall we take a look at Washington?"

Campbell pressed the foot-rest with his left foot, gave his levers a slight motion, and in a few seconds the faces of the two men were directed towards a bright patch on the clouds in the northern horizon, which they knew was caused by the reflection of the electric lights of Washington. In a minute they were flying with the speed of a railway train. The wind from their rapid motion soon began to chill them through.

"I do not think we need go to Washington," said Campbell. "I only want to show you what we can do. Let us return home."

"But how shall we ever find our way back?"

"Very easily. I have a number of lamps placed on the ground in the Coliseum which shine directly upward and can only be seen from above. Immediately we see those lamps we shall drop down upon them."

With a slight motion of the levers the chairs described a semi-circle, and the men were on the return journey. The lights of Campbelltown had been in sight all the time, and there was no difficulty in getting vertically over the Coliseum. A slight motion of the levers stopped the forward

His Wisdom the Defender

course, and the two chairs floated in the air half a mile above their destination.

"Now we have to be very cautious. Going down we have no idea how fast we may be going, except so far as we can judge by the wind we make. Draw your lever back as I do mine."

Very soon they were falling quite rapidly, and the lights in the Coliseum were plainly seen below. Then the levers were pushed slightly forward, so that the motion should be checked. They slowly approached the ground and landed outside the door of the workshop.

"Now we must be very careful in getting out of the chairs; they still press upward with our entire weight, and if we should leave them as they are, they would fly away and we should never see or hear of them again. That is what we will do to criminals in the future, instead of hanging them. We shall simply fasten a tube like those in the chairs to the criminal's body, attach a little lever, and up he will go, never to be seen or heard of again."

"I am not sure that that would be good policy with the negroes," said Gheen. "They would think they were bound straight to heaven, and would rather like to go out of the world in so glorious a way."

"Well, we need not cross that bridge until we come to it. Let us get our chairs safely into the workshop."

The levers were moved into their original posi-

The Angelic Order of Seraphim

tion and taken off. The two men loosened themselves and took the chairs into the shop. The uprights were removed and put into lockers, and the chairs placed in one corner of the room, looking as innocent as two chairs possibly could.

"I do not think we need discuss the matter further to-night. You have got as much as you can think about for the present. I am afraid you will not sleep as it is. I will merely tell you that when I fill the tubes, which you must have noticed in the daddie and centipede, with etherine, we can run them through the air as we ran our chairs to-night; we can go where we please and do what we please. I may add, for your peace of mind, that our centipedes and daddies will all be bullet-proof."

Two days later Gheen, after thinking the whole matter over, expressed to his chief his willingness to perform the duties of chief of the Angelic Order of Seraphim.

V
The First Motes

THE factories for the manufacture of aluminium, bikes, and mobies, which I have already described, were all grouped round a single nucleus near the end of the bridge connecting the mainland with Peter's Island. They stretched about a quarter of a mile along the river-bank and extended a half-mile back. To the northwest and north—that is, up the river and towards Washington—as well as back from the works, was built the residence part of the new town. The region on the opposite side of the factories remained vacant till after the first year of active operations. Then a brick wall, ten feet high, began to extend itself from the outer limit of the works, half a mile from the river, first in a southwesterly direction, and then towards the river, so as to enclose a space more than half a mile square, bounded on one side by the river-bank.

This enclosure gradually became a scene of activity. Buildings, first of wood and then of brick, were erected, chimneys grew up, draftsmen began to work, and pieces of massive machinery were trans-

The First Motes

ported from the great iron-works of Pittsburg and Bethlehem. Everything betokened the beginning of some new manufacture; but what it was to be no one but Campbell seemed to know, and he would not tell. The first output comprised the daddies and the centipede; then there was a pause, during which nothing was done but to pile up immense stores of aluminium and roll it into huge cylinders.

The policy of the establishment towards reporters and curiosity-seekers was much the same as before. "The only purpose of this wall," they were informed, "is to guard against thieves and meddlers. We thought of leaving holes here and there in it, large enough to look through, so that you could peep all you chose, but we thought you might consider that rather undignified. So we have made arrangements for letting you look in upon us at certain hours in each week. Outside of those hours we do not wish to be disturbed."

So far as possible all reporters were excluded from any permanent residence in the town, but the New York *Herald* was not to be checkmated in this way. The red-headed man was soon the occupant of one of the farm-houses which the owner had reserved from sale in the beginning and still legally held. He made it his exclusive business to pry round and find out all he could, which was, however, very little. His despatches, nevertheless, were not wanting either in length or sensation. The theory on which they were constructed was that the readers would, under

His Wisdom the Defender

any circumstances, forget all about them the next day, so that, even if their falsity were then shown up, no harm would be done to the reputation of the journal.

The keels of what looked like four ships were in due time laid along the river-bank. This tended rather to satiate than to excite curiosity. The theory was current that Campbell was going into ship-building, it being presumed, of course, that the new motive power which he commanded would be used to propel the ships. As the supposed ships progressed they became of an unusual shape, which had been tried about a century before, but had failed. It was that of a large but short cigar. The total length varied from 300 to 360 feet, and the breadth from 50 to 60 feet. The sections being circular, the height was as great as the breadth. The theory gained currency that they were to move along the sea by rolling.

As fast as the centipedes were built, they were brought to the river-bank ready for launching. Here was something new to interest the curious. The shops in which the machines were put together were two or three hundred yards from the river, but after the machines were finished they were found on the river-bank.

How did they get there? They looked as if they must weigh a hundred tons, and yet there was no possible means of transportation. It was at length discovered that they were moved during the night, but how it was done no one could find out.

The First Motes

The centipedes, as they were thus exposed, were without their feet. The latter, with all the machinery that worked them, were carefully stored inside the body.

When upwards of a hundred centipedes were built, an equal number of vessels of another kind were constructed, differing from the first in having no openings for legs. They were much like the boats of that time, with only a single deck, surrounded by a bulwark or a high railing. There was more room in the interior of these vehicles than in that of the centipedes. This was utilized to store articles of the most varied character: condensed food, beverages of various sorts, medicines, portable forges, implements and tools of all kinds, canvas, poles, tents—in fine, about every article that could be needed for an expedition to some uninhabited country. And yet, there lay the "boats" on the river-bank, still unlaunched, with no apparent means of getting them into the water.

As the rolling machinery was improved, the manufacture of a somewhat different mote was commenced. This was also cigar-shaped, differing from the motes just described only in being much smaller. The lengths varied from 30 to 100 feet, and the breadth from 6 to 20 feet. These vehicles had windows in the side, and the employees of the establishment could hardly suppress their merriment when they were ordered to design, make, and supply the mote with seats like those of the railway cars then in

His Wisdom the Defender

vogue. "What can the boss mean?" said everybody.

Four of these motes excited especial attention from the strength and care with which they were built. They were all alike in size, about 80 feet in length and 20 in breadth. They were built in cylindrical sections, each about 10 feet long, the cylinders having an arm on the edge so that they could be fastened end to end like the different lengths of a pipe for conveying water. They were screwed together in the usual way, and then, to give additional strength, were so clamped by "U's" that the junction was as strong as the cylinders themselves. Each end of the mote terminated in a hemisphere. One of these ends was completely closed and the other supplied with an opening barely sufficient to allow a man to enter in a stooping posture. Along the sides openings, about six inches in diameter, were pierced at distances of four feet. These were filled with disks of glass, cemented so as to be quite airtight.

Before the ends of the mote were fastened on, the interior was supplied with a number of longitudinal tubes extending along the walls. The three upper tubes could be filled with air or oxygen from the outside, by means of stop-cocks extending through the wall of the mote. The lower half of each of these was lined with porcelain. Holes closed by tight-fitting covers were pierced here and there along the upper part. A floor was laid along the

The First Motes

whole length, and seats to accommodate forty people were firmly screwed down.

Each vehicle was tested by pumping air into it, until a pressure of two atmospheres above that of the air outside was reached. While subjected to this pressure, every possible exit for the air was carefully searched out and closed up.

Among the numerous committees of scientific men which Campbell had, from time to time, engaged to examine special points in connection with this work, was one to experiment on the time during which human beings could live inside this air-tight enclosure. He intrusted the work of this committee to his former colleague, Professor Banks, of Harvard. The latter was charged to employ all the resources of chemistry and physiology to investigate the products of respiration in the air of a confined space, and learn how they could be made harmless.

From what I have already said of the locality, it will be recalled that the position of the vessels, when launched from the point where they stood, would not be in the open river, but in the narrow channel between the mainland and Peter's Island. This channel, while only 200 yards wide at the upper end where the bridge was built, widened down to 500 yards near the lower end of the island.

The red-headed man was very anxious to witness the launching of the vessels whenever it should take place. He made a daily visit to the factory, and was allowed by the watchmen to look into the sacred

His Wisdom the Defender

enclosure. The absence of all machinery and all preparation for launching, and the activity in other directions, completely threw him off his guard. Great, therefore, was his chagrin to arrive one morning and see the centipedes and flat boats, some two hundred and fifty in number, all floating in the channel. How they got there was quite beyond his comprehension. He vainly interviewed the workmen and all the employees of his acquaintance. Finally he had to give up the attempt to solve the mystery. This was all the easier that a yet greater one seemed to be in sight. The queer boats must be intended to sail, and the first effort in this direction was eagerly awaited by the reporters. The fact that the vessels had no visible means of propulsion heightened their curiosity. But they had seen wonders enough, among which the launching was not the least, to make them feel that this might be no obstacle to their departure at any moment. So a constant watch was kept up by day and night.

Two days after the launching there was another development. It was found that hundreds of the employees and workmen slept in the boats every night. The red-headed man bought a row-boat, and every evening went in it as far as the bridge to watch what might be going on after dark. There was sometimes a great waving of signal lights, but nothing more. The boats were evidently the sleeping-rooms for more than a thousand men; but what else?

The First Motes

One moonless evening was so cloudy that it was impossible to see what was going on. All was dark; not even a signal light was in motion. Whether the boats could sail at night under any circumstances was doubtful; that they should start such a night as this was clearly impossible. So he rowed back and went to bed instead of watching.

Next morning he was awakened by an unusual hubbub. His office-boy ran in to tell him that the boats had all disappeared. He could not believe it till he went out into the rain to see for himself. The report was true! Not a boat was in sight!

VI

Mystery on Mystery

NOTWITHSTANDING the foresight which Campbell had exercised at every step of his enterprise, he was quite unprepared for the outburst of public objurgation that followed the disappearance of the motes. Pent-up dissatisfaction with the secrecy in which he enveloped his proceedings had been constantly increasing. That he had the right to keep his secret was admitted; but men do not always like to see a right exercised. Capitalists, investors, and brokers everywhere were dissatisfied that there was "nothing in it for them." Patent attorneys and the Patent Office were almost scandalized to see the greatest inventions ever made brought into use without their protection. Manufacturers in general, and especially the great trusts of the country, were concerned for their future. The newspapers were dissatisfied because he would not tell them all about what he was doing. From these classes the leaven of dissatisfaction spread to all the people. It needed only an occasion to burst its bonds, and now that occasion was offered.

Mystery on Mystery

During the day following the disappearance of the fleet, the reporters around Campbelltown felt that a march had been stolen upon them, and they were determined to "even things up" or know the reason why. Under the leadership of the red-headed man they crowded to the gate, determined to see the manager, the secretary, or even the president himself, who was usually inaccessible. Their clamor was such that the manager had to admit them in a body, but he really could not tell them anything as to the whereabouts of the fleet. All he knew was that preparations had been going on for several days to give the boats a trial trip; but whither they were to go he did not know.

"Then we must see the president of the company."

"I doubt if he knows any better than I do."

"He ought to know, and he must know, and we are determined to see him. Our papers are all calling upon us for news, and it must be had."

Word of their demands was sent into the office of the president. He directed their admission. He seemed very cool and collected.

"Well, gentlemen, you seem to be out in force this morning. What can I do for you? I am sure the newspapers ought to be my good friends after all the news I am making for them."

The president's unconcern was like the trickling of ice-water on a much-excited man. It took a moment for the red-headed man to collect his thoughts.

His Wisdom the Defender

When at length he could command his speech, he felt that, after all, there was very little to inquire about.

"We have noticed two or three hundred boats moored in the channel for several weeks past."

"Yes, I noticed them there myself."

"This morning they are gone."

"Quite right; when I looked out of my window this morning I could see nothing of them."

He looked for all the world as if he wanted the reporters to tell him where they were.

"We wish to know where they have gone—where they are now."

"That's more than I know myself. They were under the command of Captain Gheen, and he is the only one who can give the information. Are you sure they are not somewhere behind the island?"

"But if Captain Gheen is with the boats, we cannot find him until we find them."

"That may be quite true, but it only makes clear the difficulty. Captain Gheen has, for several days, had directions to take the boats out on a trial trip as soon as he was ready. If he found anything wrong, he was to come right back. If he did not, he could go as far as he pleased, even to the north pole if the ice was not in the way. Have you seen nothing of him or his boats?"

"No, or we would not have been here. We wish to know where you think they are. What did you expect Captain Gheen to do, and where did you expect him to go?"

Mystery on Mystery

"My thoughts on the subject are worth no more than yours. I have told you where I authorized him to go. Until I hear from him I can give you no further information."

"How long before you expect to hear from him?"

"I do not know; it may be this very minute, and it may not be for several months."

"What route did you expect him to take?"

"The most direct route he could."

"Suppose he should sail to the pole, how long would it take him to get there?"

"That depends upon how fast the boats are run. As this is their first serious trial, I cannot tell you their speed, but I expect them to go very fast."

"Can you not tell us how fast?"

"If I could tell you how fast, you would not believe it. At full speed they would be out of sight and hearing long before daylight."

"You speak as if you expected them to go as fast as a railway train."

"I would certainly be very much disappointed if they went anything like as slowly as a train."

There was a look of astonishment and a great scratching of pencils.

"How many people were in the boats?"

"There were a great many, but for the moment I cannot give you exact figures; neither do I intend to do so. You may have more complete information on the subject at some future time. You must excuse my saying anything further at present."

His Wisdom the Defender

Although their curiosity was whetted by the president's expectations of the speed of the boats, they departed with the feeling that they had been unnecessarily excited by a very slight occurrence.

But the editors saw things in a different light. Thousands of men, many of them youths of respectability, had suddenly disappeared, no one knew how or where. They determined to get information on the subject and to make all the noise about it they could. Here was a chance to have their revenge, and it should not be allowed to pass. The reporters were all ordered to remain in Campbelltown that night, if they had to bivouac on the ground, and to ascertain the names of all the people who had gone on the mysterious expedition.

This work was vigorously begun by the reporters next morning, making a house-to-house canvass, and finding out what occupants had been unaccounted for during the last twenty-four hours, and where they were last seen; and farmers along the shore were interviewed to know if they had seen the boats go down the river—but all to no purpose. The keeper of the lighthouse, about three miles below Campbelltown, reported that he had seen them pass about ten o'clock. This was the last that could be learned of them. Neither of the lighthouse-keepers at Capes Henry or Charles had seen anything of them. Every steamer and vessel which was known to be on the Chesapeake that night or the following day was asked for information. Telegrams were sent to all points

Mystery on Mystery

on the coast. The *Herald* even fitted out a steam-yacht to meet schooners and ascertain if anything had been seen. Not a scrap of information could be gained concerning the fleet after it had passed the lighthouse.

The evening papers, in describing the results of the search, called upon the public for information as to friends and relatives employed at Campbelltown. The result of all these inquiries was made known in time for publication in the next morning's papers. Between two and three thousand people had disappeared from the face of the earth. In all probability the whole fleet of boats, chained together as they were, had sunk, either near the mouth of the Potomac or in Chesapeake Bay, and not a soul had been saved.

Telegrams poured in upon the president by the hundred. Every newspaper in the country called for further information, and some parent or near relative of almost every missing man begged for information as to his fate. The clamor made a public reply absolutely necessary, and the following authoritative statement was telegraphed everywhere:

"There is no reason for solicitude as to the safety of the party which left Campbelltown on Tuesday night. Every possible precaution has been taken to insure the safety of its members. Captain Gheen was ordered to report immediately in the event of any accident, or any failure of the machinery to

His Wisdom the Defender

operate successfully. The boats are practically unsinkable; even in the heaviest storm the only way in which one could be sunk would be by suddenly shipping a sea. If this accident did happen to one, she would be kept up by the others. But the accident itself seems practically impossible. If the expedition was successfully started, there was no expectation of hearing from it for several weeks. Its exact destination was left to the judgment of Captain Gheen; he was, however, to proceed as far north as he conveniently could. There is no probabilty that he would be seen by other vessels; hence no anxiety need be felt because he has not been heard from.

"A. CAMPBELL."

This statement seemed to relieve the fears of those who had friends on the expedition; but it did not relieve the newspapers in the slightest. When the *Herald* yacht failed to get news from passing vessels, people would not believe that the expedition had ever got outside the capes. So tugs were sent to dredge the river and the Chesapeake in all directions below where the boats had last been seen. The absurdity of supposing that two hundred and fifty good-sized vessels, with fifteen hundred men on board, could be sunk in so shallow a sea and not a trace be visible was pointed out by Campbell himself. But the newspapers only denounced him the louder. The whole country resounded with the outcry. Had Congress been in session it would have

Mystery on Mystery

been called upon to institute a rigid investigation. It happened that the Maryland Legislature was in session, and the pressure upon it for action was such that a committee of inquiry was formally ordered in accordance with the following resolution:

"WHEREAS, no less than two hundred and fifty floating vehicles, having on board more than two thousand men, many of them citizens of Maryland, have suddenly disappeared from Peter's Channel in the Potomac River; and

"WHEREAS, the fate of the said men is involved in mystery; therefore be it

"*Resolved*, that a committee of nine members, of whom six shall be representatives and three senators, shall be appointed by the presiding officers of the two Houses, with power to send for persons and papers, and to investigate whither the said boats have gone and what has become of the men in them."

This resolution was adopted with practical unanimity in both Houses.

Without losing a day, the chairman and two members of the committee went to Campbelltown, accompanied by a clerk, to make arrangements for beginning the investigation. They were admitted, shown into the office of the president, and received by the secretary.

"We represent, as you are probably aware, a

committee of the Legislature of Maryland, ordered to investigate the disappearance of a fleet of boats from this place. We should like, first of all, to confer with President Campbell."

"I am sorry to say that the president is not at home. He left town on Thursday evening, and is not expected back until Tuesday next."

"Where has he gone?"

"That I do not know. So far as I am aware, he said nothing to any one about his intended movements."

The chairman looked surprised.

"We have seen no notice of his departure. Does he often go away for five days without leaving any word as to how you are to reach him in case of an emergency?"

"He never did it before; I do not know why he has done it now. You know he does not encourage any inquiry into his affairs on the part of anybody here."

"What train did he take?"

"I have no idea. He simply left his office a little after the usual hour and went towards the Coliseum. That was the last I saw of him."

"I never heard of such a man leaving without his movements getting into the papers, and without any one knowing anything about it. It seems as if our first task will be to investigate *his* disappearance. However, this is Saturday, and we can wait until Monday. Monday morning you may expect

Mystery on Mystery

the entire committee to begin its investigation. We desire to conduct it here because we can so easily examine the officers and employees of the company. Can you place a room at our disposal at nine in the morning?"

"I would not like to promise you a room within the enclosure, but you can doubtless find one outside with great ease. The newspaper men have a building to themselves, as you probably know; perhaps you could get a room there in which to go to work."

The new disappearance was, of course, telegraphed to every city and every newspaper office in the United States. In this way, by Saturday evening, every person in the country was inquiring after the President of the Anita Company, with the hope that whoever might know anything of his whereabouts would speak. But not a word was heard about him.

When the committee reconvened at Campbelltown on Monday morning, the mystery was as great as ever. Before noon the work of the committee had made it yet darker. All the watchmen of the place had been examined to find out at what hour and in what direction the missing man had left. The last person who had seen him was the gate-keeper at the Coliseum. At his usual hour, about sunset, he had left his office and entered the mysterious place. No one had seen him since. Five men were in the enclosure at the time. Neither of them had again been seen.

His Wisdom the Defender

Evidently he must be hiding in the Coliseum. The committee determined to visit the place and conduct their investigations there, if they could secure admittance. The manager acceded to this course, and escorted the committee across the bridge and into the place. They noticed with surprise a number of low but rather large buildings inside, with machinery of all sorts here and there. Of course they were amazed at the sight of the suspended daddies, but no one could tell what they were for. A few workmen were found in several of the shops, but nothing of the missing men. After two hours' search and examination they left as wise as they came.

Determined not to leave until the mystery was solved, they passed the night at what was known as "Newspaper House." Next morning the committee was convened at the usual hour. The secretary was the first witness to be examined:

"I believe you said the president was to be back to-day?"

"Yes; he is now in his office."

"How did he get there? We heard nothing of his return."

"I know nothing about it, sir. All I know is he came in as usual this morning. He said he came from the Coliseum."

"It looks as if he had been hiding there all this time. Did you ever know him to do such a thing before?"

"I cannot say that I did."

Mystery on Mystery

"We must subpœna him immediately."

While the subpœna was being made out the crowd of reporters was more clamorous than ever.

"They are determined to know where you have been and what you have been doing," said the secretary. "Unless we tell them something, I do not know what is to happen."

"Very well. Tell them a rest of a few days from time to time is necessary to keep me from being worn out. So I have been vegetating as far from my usual surroundings as I can well get."

"That will only excite their curiosity the more to know where you were."

"Very well. Tell them I entered the Coliseum Thursday night and came out again Tuesday morning, and that is all I will tell them."

When he appeared in response to the summons he was so cool and unconcerned that the chairman hardly knew how to begin his questions. Had he followed the impulse of the moment, he would have asked him where he had been during the last five days. But a little reflection showed him that this would be an impertinence. So he briefly but formally set forth the object of the committee.

"We were ready to commence our investigations Saturday, but owing to your absence we were obliged to postpone it until yesterday."

He looked for an answer, but none came.

"The committee will now be glad to hear any statement you have to make on the subject before it."

His Wisdom the Defender

"I do not see that I can add anything to what I have already publicly said to correspondents and others. Indeed, the case is so simple that I fail to understand what the committee can expect of me. I authorized Captain Gheen, in charge of the fleet, to make a trial trip whenever he was ready. From his absence I suppose that he has gone on that trip. Until he returns I cannot give you more definite information."

"Why did the fleet leave in the night?"

Counsel whom the witness brought with him objected to this question as irrelevant. The committee was only empowered to inquire where the boats had gone and what had become of the men in them. No authority was given to inquire into reasons. The correctness of this contention had to be admitted, but it made the questioning rather tame. After some consideration the chairman continued:

"These boats were not propelled by steam-power, we believe?"

"No, sir, they were not."

"By what power were they propelled?"

Counsel objected. The committee was not authorized by the resolution to inquire into the methods of propulsion.

This was undeniable, and the question was withdrawn.

"The only objection I have to the question," said Campbell, "is that it is impossible to answer it in an intelligible way. I am free to say that the boats are not propelled by steam-power, but by etherine through the action of therm."

"Etherine? What is etherine, and what is therm?"

"These are terms which I have applied to certain new agencies discovered by me. I mean by etherine a new form of matter having relations to the luminiferous ether, not possessed by any other matter formerly known to men. Therm is an agent somewhat akin to electricity, also discovered by me, and still unknown to the scientific world. By these two agencies I can exercise force and produce motion in ways never before known."

"The committee admits that it has no right, under the powers given by the resolution, to inquire into the conduct of your business. Permit us to say, however, that both the committee and the country would be much gratified if you would explain the reason for the secrecy in which you have enveloped all your operations, including so important a one as sending several thousand men out on a perilous expedition."

Counsel: "My client, of course, understands that this question is quite outside the limits of the investigation. If he chooses to answer it I am not responsible."

Campbell: "I can only answer in a general way by saying that when my reasons are once fully understood I expect them to meet with universal approval. I have no interests in view but those of the

His Wisdom the Defender

world at large. These can best be secured by the policy I have adopted. When the proper time comes I shall have no further secrets, but shall gladly make everything known."

" When will that proper time be ?"

" It will be as soon as I can guard against any misuse of the power I wield. Just when that may be I cannot say, but I hope we shall all live to see the day."

" We understand, then, that in sending Captain Gheen out on this expedition you gave him no precise instructions as to his destination ?"

" I did not absolutely fix any destination for him. He was authorized to go to the north pole if he could."

" What was the object of the expedition ?"

Counsel: " Again I must make the point that the committee is not empowered to inquire into objects, but only into facts."

The question was changed.

" What provision had the party for their comfortable subsistence during their absence ?"

" They were provisioned for three months; it is the utmost limit of absence I expect. If they are not here before the expiration of that time, I shall have everything ready to send another expedition to search for them."

" But if their whereabouts is unknown, how can a search be effected ?"

" All coasts and bays where the expedition is like-

Mystery on Mystery

ly to have landed can be inspected and examined in a very short time."

"If you yourself had a son on this expedition, would you not feel a deep solicitude for his safety?"

"I should feel no other solicitude than that arising from his having gone out on an expedition of a very extraordinary kind, possibly involving unknown perils. So far as any foreseeable accident is concerned, I should feel no great fear. Of course, we are all liable to accident and death at any moment; but I do not think the liability materially greater than it would have been had they stayed at home."

This terminated Campbell's examination. He felt greatly relieved by the contrast between the courtesy and consideration with which it was conducted and the noise which the newspapers were making.

The committee left no stone unturned to gain the information expected of it. Lighthouse-keepers, residents along the coast, captains of vessels, employees of the Anita Company, and reporters were all sent for and examined at length. It was ascertained without doubt that the boats were floating in Peter's Channel on the evening of Tuesday, the 11th; that several thousand men had been sleeping on board them for several nights previous; that on Tuesday night, about nine P.M., they had cast off the ropes which bound them to the shore and moved down the river; that they had been seen to pass the

His Wisdom the Defender

lighthouse. From the time occupied in going down the river and the rate of speed in passing the lighthouse, it had been inferred that they travelled as fast as an ocean steamer. Nothing had happened to the boats within Chesapeake Bay, else the bodies of the men or the wrecks of the boats would have been discovered. It was understood that, under their orders, they had gone to sea and proceeded to the northeast. Nothing more could be learned.

A report to this effect was made on the 22d. Next day the following despatch from St. Johns, Newfoundland, appeared in all the newspapers:

"At five o'clock this evening a small boat was seen oceanward approaching this port at an extraordinary rate of speed. It entered the harbor as fast as a railroad train, dashing the water into foam on both sides. It landed a man at the wharf, who went to the telegraph office to send a despatch, and immediately returned to the boat. The man gave the names of himself and his companion as William H. Robinson and James R. Clay, both being members of the Anita Company's expedition which left Campbelltown for the north nearly two weeks ago. He reported the expedition as having safely effected a landing on the coast of Baffin's Bay, and that all were well on board. A number of letters were brought from members of the expedition for their friends, which were duly posted and will be sent by the next mail. To the great disappointment of the inhabitants the two men resisted all entreaties to re-

Mystery on Mystery

main, sailing away as soon as they had finished their errand, and before the reporters had time to interview them.

"Great curiosity was excited by the movements of their boat, which seemed to float on the water as lightly as a feather. Rapid as were its movements, no mode of propulsion was visible. When at full speed it seemed even lighter than when at rest, merely skimming the water and throwing it up into foam as it went along. It passed the lighthouse on its way out at six o'clock, and twenty minutes later was lost in the distance. Any attempt to follow it would have been useless."

This despatch served to calm the public, but it may be feared that the relief it afforded the newspapers was tinged with a feeling of disappointment that nothing so sensational as the destruction of several thousand men could be reported. They continued their attacks on Campbell with undiminished vigor. Nothing less would satisfy them than the immediate fitting out of a fast steamer which should be sent off to search for the party and report its movements. They knew well that nothing of the sort would be done unless they did it themselves, and they concluded not to try, for the new mystery of Campbell's five days' disappearance gave them ample material for discussion.

VII

And Another for the Duke

THE disappearance at Campbelltown was followed next evening by an equally mysterious appearance at Leghorn, in Italy. About nine o'clock a small steamer entered the harbor of that town and landed a slender, dark-bearded gentleman. Being recognized as belonging to the works on Elba, the customs officers allowed the boat to come in without question. The passenger went rapidly to the railway station and chartered a special train for Pisa, paying a good price in advance. There he passed the night, took the first train in the morning for Florence, and was driven to the Villa Bernaletti.

"There seems to be some comedy of errors about your movements," said the Duke. "I received a telegram from Elba a couple of days ago, telling me that you would be here this morning. But yesterday I read in the *Gazzetta* a long account of the sudden disappearance of a fleet of your boats from the place which bears your name, in which you were repeatedly mentioned as present on the spot. I therefore supposed that the despatch must have been

And Another for the Duke

sent me by error. Will you pardon my curiosity if I ask how these contradictory statements are to be reconciled?"

"I am really afraid to reconcile them, else I should do so with the greatest pleasure. You see me before you ready to take you and such of your family as will accompany me on the visit of inspection which I proposed to you last month. Doubtless that object was duly mentioned in the despatch. We may talk about news blunders some other time."

"We had made all the arrangements for accepting your invitation; but yesterday's news made us suppose that, as a matter of course, you would not be here. Still, I do not think we have made any incompatible engagements. We shall be ready after lunch."

"Your daughter will be of the party, I hope. I think something new to see will be for her benefit."

"After much difficulty I got her consent to accompany us. But how are we to reach your mountain?"

"Very easily. I came in my despatch-boat, which is kept for use between the ports of Elba, and is now waiting for us in the harbor of Leghorn."

The party, consisting of the black-bearded man, the Duke, and his son and daughter, took a special train immediately after lunch, and, passing through Pisa, reached Leghorn before dark and embarked on the boat.

They passed the night at Ferrajo, and the follow-

His Wisdom the Defender

ing morning found them on the way up Mount Campanne, or, as it is now called, Uraniberg, where the two men had driven eighteen months before. The building of the so-called convent was making rapid progress.

"The lady superior of this convent will be a Sister of Mercy to the whole world," said the conductor of the party.

The early evening found them back at Ferrajo, where the great factories were in full operation, doing for Europe what Campbelltown was doing for America. Great was the astonishment of the ducal family when told that their host could not even stop to show them the factories, but must leave immediately. The boat would be at their orders in the morning to take them wherever they wished.

"Will you excuse me if I come and go like a ghost? Be my guests here as long as you choose, but excuse the necessity which I am under of departing this evening."

He took the tug at dusk and disappeared, while his guests wondered what manner of man this was.

When the Duke arrived home with his family the evening following, he at once asked for the numbers of the *Gazzetta* which had arrived during his absence. The first thing that struck his eye was a head-line announcing the mysterious disappearance of the president of the Anita Company. Whether he had wandered away, or had concealed himself in his own

And Another for the Duke

town to evade the committee of investigation, no one could tell. To the outcry consequent upon the disappearance of more than two thousand men was added another about this new mystery. The paper for the next morning announced no really new event. It only described the continuance of the uproar which increased with every hour of the president's absence. Then followed a special evening edition announcing the equally mysterious reappearance. The missing man had quietly walked out of the Coliseum early in the morning as collected as though nothing had happened. He refused to explain his absence to any one.

As we grow old the light in which recent events are seen is not quite so clear as during the prime of life. When the Duke thought of the sudden way in which, if his memory served him aright, he and his family had been whisked away from his home, carried to the top of a mountain, shown through an almost limitless manufacturing establishment, returned to his villa by sea and land, and now found himself reclining on his comfortable sofa as if nothing had happened, it needed some assurance from his family and some examination of his own memory to be sure he had not been dreaming.

"Is it really you who stand before me?" he said to his wife. "I am not dreaming?"

"What a question!"

"You and I and all of us have been on a voyage to Elba, have we not?"

His Wisdom the Defender

"Of course we have. Why do you ask such a question?" She looked alarmed.

"Who took us to Elba?"

"My dear husband, what is the matter with you? If you ask such a question as that I must telephone immediately for our medical man."

"There is not the slightest need of that. I just want to hear you repeat the name of our leader and tell me all about it."

"Why, you must know. It was Professor Campbell."

"The president of the Anita Company?"

"Of course. Who else could it be?"

"Now look at the *Gazzetta,* and you will see why I asked you. President Campbell was reported as at his post in America only last Wednesday morning, and he was there again this morning. Did you not notice something very odd about him while he was travelling with us—as if he were made up of some ethereal substance which might vanish into thin air at any moment? It is true that he made no such impression upon me at the time; but now, when I recall his visit, I cannot help thinking of him as a sort of ghost that had never existed until he reached our house that morning."

"I certainly formed no such impression."

"You recall the sudden and mysterious way in which he took his departure?"

"Yes, very well; it was sudden and mysterious, as you say, but that was all."

And Another for the Duke

"I cannot help feeling that no human being made of ordinary flesh and blood could have departed in such a way. I cannot altogether get rid of the idea that he dissolved into thin air the moment he was out of our sight. How else could he have been in America thirty-six hours later?"

"I shall really be alarmed if you entertain such a notion."

Another question presented itself to the Duke's mind. The student whom he had entertained at his house long ago—the professor who had visited them—the owner of one-half of Elba—the mysterious president of the Anita Company, and his guide of the past three days—were they all one and the same person? If the telegraph was to be believed, they certainly could not be; but who was who? The deference shown his guide at Ferrajo during the whole visit to the works was such that he could not be less than lord and master. So there was nothing to do but wait for light.

Let us now return to the Potomac. During the next weeks the building of the queer boats went on as if nothing had happened. No explanation of the mystery was vouchsafed; the president of the Anita Company answered all inquiries as if he saw nothing unusual to inquire about; reporters searched in vain; editors exhausted themselves in declamation and discussion without reaching any conclusion. Reporters were now freely admitted nearly every day.

His Wisdom the Defender

Occasionally, when some public man or well-known editor paid a visit to the works, Campbell himself would accompany him to show him what was going on and explain the luxury of the future traveller in these new vessels.

Entering a mote and climbing to the upper deck, Campbell would show the visitor how beautifully the light would come through the magnificent arch formed by the upper part of the " ship," and how luxurious all the arrangements for passengers were to be. While this was being set forth at such length the visitor's thoughts were elsewhere.

"But how are you going to propel this vessel through the water?"

"By etherine."

Then the visitor would smile in silence. If he had not known that the boats were actually going in a very mysterious way, he would not have believed. Knowing what he did, he wondered in silence, and left no wiser than he came.

A month had elapsed since the disappearance of the fleet. The press had continued to pour vials of wrath on the report of the Maryland committee as hot as those with which they had been visiting the Anita Company. During this interval the letters which had been mailed at St. John's reached their destination. To the great embarrassment of the reporters there was no indication as to the friends to whom they might be directed. To get hold of them, their only course was to learn the names of

And Another for the Duke

those persons whose relatives at the works were supposed to have gone on the expedition, and to ask them for the letters when they arrived. Several were thus obtained, and, of course, immediately published. They were, however, so tame as to lead to a very strong suspicion of having passed a censorship, a suspicion which our readers will not be slow in believing well-founded. There were glowing accounts of the rapidity with which the voyage had been made and the pleasure attending it. But no events were related. There was nothing about wind or weather. The coast where they landed and the country in the neighborhood were described, but nothing was stated by which the location could be determined. A very interesting experience had been gained, but no one told what that experience was. The really good news, though bad for the newspapers, was that all were well, barring a few accidents to the men arising from the unusual character of the boats in which they sailed. All were happy, but did not know when they should get back to their friends.

The daily visits of the reporters to Campbelltown were almost futile so far as any new results were concerned. Every day the same story: " Nothing more has been heard from the Northern expedition, and nothing is expected to be heard for several weeks to come. If anything is heard you will be duly informed. These queer, cigar-shaped boats are being completed as usual. When they are finished and ready to proceed on a voyage, you will be notified.

His Wisdom the Defender

The veil of secrecy will then be lifted, and you shall see how the boats are propelled."

The next development was the issue of a large, beautifully engraved invitation, to the following effect:

" The Owner of the Motes requests the pleasure of * * * * * * * *company on Tuesday, May 29th, to witness the first public attempt to run the Motes."*

This invitation was sent to the President and the heads of departments, the diplomatic corps, both Houses of Congress, the leading officials at Washington, including the judges of the Supreme Court, and a few officers of high rank in the army and navy. The press came in for a liberal supply, each addressed to the editor of the journal in his official capacity. Presidents and professors in the universities and colleges were remembered.

With each invitation was a card stating that a train would leave Washington for Campbelltown at 2.30 P.M., on the appointed day, and start on its return about seven.

In addition to these general invitations, a select number received invitations to dinner, at 6.30, with the information that the owner of the motes would take advantage of the occasion to make a statement respecting his policy.

There were some half-dozen people whose presence, for various reasons, Campbell especially de-

And Another for the Duke

sired. Among them were Winthrop, the Speaker of the House of Representatives, and the French Ambassador. Fearing that the latter might have some previous engagement, a private note of explanation was sent him in advance, to the effect that the exercises would be of the highest order of interest. The ambassador took the hint and accepted both invitations. The British and German ambassadors both sent regrets. It happened that the former had a ball and the latter a dinner on that very evening. Campbell was not in the least dissatisfied at this, as the presence of the Frenchman and the absence of the other two would serve a purpose in the intricate game he expected to play.

Outside the press, the amount of public curiosity excited was less than would have been expected. The word " mote " had never been publicly used until it was printed in the invitation. People could only guess that it meant the queer, cigar-shaped boats. " Who wants to see a mere attempt? We may as well wait until they run; then we shall see them without doubt." Influenced by such considerations as these, about one-third of the invitees either declined or failed to appear.

The great body of the Angelic Order had gone with the expedition. Some twenty neophytes had been kept at home to take part in the unveiling.

VIII

The Great Unveiling

ON the morning of the great day all was bustle and activity in the works of the Anita Company. The few remaining daddies and centipedes were taken down, supporting ropes were removed, and they were allowed to rest upon the ground. Then, instead of being tied as before to the top of the tower, they were fastened to the ground, as if to prevent them from flying away. When the Seraphim commenced their practice, they were astonished to find that the motes ran just as well without the supporting cords as they had done with them. The difficulty now was to prevent their flying away altogether. When the proper lever was removed, they rose in the air and could be directed at pleasure so far as the tethers by which they were bound would permit. It was a repetition, on a larger scale, of the scene in the uncanny workshop.

Three of the best-trained Seraphs were then taken on board the loomotes, where they were shown how

The Great Unveiling

the mote was to be managed and run. Thus everything was ready for the exhibition before the appointed hour. Trains were kept running all day, and a large body of visitors besides those who had been specially invited availed themselves of the occasion to see the town and, if possible, witness the unveiling of the mystery. When the two trains bearing the invitees arrived, they were shown into the enclosure, where the motes, now two hundred in number, lay.

The regular guests were followed by the crowd of sight-seers, who were freely admitted. All were requested to arrange themselves round the borders of the enclosure.

The gate by which the guests entered was near the middle of the northern wall. About a hundred yards in front of the entrance was a grand-stand, erected for the accommodation of the specially invited guests, the crowd being kept in the rear. As the stand was filled, the scene presented to the eyes of the occupants excited their curiosity to the highest pitch. Immediately in front of them was one of the huge structures we have already described—a cylindrically formed " ship " built of aluminium, 300 feet long in the body, and towering 60 feet above the ground. One end terminated in a hemisphere, the other in a round, blunt projection in the shape of a rifle cannonshot or the end of a cigar. The whole was painted light green. On this background was painted in immense letters the words:

His Wisdom the Defender

"To the ocean now I fly—and the happy climes that lie
  Where day never shuts his eye—up in the broad fields of the sky."

This inscription extended along two-thirds the length of the mote, and might have been read half a mile away. Above everything towered what was evidently the pilot-house, in which could be seen several men, looking for all the world as if they were on ship-board, waiting for the engines to start. And yet, not only was the ship not launched, but there were no visible means of propulsion if she had been. On each side of the pilot-house was painted the name *Hesperus*.

Beyond the *Hesperus* was a sister-mote of the same size, the *Cynthia*. She also had her poetic inscription:

"Nature, that heard such sound, beneath the hollow round
  Of Cynthia's seat the airy region thrilling,
 Now was almost won to think her part was done,
  And that her reign had here its last fulfilling."

To the left of the *Hesperus,* and yet farther from the river, were two motes of somewhat smaller size, which were being fitted up most sumptuously. The nearest bore the name *Concordia* and the inscription:

"Hoch überm niedern Erdenleben soll sie im blauen Himmelszelt
  Die Nachbarin des Donners schweben und grenzen an die Sternenwelt."

The other bore the name *Friede*.

The Great Unveiling

As the guests faced the *Hesperus* the river was on their right. The space between the huge mote and the river had been cleared away, as if to make room for the expected launching. But every appliance for such an operation was wanting. The only noticeable object was a small cannon, pointed towards the river. What could be coming?

To the left, on each of the great motes, were the two hundred or more smaller ones we have described. Individually they looked insignificant alongside their huge neighbors, but collectively excited as much curiosity as the others. What possible object could there be in building so many of these vessels in advance? The name of the nearest one excited special attention. This was the air-tight one we have already described, which now bore on its side the words

THE GOLDEN AGE.

It seemed to the guests that if any of the "boats," as they called them, were worthy of this appellation, it ought to be the largest ones. They changed their minds in less than forty-eight hours.

The attention of Campbell was principally occupied with the *Hesperus*. He stood outside of her, giving directions to and hearing reports from a number of assistants who were continually running in and out of her, and talking with the men in the pilot-house. It was at length noticed that this bustle ceased. The spectators held their breath as they saw the central figure of the whole scene walk slow-

His Wisdom the Defender

ly to the stand, ascend the steps, and take one of the seats which had been reserved for his party in front. On his right sat the French ambassador; on his left President Winthrop and Mr. Justice Geary of the Supreme Court. He first looked intently at the men in the pilot-house, then, rising from his seat, he leaned forward towards the right and made a signal to the man at the gun. The report of the latter was echoed from the sides of the motes.

Immediately a scene was presented to the spectators which made each feel that he must either be dreaming or was being treated to a theatrical exhibition. The mighty *Hesperus,* with its thousand tons of weight, began to move, then rose slowly and majestically in the air to a height of several thousand feet, swung in a vast circle, including half the breadth of the river in its radius, returned to its starting-point, and slowly settled down in its place.

Then, one after the other, three or four of the lesser motes rose in the same way, described a yet wider circle, and returned in like manner.

A herald cried out a request to all the guests who wished to take a sail to enter the *Hesperus* and climb to her upper deck. Campbell entered first, followed by some fifty of the boldest of his visitors. Among the latter was President Winthrop. The opening in the bottom through which they had entered was closed and the word of command was given. In a moment all on board felt themselves in motion, and, looking through the glass sides which enclosed them,

The Great Unveiling

could see the ground about them and the thousands of upturned faces sinking rapidly downward. In three minutes the broad Potomac was below their feet, and a rushing, whizzing sound gradually increased. This was caused by the rapid motion of the mote through the air. Five minutes later the whole breadth of the Chesapeake was spread out to view, as the vessel rushed forward in her swift course of more than two hundred miles an hour. A great swing was made which brought Fortress Monroe in sight. A broad curve was then taken towards the north, and in less than an hour, with the increasing height, Baltimore and Washington were seen through the air.

The emotion felt on board was such that scarcely a word was uttered. The passengers looked on in almost breathless expectancy, not unmingled with apprehension.

When the mote returned and was safely landed, Campbell and Winthrop approached each other. Both recalled a conversation they had held four years before. Campbell spoke first:

"Do you remember what I said to you at that interview when I asked leave of absence from my professional duties?"

"Yes, I have never forgotten it."

"I have often been curious to know what you thought of my remark at the time."

"I was simply perplexed beyond measure, and had serious fears for your mental condition. Not

His Wisdom the Defender

before you began to astonish the world by your inventions was my uneasiness removed. Now it looks to me as if you might very well claim that this is the greatest day in the history of the world."

"Perhaps it is the greatest day the world has yet seen, but I hope for a yet greater one hereafter."

A crowd had gathered round, listening with intense interest to the conversation. "Excuse us a moment," said Campbell, "I wish to say a word in private to Winthrop. Come with me." Then, when they had retired into a corner:

"This is only the beginning, and is not the day I had in mind when I spoke. The greatest day in the history of the world, if I can bring it about, will be that when war shall have ceased forever, armies and navies exist no longer, and universal peace reign over all the nations. Not till then will all my hopes be fulfilled."

"That looks hopeless, and yet I must admit that if any man can bring it about it's you."

"Be sure you do not drop a whisper about it to any one; but I mean to bring it about."

The dining-table was spread in the Coliseum, in the north end of which had been erected a large banqueting-hall.

After the table was cleared Campbell made an address, which is of such historic importance that we shall reproduce its main features:

"FRIENDS AND FELLOW-CITIZENS, — I do not

The Great Unveiling

think you will look for any apology from me for making some remarks on what you have to-day seen. Many questions must be presenting themselves to your minds. I fancy that one of the foremost of these questions is why I have proceeded so secretly in the work of perfecting the application of certain forces of nature, the result of which you have seen before you to-day. This question will be answered when I set forth to you the state of things as it has presented itself to my mind.

"It is now a little more than four years since I found myself in possession of a natural agent of which man had never before suspected the existence, an agent by using which, instead of being confined to the earth as heretofore, he could fly from continent to continent with a speed which the wildest imagination of the poet never conceived. The inauguration of the golden age seemed quite within my power. No part of the earth would hereafter be difficult of access. Men could fly above the air and, in the pure ether, make the circuit of the earth with almost astronomic speed.

"As a scientific investigator, the main object of whose life had been to benefit his fellows, my first impulse was to make known my discovery to the world and invite all men to share in its beneficent results. But a little consideration showed that this course would be productive, for a long time to come, of irreparable disaster. A situation would at once be created with which the laws and customs of

His Wisdom the Defender

men would not enable them to cope. Universal confusion would have followed the demonstration of my discovery. I can hardly describe to you in detail what would have happened. First of all, it is clear enough that the stocks and bonds of all existing railway and transportation companies would, at a single stroke, have become nearly worthless, were the building of the new vehicles allowed to go on as rapidly as enterprise could produce them. A year or two only would be necessary to do away with railways, unless for local transportation, and steamships would have ceased to run within another year. The fall in railway stocks would have produced a universal panic and a corresponding fall in almost every other form of investment securities. Universal bankruptcy, with all the calamities attending upon it, would have been the immediate result. Almost every form of industry would have been stricken as by a paralysis. Widespread starvation among the masses, now deprived of employment, could have been averted only by an almost universal system of gratuitous distribution of food and other supplies. The work of recovering from the cataclysm would have been that of making a new world.

"Must I then abandon the project of doing to my fellow-men a great good, because they would convert it into a great evil? Must the secret be allowed to die with me, perhaps to be revived in some future generation? After a long and careful reflection it became evident to me that if I could retain

The Great Unveiling

in my own hands the power to guide the revolution, I could bring about all its benefits without its attendant evils. To do this my power must be absolute. To gain absolute power I must acquire the means of carrying on my enterprise before the public should be made acquainted with its nature. Had it been known when I founded this town four years ago that I was building vehicles which would do away with railways and steamships, the whole country would have been thrown into a panic. The pressure on me and the crowd around me would have been such that it would have been impossible for me to go on with the work in the quiet and systematic way which was necessary to success. I must, therefore, whenever my object became public, be able to say to my fellow-men, see what I can do for you, but do not crowd upon me to seize what I have got, and thus bring disaster upon your fellows.

"The key-stone of my policy is that the power of the flying motes, which has been exhibited to you today, shall be used solely for the benefit of the entire human race. From this day forward no person, not even myself, shall derive any emoluments from it except those to which they shall be entitled as compensation for services rendered.

* * * * * * *

"I propose to call the vehicles which you have today seen running through the air by the general name of *motes*. It is brief and significant, and will not fail to strike you favorably. The motes, so far

His Wisdom the Defender

as I have yet built and projected them, are of three kinds. I propose to call them loomotes, weemotes, and himotes. These little syllables are short and easily distinguished. The loomotes are the largest of the kind. The *Cynthia* and the *Hesperus,* on the last named of which many of you to-day have made a wide circuit, are examples. They are several hundred feet in length, and so fitted up that passengers may easily eat and sleep during their journey, as they do on steamships."

We spare our readers his description of the weemotes and himotes, with which they are so familiar.

"The radical change which the running of the motes will make in the relations of nations cannot avoid having its political side, which must be taken account of in framing all plans. I propose as soon as possible to send a mission, in one of the smaller loomotes, to each of the principal European capitals. I desire that this mission shall invite one or more leading publicists in each country to a general conference with me at the earliest possible date. Perhaps this conference may assume a certain permanence in its deliberations. Its main purpose will be to advise me as to the political effects of the mote service. I cannot at the present time go far in anticipating the conclusions of these deliberations. One conclusion, however, seems clear: the mote service should be able to assume a position of political in-

The Great Unveiling

dependence, so far at least as the international service is concerned. This end must be kept in view from the beginning.

"Whether this end be gained or not, it seems desirable that the supreme authority in directing the policy of the motes should have a special title. I propose that 'Owner of the Motes' shall be that title, until a better one is devised.

"I now wish to read one general regulation which I have established for the special benefit of the gentlemen of the press, with whom I desire to hold the most friendly relations. The profession of journalism is a trying one, in that it is necessary to publish every piece of news as soon as possible, which frequently makes errors unavoidable. It is embarrassing to have such errors speedily pointed out by those in authority. To guard against this the rule I have made is as follows:

"'Neither the Owner of the Motes nor any one connected with their management shall contradict any false report that may be published respecting the views or proceedings of those in charge of the mote service.'"

After reading this he hesitated a moment, and, for the first time in the course of the day, a humorous smile began to spread over his features.

"I notice," he said, "that there is a curious feature about this order. It forbids the contradiction of a false report, but does not forbid the contradic-

His Wisdom the Defender

tion of a true one. The inevitable conclusion is that, in case any report is contradicted, that very fact will give evidence of its truth. It is no doubt a pity that the order is so worded as to make this possible, but the difficulty may be avoided by simply not contradicting any report whatever. I am sure such a policy will relieve our journals of all embarrassment."

It is questionable whether even the red-headed man saw how astutely this order was contrived. The pleasure of publishing authoritative confirmations and contradictions could never be enjoyed so long as the order was enforced. The public would have to take what the newspapers said with just as many grains of salt as it thought proper.

Our readers will not fail to note that in all this address the uppermost thought in Campbell's mind was evaded. This was the relation of the motes to warfare. He judged it best not to let the public know that he had this aspect of the case in mind until it had at least seen the importance of the problem by itself. His solution, as our readers have already seen, was completely worked out, but he wanted to see what conclusions the world would reach on the subject by its own motion.

After thanking the guests for their attention, Campbell invited them to follow him to a scene very different in its character to that which they had witnessed, but which he hoped they would not consider inappropriate. As they left the structure in

The Great Unveiling

which the banquet had been held they saw in the starlight an immense curtain spread before them, through the folds of which glimmered what looked like moonlight, though there was no moon in the sky. As their leader approached, the curtain opened and exposed what seemed to be a Grecian temple. Its end was turned towards them, and its pediment was supported by a row of Corinthian columns. It was built entirely of phosphorescent ware, and was seen only by its own glow, which gave it the appearance of masses of transparent alabaster illuminated through their whole interior. Its walls seemed higher than the Coliseum in which it was built, and the surrounding gloom was made impressive by the soft light which it shed. The steps and the floor were of wood, and therefore dark—else the guests would have hardly dared to mount them. Entering, the shining walls on each side, strengthened by rows of pilasters, seemed to extend more than a hundred yards, and to be a hundred feet in height. These dimensions were partly the result of a cunningly devised illusion in perspective. The light shed from all sides illuminated the whole interior without casting a shadow. Looking up, it was seen that there was no roof, and the sky, with the few stars whose light was not extinguished by that of the walls, added to the impressiveness of the scene. On each side were rows of seats, which the company were invited to occupy.

Presently strains of sacred music were heard, though no organ was in sight. Commencing as if at

His Wisdom the Defender

a great distance, its tones grew louder and louder. Then, above the farther end of the temple, was seen approaching in the air a crowd of beings attired as angels in robes, which seemed to shine even brighter than the walls of the temple. Soon the great song of praise was heard, sung by the whole chorus of Seraphim and their companions in the language in which the largest part of the Christian Church has listened to it for centuries:

" Te Deum laudamus, te Dominum confitemur,
Te æternum Patrem omnis terra veneratur."

The song of thanksgiving concluded, Campbell took leave of his guests, after inviting four of them to accompany him to his private office.

" Never in my life have I seen anything so impressive," said Winthrop. " It makes me feel as if all things sublunary were, for the time at least, unworthy to occupy our thoughts. And yet you have given us more to think about than the world ever gave before. That is, if I am not dreaming. I cannot feel quite sure that I am not, for the dreamer is often sure that he is awake."

" Let us dream on, then; I would feel as you do if I had not had this picture before my mind for years. Now let me tell you something. I want you to be nearest to me for some time to come; perhaps for good. And yet, I do not dare to tell you all that I have in mind. You perceive what a terrible responsibility rests upon me in so conducting

The Great Unveiling

this enterprise that the ends I have in view shall be reached."

Then, turning to the others:

"I desire to have your frank opinions from time to time, either individually or collectively. I desire your help in getting the best men for each high and responsible station that has to be filled. In the case of the highest positions the responsibility will be too great for the place to be sought after and the honor too great for it to be declined.

"I am not sure that you fully appreciate the gravity of the situation which has been created. In my speech I have purposely omitted the main point, because I considered it best to say nothing about it until the public should see and inquire for itself. It is evident enough that the first power which can get possession of a fleet of motes can land an army in its neighbor's capital, take possession of its government, devastate its cities with dynamite, blow up its fortifications, and do anything it pleases. It can make itself master of the world. The turmoil which the mad rush for money will make will be of small importance alongside the public danger from the use of the motes as instruments of conquest.

"What is my duty in this conjuncture? I feel myself responsible to God and man for taking such measures that the power I have created shall be used for good and not for evil. What must I do to secure this end? On this matter I want the advice both of yourselves and of the wisest men of the world.

His Wisdom the Defender

My own opinion I will state only in a general way. Every consideration forces me to the conclusion that the more aggressive my policy, and the more fearless my determination, so long as I keep within the bounds of law, the better it will be for humanity. And when I say the bounds of law I do not mean the law of the past, but the law that must govern the future.

"I have spoken of the mission which I propose to send immediately to the leading capitals of the world. I wish President Winthrop to be the leader in this mission. I regard this duty as coming into the category of those I have described which are neither to be sought nor declined. President Winthrop, do you accept this view?"

Winthrop asked for time to think over the matter. No one knew what a day might bring forth.

Campbell resumed:

"My policy, whatever it may be, must be pursued unflinchingly to the end. I want you to sustain me in this, and not to let me give way at a critical moment. One last word. It is necessary that the dignity of my position as the leader in this enterprise shall be sustained. I trust that you will do what you can to assert it.

"Please keep within call. Perhaps you did not notice out there in the field a few motes smaller than the others, and shaped quite differently. These I call 'messenger motes.' They are intended for the rapid conveyance of envoys or of despatches from

The Great Unveiling

one point to another; hence their name. One of these will be at the service of each of you from and after to-morrow. By their aid you can go where you please and confer with whom you think proper. I ask you to be my guests for to-night. In the morning, after breakfast, your motes will be at your disposal."

IX

A Voyage Through Space

AMONG the Seraphim, one who had especially attracted Campbell's attention by his coolness, nerve, and silence was the since famous Captain Rogers. He had therefore been selected to run the *Hesperus* on the day of the unveiling, and was to take the *Golden Age,* the first of the himotes, on her trial trip next morning. This venture gave Campbell more real anxiety than the short trips of the *Hesperus,* because his experiments had already demonstrated what the latter could do, while the possibilities of the himote were still untried. Nothing less was projected than sending the *Golden Age* round the world above the atmosphere. So daring a conception, and one fraught with such possibilities, might well appall even the courageous author. No human being had ever mounted more than four or five miles above the earth's surface, not only from the impossibility of the ascent, but because the air got too rare to breathe. How could men ascend entirely above the air—into the celestial spaces, in fact—by the newly discovered force? Only one way

A Voyage Through Space

was possible. They must be hermetically sealed inside an air-tight tube, and carry the air to breathe with them. The contrivances for enabling them to determine their height and position, guide and direct the mote, purify the small supply of air at their disposal, and guard against the dangers they might incur during their flight through the celestial spaces had long occupied an important part of Campbell's attention.

It was a prime condition with him that the first experiments in so perilous an enterprise must be made by men who had no near relatives. Another was that no one should be allowed to go who did not volunteer to do so after fully understanding the possibilities of the case. Rogers, having, in his own words, " neither parents, wife, chick, nor child," was quite ready to be one of a party who could always thereafter say

> "We were the first that ever burst
> Into that silent sea"

of the celestial spaces. With the knowledge only of his chief, he had, on several previous nights, risen from the Coliseum in the *Golden Age* to a height, first of fifty, and then of a hundred miles, in order to insure that all the contrivances were in proper working order. Being satisfied on this point, he was eager to make the trip.

With no resistance from the air, there was no limit to the possible speed of travel except that set

His Wisdom the Defender

by the limit to which the etherine within the tubes of the mote might be thermalized. The energy from five hundred tons of coal had been infused into the etherine, and this, Campbell had calculated, would suffice not only to carry the mote to a height of a hundred miles or more but to set it flying with a speed of at least two miles a second. But he warned his captain against attempting any such speed at first; he must find, by careful watching, what effects might be produced by the speed. Even the thinnest air would speedily burn the hardest body passing through it at such a rate.

Rogers had two companions to go with him. The duties of all three men were strictly defined. The captain was to occupy himself principally with the levers by which the vibrations of the etherine were directed and controlled, and thus guide the mote and fix her speed.

A second, called the "Sounder," was to occupy himself with the optical instrument by which the height of the mote above the earth's surface at any moment could be ascertained. This consisted mainly of a slender telescope which passed through a vertical tube and through a small round opening in the bottom of the mote. At the bottom of the telescope were two reflectors so arranged that, when the mote was high above the earth, the man at the telescope could see a portion of the horizon on each side in his field of view, and, by the angle between them, determine the height. All the fittings of the tele-

A Voyage Through Space

scope and of the tube in which it slid had to be airtight, so that no air could escape from the mote through them. The upper parts of the tube and telescope were contained in a vertical case, about six inches square, which rose from the floor, to which it was fastened. In front of it was a seat for the observer, who sat with the case between his knees, and his body bent forward, so that he could look vertically downward into the telescope. He was not to leave his seat while the mote was in rapid motion, except in an emergency, but was continually to report to the captain the varying height.

The third man was to keep a lookout generally, especially at and through the glasses which closed the port-holes, and at the barometers which indicated the internal and external air-pressure. He was to watch the air-blowers, to see that they kept the air passing through the sulphuric-acid tubes, and regulate the flow from the tubes of compressed oxygen, by which that element was added to the air so as to keep pace with its exhaustion by the breathing of the party. In case of the fracture of a window, or any leak of the air, he was instantly to spring at the point and cover the leak with the nearest cushion.

A bundle of New York papers was taken on board, to be thrown out when over some of the great cities, especially London. Rogers was apprised that it would be of no use, even were it practicable, to do this at the greatest heights, because the velocity acquired by the papers in falling through the vacuum

His Wisdom the Defender

would be such that they would take fire on reaching the thinnest air, and never reach the ground.

Next morning it was after sunrise when Campbell, two laborers, and the three ambitious voyagers met at the entrance of the *Golden Age*. There was a warm shaking of hands. The chief was so affected by his emotions that he embraced the captain before parting with him. Then, one after the other, the three men lay themselves inside the entering-tubes and were pushed into the mote by the two workmen. The door closed after them, shutting them out of all communication with the world of men. A few moments of breathless suspense, and the mote rose from its supports; then, when all was clear, darted forward and upward. In five minutes it was a black speck high up in the blue sky to the southeast. This speck grew smaller and grayer every moment till it vanished from sight. Then Campbell slowly walked to his home to hear what the world had to say.

The sailing orders of the *Golden Age* were that if everything went right she should make first for the Cape of Good Hope and land there in order to make a careful examination to see if she had suffered from the effect of her voyage. What to be done next was left mostly to the judgment of the captain. He could go around the world if he chose, but was warned not to go far into the shadow of the earth, but keep within sunshine, lest the intense cold of the celestial spaces might injuriously affect the walls

A Voyage Through Space

of the mote. Let us accompany the party and share its experiences.

For twenty minutes hardly a word was spoken. Then the sounder, looking up from his instrument, made his first announcement:

"Fifteen miles high!"

"How dark the sky is getting!" said the lookout.

In fact, the windows on the right-hand side were rapidly growing darker, as if night were coming on. On the left the sun shone through the openings with a strange tinge, its rays seeming hardly to illuminate anything on their passage, but, falling on the walls of the other side, made a long row of bright bluish circles.

In front of the captain was a white circular disk, about a foot in diameter, something like a large aneroid barometer. Figures went round its circumference — 0, 5, 10, 15, 20, etc., up to 150. Through the centre passed a pointer, which, at the start, marked 0. This was part of a contrivance so connected with the etherine as to show the speed of the mote in miles a minute. When the sounder called out fifteen miles high, the pointer had got more than half-way from 0 to 5, and was making visible progress towards the latter figure every minute.

The rush of the mote through the air could be heard. The sound increased to that of a strong gale, then slowly changed to the roar of Niagara.

"Twenty miles!" said the sounder. The pointer

His Wisdom the Defender

was nearly at 5. The roar was diminished in volume, but taking a higher key-note.

"Twenty-five miles!"

"I see the stars," said the lookout. "The sky is as black as night."

But the row of circles made by the shining sun still illuminated the interior, so that they could see as if by a row of electric lights. The roar of the cataract was rapidly changing to the base note of an organ-pipe. Soon the pointer had passed 5 and was hopefully on its way towards 10.

Up to the present time the mote kept the same inclination with which it was started—that is, its prow was so much higher than the stern that to go towards it was like climbing a steep hill. One had to hold on to the seats on each side. The object of this inclination was that her motion through the air might be end on, so that the resistance should be the least possible. Now the air had got so thin that its resistance was of little account. So Rogers called on the lookout to come and help him operate the machinery by which the mote was to be brought to a horizontal position. This was worked by a double crank, of which both men took hold. Two minutes' pretty hard turning of the crank brought the mote into the required position, so that one could walk on a level from end to end.

"Thirty miles!"

The voice of the sounder had a metallic sound, as though coming from a throat of brass. The tone of

A Voyage Through Space

the organ was changing to a musical note of a high pitch, growing higher and yet feebler every moment.

Rogers went to the nearest window, put his face close to the glass, and peered out. The sky was blacker than night, and, though the sun was shining brighter than ever, the constellations all sparkled as he had never seen them sparkle before. The number of the stars seemed countless. The horizon was not that of the sea; it was a foggy white border to a sky below. For now there did seem to be a sky below. It was of a dark blue, almost black tint, over which, scattered here and there, were bright clouds, thirty or forty miles below, and increasing their distance every moment. This blue-black sky was the Atlantic Ocean. Some bright patches near the horizon, less bright, however, than the clouds, were the Bermuda Islands.

"Forty miles!"

Notwithstanding that the pointer was now well past 10 and still advancing, the sound of passing through the air had completely died away, and a silence the like of which man had never before known took its place. By each of the voyagers, not only the beating of his heart, but the pulsations of the blood through his arteries, its coursing through the veins of his head, the contraction and expansion of his chest, the inspiration and expiration of air from his lungs, were all heard with startling distinctness. They dared not speak much above whispers, for when they did the brazen ring of their

His Wisdom the Defender

throats was frightful. The sky was black as ink, and the illuminated circles of the sunshine filled the interior of the mote with a light so blue that their faces looked to one another like those of corpses. A superstitious dread nearly overcame the sounder and the lookout; and the captain, to whom, as a trained physicist, the reason of the singular phenomena was clear, required all his nerve to keep up. They were now, to all appearance, above the atmosphere, with nothing about them but the pure ether of infinite space.

"Fifty miles!"

"We must be completely above the upper limit of the atmosphere," said Rogers. "I think it will be safe to put on speed."

And they were already going fifteen miles a minute, leaving a mile behind them every four beats of the clock! There seemed to be two men within the captain, of very different sentiments. One was filled with speechless dread at the awful situation in which they were placed, and the yet more awful one into which they were running. The other was cool, collected, and fearless, so much the stronger of the two that he had his frightened companion completely at his mercy. The strong man reached for a lever which had been set and clamped when first they started, and had remained untouched. He unclamped it, slowly turned it, and again clamped it. All felt the mote spring forward like a fiery horse when his driver has touched him with a whip. Then

A Voyage Through Space

a singular change was felt. The prow seemed to have risen up into the same position as when they started. All had to hold on to keep from falling down into the stern. Rogers looked through the window. The horizon, now nearly a thousand miles away, had in appearance the same inclination as the mote. The earth and the ocean far below were tipped up as if by some cosmic convulsion.

The explanation was evident to his trained mind in a moment. The speed of the mote was being constantly accelerated; and this had a tendency to force everything towards the stern, and thus change the apparent direction of gravity. He called to the lookout to come again to the crank. A few more turns brought the mote once more into what seemed a horizontal position, though, in reality, the stern was now higher than the prow.

"Seventy miles!"

"I shall keep her at about that height," said the captain. "Let me know when she deviates." He took hold of a lever which regulated the height, and set it at 0.

Now for fifteen minutes they seemed immovable. Not a quiver was felt. And yet the magic pointer was seen slowly creeping round. It passed 20, then 30, more than keeping pace with the passing minutes. 90 was at length passed, 100 would soon be reached. The captain felt that the speed had reached if not passed the prudent limit, so he again unclamped the speed lever and set it at 0.

His Wisdom the Defender

There was again a shock, but this time in the reverse direction. The mote seemed to jump backward, and her prow to fall with a suddenness that alarmed them all. In fact, the prow had really been down all the time, but they only felt it when the elevation ceased to increase and the speed became uniform. The two men again turned the crank, now in the reverse direction, and the mote was again brought into a horizontal position.

So complete became the stillness that all motion seemed to have ceased. The men felt as if afloat in the ether. But when they watched the clouds and ocean seventy miles below, the latter seemed to be slowly moving under them, passing behind, and disappearing one by one at the horizon. More than an hour passed thus. A gray streak was seen coming out of the horizon ahead. It was the island of St. Helena.

" Sixty-five miles!" said the sounder. " We seem to be getting lower."

A squad of soldiers at St. Helena noticed one of their number looking up at the sky.

" What are you gazing at ?"

" In the name of all that's holy, what's that up there ?"

A sergeant, more intelligent than the rest, saw the men gazing, and looked up also.

" I'm blessed if there's not a comet—in broad daylight, too! Did you ever hear of such a thing ?"

A Voyage Through Space

Soon the whole garrison, commissioned officers included, were gazing at the strange sight.

"It must be moving," said the sergeant. "When I first saw it it was right over Simmons's Rocks. Now it's over the guard-house."

He was right. It seemed to keep slowly on, then grow smaller, and finally disappear from view entirely. One of the officers proceeded immediately to write an account of this strange comet or meteor —he could not tell which—and send it to a scientific journal. But he did not know that there were three human beings inside the comet. He could only tell how it was first seen in the southwest, almost forty-five degrees above the horizon, and had a tail half a degree long. Indeed, this tail was all that was visible. It moved slowly towards the south, increasing its altitude, and in five or ten minutes faded away from view.

Let us return to the men inside the mote. When the captain heard the announcement, "Sixty-five miles," he gently drew down the elevating lever to check the fall. The lookout happened, while this was being done, to be gazing out of the stern window.

"We are getting down towards sixty," said the sounder.

The captain drew the lever yet farther down, and clamped it. As he did so the lookout exclaimed:

"Do come here! What does this mean?"

"What is it?" said the captain, as he hurried aft.

His Wisdom the Defender

"A big ball of light as big round as the mote itself."

The captain peered anxiously through the window. Sure enough, there was a round sheet of yellow light, quite bright at the centre. The cause was evident in a moment. The atmosphere, which he had been taught extended only to a height of forty-five miles, must really be much higher—over sixty miles. Darting through it at the rate of a hundred miles a minute, rare though it was, it was burning off the material of the mote, which was being left behind in the form of a long flame. This flame he saw end on, so that it looked like a round sheet of light. It was bright in the central part, because there he saw the light through its whole length, which might be several furlongs. In a word, the frail vehicle which contained them was a shooting-star!

Such a consciousness, in connection with the general situation, might have paralyzed the faculties of an ordinary man. But, fortunately, Rogers was not an ordinary man. He jumped like a tiger over the space that separated him from his station and pulled the elevating lever to its lowest limit. They felt the mote take an upward bound; in two or three minutes the sounder called "Sixty-five miles," then "Seventy" and "Seventy-five." Before this the flame had disappeared, and probably the danger was past. But there was still room for anxiety. How much of the walls of the mote had been burned away, it was

A Voyage Through Space

impossible to conjecture until a landing should be effected. Worse yet, who knew but the burning might still be going on, but too slowly to be perceived? Not till one hundred miles was announced did he dare to stop the upward flight.

After a half-hour of suspense the coast of South Africa was seen rising out of the horizon. The speed was gently slackened, and the mote at length brought to rest at a point, as near as could be judged, above Cape Town.

Now came the greatest trial of the nerves, the fall through the eighty miles which separated them from the earth. True, the arrangements for commanding the motion were so carefully devised that there was no real danger. But who could feel safe when falling, falling, mile after mile? Whatever the feeling, it had to be done. The elevating lever was raised, and all felt the floor falling from under them. The sensation of falling continued, whereas in the previous experiences there was no sensation of motion except for a few moments at a time after a sudden adjustment of some lever. Now, however, the continuance of the sensation produced an attack of nausea, quite like that which our ancestors had to suffer in crossing the ocean, and which they therefore called "sea-sickness." Rogers returned the lever to the zero point when a minute had elapsed, but the stomach of the lookout went through a gymnastic performance of a very disagreeable kind. Although the falling sensation now disappeared, they

His Wisdom the Defender

were really approaching the earth at the rate of a thousand feet a second, and the sounder went through his calls, " Sixty-five miles," " Sixty miles," and so on, in regular succession.

" Forty miles," said the sounder.

Now a gentle wind began to be heard. It was caused by the rush through the air. The lever was depressed in order to diminish the speed of the drop. The effect was to make them feel as if a sudden addition of thirty pounds had been made to their weight, and to bring on a return of the nausea. But the lever was turned back a little by the watchful captain as he saw that the speed of the drop had been brought within a safe limit.

But how was he to know how heavily he might strike the earth so long as he was hermetically sealed in the mote? On each side of the latter, below one of the windows, a small tube projected, through which a little air-vane could be pushed. A simple contrivance enabled the speed of the fall to be seen at any moment by the motion of this vane.

In due time the mote touched ground at a point just east of the limits of Cape Town. Then, for the first time since he started, it occurred to the captain to note the time by the chronometer that had been ticking alongside of his station during the entire journey. It read 9.50. He had arisen from the ground at 6.45. The entire journey had therefore occupied little over three hours.

The uppermost question now in his mind was how

A Voyage Through Space

much the mote had suffered during the few minutes that it had been playing the part of a meteor. The exit was opened. He got into the sliding-tube, was pushed out, and, springing to his feet, began inspecting the mote, heedless of the crowd that was gathering around. At the first glance he was thunderstruck. She was white when they started; now she was black as coal from end to end, except on the hemispherical stern. Not only had the paint been completely swept or burned away, but the wooden casing beneath it was charred over its whole surface. On scraping the surface it was found that the charring was less than an eighth of an inch deep, even around the bow, which must have suffered most. Below this the oak casing, an inch thick, was quite intact, and as hard as ever.

Relieved by this discovery the captain consulted with his two assistants as to what had better be done.

"Count me out, whatever you do," said the sounder, who had borne what was really the most trying duty of the three, that of sitting constantly at his post while the most exciting experiences were going on. "The mote may rest here and rot, so far as I am concerned. I am going back by the ocean, even if it takes a month."

The captain proposed that, before reaching a decision, they should lunch. They had only taken a bite since starting, and their minds had been so much occupied during the passage that the wants of their stomachs had been unfelt. There was a supply

His Wisdom the Defender

of food and drink in the mote, but it seemed best to leave this intact, and go to the nearest restaurant for breakfast. His two assistants went first, guided by the crowd, while he kept guard over the *Golden Age,* now minus its name, during their absence. They were asked to send him a pot of coffee and lunch from the restaurant.

I need not describe the scenes around him while he was waiting. He had, of course, to talk with reporters the whole time. He had humor enough in his composition to talk of his journey as if it were a very commonplace affair, and to affect wonder at their interest in it. He talked of sixty, seventy, or ninety miles a minute, much as a railway engineer of the time would have talked of sixty, seventy, or ninety miles an hour. Only one little word was changed; why wonder so? As he was taking his coffee, which he did astride of the entering-tube, with a plank thrown across it as a table, his humor and his inability to see why his arrival caused so much interest and commotion both increased. To questions what he would do and where he would go next, he replied that he must get home to dinner. "My wife" (an imaginary quantity, as our readers know) "is very precise in her household arrangements and always complains if I am late to meals. However" (looking at his watch), "it is hardly eleven o'clock by our time, and I intend to take a spin round the south pole on my way home. If I then find that I have time, I shall also take a look at the

A Voyage Through Space

Pacific Ocean, and make a little run over the north pole during the afternoon. I would return by way of Australia and China; but just now it is night in China, and we should suffer from the cold."

"But you don't mean that you can visit both poles the same day, or reach China before the sun rises there?"

"Why not? I can go where I please as long as I am back to dinner. You have learned geography, and know that it is only twenty-five thousand miles round the world. Running one hundred and twenty-five miles a minute, you can soon cipher out that I have plenty of time to get round the world, and wash and dress before six o'clock."

All this talk was recorded by nimble pencils as it advanced, and immediately cabled to the leading journals of the world, with results that we shall see in the next chapter.

A good breakfast and a sight of the wondering crowd, which now included almost every inhabitant of Cape Town old enough to walk and well enough to leave his bed, had a wonderful effect on the sounder. He had heard some of the captain's talk, and felt ashamed that he should have to say, "We cannot move, after all, because one of my assistants is afraid to return." So he agreed to try again, if only he could be relieved by the lookout during a part of the run—change places with him, in fact, from time to time. As Campbell had taken the precaution to have each of the three men trained in the duties

His Wisdom the Defender

of the two others, so that the mote would not be crippled by any disability of either during the run, the proposed arrangement was readily acceded to by the captain.

The latter had telegraphed his arrival to the Owner as soon as possible after landing, and now made preparations for continuing his journey. We spare our readers the details of the start. The curiosity with which the crowd watched the three men as they lay down one by one in the entering-tube and were pushed or drawn in by the others, their amazement when they saw the forward end of the huge vehicle raise itself up as if alive and turn round so as to point towards the south, and their bewilderment when it darted away, all go without saying. It was now by the local time four P.M., though the chronometer in the mote only marked eleven.

The experiences of the voyagers were, for the most part, so like those of the outward journey that we need not detail them. Extracts from the captain's log, which he now kept and embodied in his report, will show the salient features of the trip:

11.30.—Height, twenty miles. Speed, moderate.

11.40.—Height, forty miles. Begin to put on speed.

12.—Height, one hundred miles. Have driven speed nearly up to its limit—one hundred and twenty-five miles a minute. Deem this quite safe so long as the height is maintained. Keep up a good lookout for any sign of meteoric combustion.

A Voyage Through Space

12.5.—A bright line of white on the south horizon. The Antarctic ice.

12.15.—All below is dark. The sun is shining on the horizon only. Curving course as fast as possible for speedy return to sunlight after passing pole. Continuous observations of zenith tube kept up.

12.18.—Passing south pole; height one hundred and ten miles; speed one hundred and twenty-two. All is now darkness, except an illumination of the horizon in the direction where the sun has set. Direction of passage, from meridian 10 degrees east of Greenwich to 170 degrees west. Course still curving, so as to reach 160th meridian, where sunlight will be reached.

12.22.—Sun rising, but all is darkness above and below. Now curving course towards the west, so as to run as nearly as possible on the 160th meridian.

12.40.—A curious spectacle. On the left all is darkness; on the right the clouds below are brightly illuminated by the sun. They almost cover the ocean, which can be seen only in black patches. The silence is complete and awful. The mote runs itself, except as the elevating lever has to be touched from time to time to regulate her height. Do not deem it safe to fall below one hundred miles.

12.50.—Clouds below getting thinner, so that the dark ocean is seen between them.

1.30.—The Sandwich Islands are sighted by the lookout. Must curve towards west, so as to take an

His Wisdom the Defender

S-shaped course to the north pole, and not get into darkness after passing it.

1.50.—Passed the Aleutian Islands and Bering Strait.

2.7.—Passed over the north pole, now running on a meridian 15 degrees east.

2.25.—Over the Baltic Sea. Slowing down and making a sharp curve to west to pass over London.

2.36.—Speed, eighty; height, one hundred and five.

2.45.—Speed, thirty; height, seventy.

2.50.—Speed, twenty; height, forty.

3.—Speed, twelve; height, thirty.

Getting dark; twilight below; England in sight. Preparing to throw out papers.

3.10.—During the last five minutes supposed to be passing over London; throwing out papers; cost some air; barometer reduced two inches, one inch of which will be made up by oxygen from tubes. Shall now start on the home stretch.

3.25.—Height, thirty-five; speed, twenty.

3.50.—Height, ninety-five; speed, ninety. Ireland seen far behind in the light of the setting sun.

3.53.—Losing sight of Ireland.

4.10.—Lookout reports patch of land ahead—Newfoundland.

4.30.—Over the Nova Scotia coast, Massachusetts Bay coming into sight. Put on the speed-break with as great force as is prudent. Can hear the joints squeak under the pressure.

A Voyage Through Space

At this point the log suddenly ceases. The report of the captain tells us why:

"A few minutes, not more than three or four, after putting on the brake-lever to stop the mote, we were startled by what we all supposed to be a flash of lightning, accompanied by a single crack of thunder so sharp that I felt it as a slap in the face, and, for a moment, thought I was deafened. At first none of us supposed it to be anything else than an electric discharge, probably caused by the rapid thermalization of the etherine which was now going on through the loss of kinetic energy by the mote. Soon a faint whistling sound was heard, the origin of which was obscure. After some examination to learn whence it proceeded, I found that it came from a minute hole in the wall of the mote, about two or three millimetres (one-eighth to one-twelfth of an inch) in diameter. As this hole seemed quite dark on looking into it, I supposed at first that it was a shallow one, which some workman had bored by mistake. Yet, when I put my finger over it the whistling ceased, showing that air was escaping through it. Further examination showed that it passed in a straight line quite through the metallic wall of the mote and the wooden sheathing, looking dark only because of the blackness of the sky outside. Putting my eye near it, I could see a star through it. I whittled a piece from a stick of wood and plugged up the hole.

"Then we noticed that the sound had not quite

His Wisdom the Defender

ceased, and soon found a similar hole on the opposite side of the mote, which was also plugged up. The holes were so small that the escape of air was too slight to cause trouble."

The report then goes on to explain how, forgetting that a himote at full speed would run a thousand miles before she could be brought to a standstill, the captain had omitted to put on the brake till he was over the coast of Nova Scotia. In consequence they were carried to the southwestern part of Virginia before they could stop.

After hearing of the departure of the *Golden Age* from Cape Town for home, Campbell looked for her return with the greatest solicitude. The mishap by which her name had been swept away, and her color changed from white to black, which had been telegraphed to all the world, made him feel that Rogers had been imprudent in venturing to return after so slight an examination of the damage as he could make. Great, therefore, was his relief when, a little after five o'clock, an object was sighted in the sky which could be no other than the mote so anxiously awaited. She landed without further accident, and all was safe.

Campbell's scientific commission had no difficulty in demonstrating the cause of the strange stroke which the *Golden Age* had received. "It is well known that shooting-stars are caused by minute bodies flying through space at the rate of twenty, thirty, or even forty miles a second. Though no

A Voyage Through Space

larger than a pebble, one of these bodies, striking a plate of metal, would bore a hole through it as a bullet would go through a plank. As they actually strike our air, they first pass through many miles of the rarest air of the upper regions, and are thus dissipated before reaching the dense air below. But, on passing through the side of the mote, the meteor instantly encountered the dense air within, where its high speed cleaved the air like a stroke of lightning. We find that the two holes are exactly in the same line, so that an eye outside the mote looking into one can see quite through the other also."

X

How the World Received the News

TO narrate the events following this memorable 20th of May would require volumes. In fact, so many volumes have been written on the subject that our readers would not be interested in the repetition of the details, even if we had room for them. We shall confine our narrative to a few leading features of the case, personal to the great actor, to which publicity has not yet been given.

The first sentiment, especially in Europe, was one of combined amazement and incredulity. It was late in the evening in London before the American correspondents of the leading journals could cable the final event. The newspapers were nearly ready to go to press, and there was little time for comment. The general feeling was accurately expressed by the London *Times,* which commenced a leader on the subject in the following way:

"Has the order of nature changed? Or is some demon playing with the Atlantic cables, sending messages in both directions at its own good pleasure without regard to the signals which the operators

How the World Received the News

are making? The readers who peruse our columns this morning will be forced to the conclusion that one of these questions must be answered in the affirmative. A succession of despatches which have the self-consistence and every other external appearance of truth poured in with the signature of our Washington correspondent during the afternoon and evening. The general press despatches were equally explicit and consistent. All told the same story. A thousand people assembled to witness a long-expected event, the exact nature of which was left in doubt. They gazed on immense structures of metal, sixty feet in height, hundreds of feet in length, weighing thousands of tons. These structures were visited from end to end and examined inside and out without the discovery of any source of power or any possible means of setting them in motion. Suddenly one of them rises in the air, ascends to the height of a mile, and sweeps in a vast circuit over land and water, hill and dale, carrying hundreds of people with it. A circle nearly two hundred miles in circumference is described with a speed far exceeding that of the swiftest railway train, and the structure then returns and settles down into its former place without the slightest evidence that it had ever been moved.

"If the cable is conveying real intelligence, our correspondent was himself on the structure and was carried round with it in its aerial course.

"That such a story could be anything else than the

His Wisdom the Defender

outcome of some widespread hallucination or diseased imagination few will be disposed to believe. Are all the cables, then, operated by demons? Several despatches of inquiry sent by us over two different cables to our correspondents were promptly answered in such a way as to show that they must have been correctly understood by the agency answering them. All our expressions of surprise and incredulity found an answering response from the other end of the wire."

* * * * * * *

These words well expressed the feeling of that small portion of the people who were up till midnight and in receipt of the news. The great majority had retired to bed after hearing vague rumors that something of a very unusual nature was transpiring on the banks of the Potomac. They would naturally wait for their morning papers to see what it was all about.

But before people had finished breakfast the morning papers were behind the age. About one-half the directors of the Atlantic cable companies had spent the last hours of the night in the telegraph offices, or at the cable landings when they could be reached, to see if any signs of the cables being bewitched, other than the extraordinary statements they were carrying, could be discovered. By morning they received messages in such number and of such consistency that further doubt seemed scarcely possible. All day the newspapers kept issuing an unbroken stream

How the World Received the News

of extras, without being able to supply the great demand.

Of course, when Parliament met in the afternoon his Majesty's government was overwhelmed with inquiries as to what had happened. Much chagrin was expressed when members had to be informed that the government was without any important information not already found in the public prints, owing to the fact that his Majesty's ambassador in Washington had been otherwise engaged during the reported event. The ambassador had been constantly telegraphing all the morning, but his despatches were based entirely on the reports of the news-gatherers, without adding anything new. They only confirmed the truth of these reports by showing that he saw no reason to doubt them.

Scarcely had this been said when new fuel was added to the flame by the reported arrival of the *Golden Age* at the Cape of Good Hope, with the story of its captain and crew that they had left Campbelltown that morning, and had made the passage in three hours. The first effect of this news was to renew the suspicions of some demoniac illusion, because it seemed to involve, if possible, something yet further beyond the bounds of credibility than the sweeping of the *Hesperus* through the air. Among the scores of scientific experts interviewed was Professor Gale, of the University of London, the leading physicist of England. He said:

" Accepting the laws of nature as they have always

His Wisdom the Defender

operated from the beginning of time, what is reported is a simple impossibility. From the Potomac to the Cape of Good Hope is some 7000 miles. A very simple calculation will show that to make this distance in three hours a speed of more than 3300 feet per second would have to be maintained. An object like that described going through the air at such a speed would be heated red-hot during the first half-hour, and would be completely dissipated —burned up, so to say—by the friction of the air during the next half-hour."

"The report says the mote was completely blackened and had all her paint swept away," said the reporter.

"I can hardly regard that statement in any other light than as a concession to plausibility," continued the professor. "Just think of the absurdity. The mere air pressure would have been a thousand tons or more, enough to sweep away any possible wooden casing and burst in the end of the mote. And where is such a power to come from? Either, as the *Times* said this morning, the order of nature has changed or some singular deception is being practised."

We do not wish to harrow the reader's feelings, and therefore draw a veil over those of Professor Gale when it dawned upon his intellect that a mote flying above the air would evade his seemingly insuperable objections, and that one which could rise a foot might as well rise a hundred miles. In fact, when he learned the truth he could not help making

How the World Received the News

a disadvantageous comparison of his own wit with that of a French lady who, when told that some decapitated martyr (I forget who) had picked up his own head and carried it half a mile, promptly replied: *"C'est le premier pas qui coûte!"*

It happened that Professor Gale had a colleague whose intellect bore a remarkable resemblance to that of Campbell. He was not only one of the most eminent mathematicians of England, but in his writings were found the profoundest researches that had ever been published in the hidden realms of philosophy. When he first heard the news his brain was racked to imagine how such a thing could be. The theory which he thought out was only confirmed instead of being shattered by the news from the Cape. It was set forth in the following letter:

"To the Editor of the Times:

"The event said to have occurred yesterday on the banks of the Potomac is not so incredible to me as it appears to you. It is only its suddenness that makes it appear so. How would it have been if neither telegraph nor telephone had ever been known to us until some enterprising expert had secretly stretched wires and cables under land and sea around the globe, perfected his apparatus, trained his operators, and then asked us to come to see the result? The leading men of the empire are invited to the newly founded telegraph and telephone office, and the King himself is invited to step to the 'phone and

His Wisdom the Defender

address his cousin in Berlin. The latter answers in a clear voice, which the King at once recognizes. He carries on a conversation. Presently a ticking is heard and a printing-machine begins to operate. The distinguished assembly is told that the machine is worked by an operator in Australia.

"Would one of those present cease to believe that the whole affair was a delusion until the mechanism was explained to him? I trow not.

"Now let us see if we cannot conceive a way in which the results reported the last two days might be brought about. It has long been well understood by physicists that the luminiferous ether, which, so far as we know, fills all space, has the properties of an elastic solid, clear and invisible, like an absolutely transparent crystal. Why matter should move through this solid as it does, without encountering the slightest resistance, is a mystery which fails to strike us in its true character because of the familiarity of the fact. Professor Campbell announces that he has succeeded in producing a kind of matter which exerts a new reaction upon the ether when made to vibrate in a certain way. If he has done this, then nothing is simpler than to produce the result described. A mass of matter of this kind might be made to fly through space, carrying any burden whatever as lightly and easily as a bird flies through the air. The motion may be swifter than that of a bird, as the propagation of light through the ether is swifter than any motions we see on the earth.

How the World Received the News

These considerations lead me to look for a complete confirmation of everything reported by your correspondent.
"W. K. CONSTANT."

The excitement in the business world on both sides of the Atlantic beggared description. The exchanges and brokers' boards were everywhere in a state of such wild uproar that business had to be suspended as a measure of public safety. But for the assurance given by Campbell that the interests of all holders of stock in railways and other transportation companies should be carefully guarded, a vast amount of these properties would have been sacrificed by their owners in a moment. The form of the announcement tended to discourage sales, because he had stated that only original holders on the date in question could look to him for aid.

Campbell had been planning everything for years with such minute attention to details that he had little to do but select the men who were to act and send them on their several errands. Sites for mote stations had already been purchased in the principal cities, and two weeks had not elapsed before motes began to run between New York, Philadelphia, Chicago, and San Francisco. The *Hesperus* and the *Cynthia* were designed to ply between New York as one terminus and Paris and London as the others. But, foreseeing the temptation to which governments might be exposed, they were not sent on their first voyage until arrangements could be made with the

His Wisdom the Defender

respective governments of France and England to guarantee their neutrality.

The mission to the principal nations of the world foreshadowed in his speech at the banquet was organized in the course of two weeks. The principal capitals of Europe, as well as those of China and Japan, were to be visited. In each country one or more citizens learned in international law were to be invited to take part in a general council as to the policy to be pursued by the Owner of the Motes in order that the beneficent end he had in view might best be carried out. These gentlemen were expected to deliberate during the voyage from place to place, and upon their conclusions would depend to a certain extent the future policy of the Owner. At each capital a personal representative of the Owner was stationed, whose business it was to establish the closest relations both with the government and with commercial bodies of every kind, with a view to reporting on public feeling as to the policy best adapted to each country. The head of the whole expedition was President Winthrop, who had been selected by Campbell for the duty, not so much on the score of friendship, as of confidence in his general fitness for the work.

A somewhat embarrassing question was to devise a method of procedure which would not sacrifice Campbell's independence and would at the same time not ignore the functions which the government of the United States might legitimately expect to assume

How the World Received the News

in the affair. To secure the latter object, a formal letter was written by the Owner to the Secretary of State informing him of the purpose and objects of the expedition, and asking that special arrangements for its visit to each capital should be made by the representative of the United States there resident. In this way Mr. Winthrop was placed in direct communication with each American ambassador, whom he apprised of his intended movements.

The mote *Friede* was chosen to carry the party, doubtless on account of the significance of its name. It left on the morning of May 31. Its arrival at London next day was looked for with breathless interest, not unmixed with incredulity and fear. A point in Hyde Park had been offered the American ambassador by the British government as a place for its landing. At ten o'clock in the morning a black-looking speck was sighted in the clouds. It speedily grew larger. When no doubt could remain the police cleared the crowd from the chosen spot, and the large object slowly and majestically descended towards the ground. The American ambassador was on the spot and was received by Winthrop at the door of the mote. Arrangements were soon made for a visit of the King, pending which no other visitors would be received. His Majesty was duly advised and fixed on the hour of five o'clock that afternoon. Campbell would have been impatient of the delay; but Winthrop was well enough trained

His Wisdom the Defender

to make due allowance for the dignity that must hedge the person and movements of a monarch. At the appointed hour the King and his suite arrived, escorted by the American ambassador. The royal party was welcomed by Winthrop at the door of the mote and taken to the upper deck. Here the following address was made to the King:

"May it please your Majesty: I am directed by the Owner of the Motes to assure your Majesty of his high appreciation of the honor done him by this visit. He trusts that the determination he has expressed to administer his extraordinary powers in promoting the welfare of the entire human race will be favored with your Majesty's approval. Animated by this motive, he has deputed an able and distinguished citizen of the United States to reside in London as his personal representative. The functions of this representative will be to invite the closest relations with representatives of British interests, and acquaint himself with the needs of commercial bodies and other organizations, in order that he may report from time to time what policy and what measures on the part of the Owner of the Motes will be most conducive to their usefulness as an agency for promoting the welfare of your Majesty's subjects."

The King was quite unprepared for so formal an address, but was well enough trained to make a very brief but quite proper reply, expressing his apprecia-

How the World Received the News

tion of the sentiments and intentions of the Owner of the Motes. There was then a somewhat embarrassing pause. The King was naturally interested to see the distinguished representative alluded to, who was to fulfil so important a part in acquainting himself with the views and wishes of the British people. Mr. Winthrop and the citizen himself were quite desirous that the latter should be presented to the King. The privilege was then asked of presenting him, which was accordingly done.

We mention this proceeding because it looked so much like the presentation of an ambassador from a foreign power to the Court of St. James. It looked a little that way to the American ambassador himself; while the procedure was so adroitly managed that an escape from the conclusion was very easy.

One great and indisputable fact had begun to dawn on the minds of men. The motes might be new and terrible engines in future warfare. As this fact became more and more evident, it caused universal alarm. The impossibility of defence from an attack of a fleet of motes was felt on all sides. It was clear to every one that something must be done to guard against the danger, but what to do no one knew.

On the problem thus presented, Americans, as represented by Mr. Secretary Bayne, looked with less concern than others, because they felt that the motes belonged to their country, and would therefore be used for no purpose antagonistic to its own interests.

His Wisdom the Defender

True, this view of the case was a little weakened by the knowledge that several hundred of these vehicles were in the course of construction on the island of Elba; but, although this island was still under the jurisdiction of Italy, the danger was minimized by the fact that the motes still belonged to one of their own citizens, who alone would be likely to control them. On the other hand, the citizen repeatedly speaks of himself rather as a citizen of the world than of the United States. What will be his policy as regards the great political power which he wields?

The second morning following the arrival of the mote in London and the ceremonies we have described, a messenger arrived at Campbelltown from the Secretary of State, bearing the following note:

"STATE DEPARTMENT, *June 11, 1945.*

"DEAR SIR,—I am directed by the Secretary of State to say that he will esteem it a very great favor to have you call on him at your earliest convenience—this afternoon if possible. He wishes to consult with you on a matter of the highest importance both to yourself and to our government. If not convenient to come this afternoon, please state the time of your arrival in order that the Secretary may arrange his engagements to suit your convenience.

"Very respectfully,
"JAMES B. SMYTHE,
"Private Secretary."

How the World Received the News

An answer was immediately despatched that the Owner of the Motes would call on the Secretary at three o'clock that afternoon. He arrived promptly on the hour and was at once ushered into the private office of the Secretary, whom he found awaiting him.

"Mr. Campbell, I have requested this interview because it must be quite evident to you that the enterprise you are inaugurating has an interest not attached to any ordinary affair, since it concerns not only the welfare of every citizen of our country, but must be intimately associated with the international relations of nations, our own included. You will, therefore, see that it is a part of the duty of our government to assure itself that your proceedings shall not either imperil its relations with other governments, compromise this government, or prove in anyway detrimental to the interests of our country. Acting on these considerations, the President and his advisers have been deliberating on the measures to provide against any evil of the kind to which I have alluded. Naturally you are yourself a very important factor in any arrangement that may be made. The responsibility which you have assumed is fully recognized by all. It is therefore the desire of the President that you be consulted as to every measure taken and duly informed of all that may be done. On the other hand, it is expected by this government that you will with equal frankness recognize its superior responsibility in the case, especially its responsibility to foreign nations for your own acts. I must, therefore, ask your permission to make some inquiries, which I should have no right to make of an ordinary citizen, as to your future policy in organizing a mote service."

"Mr. Secretary, I fully recognize the propriety of all you say. I shall be glad to answer any questions you may ask so far as I am able so to do. At the same time, you will observe that it would not be a mark of the highest wisdom on my part to reach any absolute conclusion as to what I shall or shall not do in advance of the contingencies that may arise. I have certain great things in view; I mentioned these in a speech at a banquet which I regret that you were unable to attend, but which you have perhaps done me the honor to read."

"I have done so, and there are a few points in it about which I wish first to inquire. You spoke of the desirableness that the organization for running the motes should enjoy a position of political independence. Will you kindly explain the exact meaning which you attach to that phrase?"

"The meaning attached to the phrase seems to me as clear as circumstances permit it to be. It must be evident to you, Mr. Secretary, that the control of the motes carries with it enormous power, the power of doing not only a good heretofore unknown, but of bringing about untold miseries—in a word, the power which controls a fleet of motes can land armies where it chooses and conquer whom it chooses.

How the World Received the News

Moreover, the commercial relations of nations will be made much closer when intercourse is carried on in so easy and rapid a way, as it soon will be. Under these circumstances it seems very desirable that the motes be controlled by no one nation, because that nation would practically command the world. My view, therefore, is that the control should be exercised by some neutral and independent power, obliged to provide positively against the use of the motes for the purpose of conquest of any people whatever, or in the special interest of any nation at the expense of other nations."

" You have partly explained the other question I was going to ask you as to your intended use of the motes for the benefit of the entire human race; your own country, apparently, having no higher claim on you than any other? If I understand correctly, this is your view."

" I tried to make that view perfectly clear in my address, and I do not see how anything can be added to what I have stated. Please remember that this country will necessarily have enormous advantages at the start, which may well become permanent. Such being the case, I cannot feel under any obligation to favor it at the expense of other nations."

" Now, a third point. The attention of the Department has been called to the proceedings at the presentation of your personal representative to the King of England, which are said to have been conducted in such a way as to imply that you were your-

His Wisdom the Defender

self an independent sovereign, sending an ambassador to a foreign court. I trust you will deny any such intention."

"I certainly had no such intention. I suppose my right to have a personal representative at the capital of any country is unquestioned. The presentation of Mr. Robinson to the King had no more significance than the presentation of any other citizen of the United States. It was done simply because he and the King were both on board the mote, and the King was willing to make his acquaintance on account of the very important position which he occupied."

"That is quite satisfactory. But I am not satisfied with the sentiments you express as to your duties towards your own government. You must be perfectly aware that this government cannot for a moment tolerate any act of one of its own citizens looking to the formation, by his own will, of an organization independent of it. It is responsible to foreign nations for your acts. It is therefore imperative that you act only as authorized by it. So far as I am aware, you have not yet done any overt thing calling for repression. At the same time, you must be quite conscious that one of your proceedings has caused and is causing great anxiety throughout this country—that is, the sending of an expedition, several thousand strong, to some unknown point in the northern regions, and refusing to give any information as to its purpose or object."

How the World Received the News

"The reasons for sending the expedition out were implied in my address. It was necessary to train a large body of men in the use of the motes, and to have their training carried on without the public knowing anything about it; otherwise, the calamities which I described would have at once been brought on, and unending confusion would have been the result. At the present time there is no object in bringing the expedition away from where it now is until I shall need the services of its members."

"You will, I trust, deem it right that I should speak with perfect frankness. I must say that your explanation for still keeping the force out of sight seems to me unsatisfactory; but it is useless to go into details. I can only caution you once more against taking any measures which will call for repressive action on the part of the government.

"Meanwhile, there is another point which I have to mention. The President contemplates calling an international conference to negotiate and deliberate on the measures to be taken by the various governments of the world to protect them against the dangers you have pointed out. It seems to me eminently proper that you should be named as one of the conferees. I apprise you of this because the President has expressed a special desire to hear your views on the subject."

"Will the specific purpose and end of the conference be named in the call?"

His Wisdom the Defender

"I cannot say; that matter has not yet been decided upon. At present the idea is only assuming shape."

"I do not think I ought, under any circumstances, to take part in such a conference. For me to do so as a representative of this government, with all due deference to your views, would not be wholly compatible with the responsibilities which you have, in part, recognized in my position. What interest I shall take in the conference will depend upon its objects; if you will allow me a moment to put my views of the matter in writing, I will do so."

A tablet was handed to him and he wrote as follows:

"Call a conference to agree upon the immediate and complete abolition of the military and naval establishments of all the powers taking part in it, and the disbandment of all troops, wherever employed, not absolutely necessary to the protection of life and property against unlawful violence."

He handed the paper to the Secretary, who read it and reread it slowly and carefully.

"This is going altogether too far. It cannot be thought that any of the great powers would consent to entering into a conference on such terms. This government would not do so itself. It must keep the influence due it as one of the leading military powers of the world. All it can agree to is that this power shall not be so used as to imperil the interest of any other independent nation. If all na-

How the World Received the News

tions shall agree, the power shall be restricted so far as the concensus of opinion may deem proper."

"I fully concede," replied Campbell, "that the leading nations of the world would not be likely to agree to any such proposal. For that reason I shall feel little interest in the proposed conference. My own private opinion is that the interests of humanity cannot be guarded by any measure less drastic than the one I have suggested. Meanwhile, all I can do is to prevent, to the best of my ability, the power which I wield being used in an attack on the rights and liberties of any people whatever. More than that I cannot say. Is there anything to be added? If not I have only to thank you for your kind consideration in all that you have stated."

The two men shook hands and took leave of each other. The interview had greatly increased the solicitude of each as to the intentions of the other. The fears of the Secretary that Campbell contemplated some move incompatible with the duty of a citizen to his own country, and likely to complicate international relations, were not allayed. Campbell saw that the policy he had in contemplation would meet with no sympathy in the Department of State. But a voice sounded in his ears:

"He who would wield the power of a god must bear the responsibility of a god."

Besides the personal representative who had been presented to the King, and who was not expected to take any active part in business negotiations, Camp-

His Wisdom the Defender

bell had sent out in the mote a skilled attorney and a man of business, with a view to making arrangements with the British and French governments to run the two great loomotes between New York and their respective capitals. The great point aimed at was that each government should agree to respect the neutrality of the motes under all circumstances. In the course of a week a contract was made with a duly authorized representative of his Majesty's government, in which occurred the following clause:

"It is agreed by the party of the first part that the mote to be run under the present contract is guaranteed against detention or seizure by any power whatever while within the jurisdiction of his Majesty's government, except as provided in the following clause: If it should appear that any persons or parties in an arriving mote design to inflict unlawful injuries upon his Majesty's subjects or upon their property, or to make war upon the forces of his said Majesty, then his Majesty's forces shall have the right to enter said mote and seize and remove all such persons. The mote shall then be released and restored to the Owner."

Under these arrangements the loomote *Hesperus* started on its first voyage to London, and the *Cynthia* left for Paris on the day following. In the meantime the expedition under Mr. Winthrop had nearly completed the tour of the capitals of Europe, and was about to start for Pekin, when an unforeseen event disturbed the current of the Owner's plans.

XI

The Red-headed Man Scores the Greatest "Beat" in the History of Journalism

IF telegraph wires could feel the weight of the messages they were conveying, the whole line from Washington to Campbelltown would, within a week after the interview with the Secretary of State, have bowed beneath its burden. Long before Campbell was up, despatches came in so rapidly that the operators found it was almost impossible to take them. The messengers carried them to headquarters in handfuls. The purport of all was a good deal the same:

"Please deny report in New York *Herald* this morning."

"Please allow our representative an interview on the subject of your intentions, as stated in the *Herald*."

"Please explain situation. What authority has the *Herald* for its statement? The Bungtown *Banner* will gladly publish anything you have to say on the subject."

And so on, in an endless chain.

His Wisdom the Defender

During breakfast it was Campbell's habit to read, before their classification by his secretary, both the newspapers and such despatches as might have arrived. The moment he entered the room and took his seat at the table, he saw that something extraordinary had happened. There was such a stack of despatches that it seemed hopeless to attack them. They were still falling like snow-flakes. A glance at two or three was sufficient to show that the issue of the New York *Herald* that morning must contain something of a very striking character. As soon as the paper arrived, he called for it and examined it with eagerness. The very first page, usually devoted to advertisements, was taken up with a blazing article in double-leaded type, with the most striking phrases printed here and there in red and blue colors. The heading took up about half the page, and the first line was printed in red letters an inch high:

THE SECRET OUT!

What Archibald the Great has been doing and thinking!

What he is going to do!

The armies of the world to be swept from the earth!

The navies to be sunk!

The United States of the World to be organized!

King Archibald the First to assume the reins of Universal Government!

A Feat of Journalism

Full account of his plans from our special correspondent!

This was the prelude to a despatch from "our correspondent" at Campbelltown. It was a paper such as no one but a *Herald* reporter could write. The phrases in red or blue were in type twice as large as the pica of the rest of the article. Glancing down the page at them, such expressions as these caught the eye: "Machine-guns," "Dynamite Earthquake-makers," "Hailstorm of bullets," "His Most Gracious Majesty, Archibald the Great, Ruler of the World." The despatch extended over to the second page. Each of the six columns on this page was headed with the words "The Secret Out" in red letters.

Campbell read the first two columns, then threw the paper down in dismay and disgust. The words which he read were these:

"The whole human race may well tear its hair when it sees its stupidity in failing to divine the objects of the man who, during the past four years, has filled so prominent a place in its eyes. That no one should ever have guessed his motives and seen through his purposes will hereafter seem incredible. All that was dark is now light. Everything that was concealed is made known. All the eccentricities of his conduct, his singular ways of doing business, his constant refusals to accept even the most advantageous offers of co-operation, the mystery

His Wisdom the Defender

which enshrouded all his movements, his regal inaccessibility to the public—all are now explained. When he invented his thermic engine, people wondered why he did not patent it and proceed with its manufacture on the largest scale. For a long time they did not even guess that he had anything else in view. Then his secrecy was explained by showing that he had something else in view—no less than the building and running of the motes. Even these were enveloped in mystery until it was absolutely necessary to his plans that they should be shown to the world.

"No one could for a moment believe that the excuses he made were his sole reasons for secrecy. No one has given any credence to his explanation why, at this day, thousands of his men and hundreds of his motes are still practising at some unknown, uninhabited point in or near the Arctic zone.

"Now all is clear, as it should have been from the very beginning. He has intended all along to become the ruler of the world. In a few weeks everything will be ready for the final move. Is it not singular that among the few people who managed to see the strange port-holes pierced in the sides of more than a hundred of the motes, no one suspected what they were for? Out of each of these holes now peers a machine-gun. Flying through the air, taking up any position they please, dodging every weapon that can be aimed at them, taking every hiding-place within their range of vision, these phantom ships

A Feat of Journalism

are invincible. Under the hailstorm of bullets from their artillery, every army in the world will melt away like snow-flakes under a tropical sun. Helpless as sheep, soldiers can escape their fate only by hiding in casemates or hurrying themselves out of sight in caverns and cellars. Any city that refuses to submit can be brought to terms by dynamite shells. Any ruler who objects to the new order of things can be carried in chains before the higher than imperial throne of the modern Jehovah.

" The great problem before him has been to keep his plans secret until he was ready to act, and thus prevent not only the seizure of his person and his establishment by the government in self-defence, but the danger of any combination among the nations to defeat his plans. This is the real reason for the great Arctic encampment being still kept out of sight. That he really has communication with it every night no well-informed person can seriously doubt. He awaits the report that all is ready..."

There was also an editorial, in double-leaded type, calling attention to the discovery made by the correspondent and to the achievement of the *Herald* in being the only journal to make known the secret. It was written in as light a vein as if it had commented on an every-day subject. It spoke rather breezily of King Archibald I. " He will be a fairly good monarch, after all, and the world may not have much occasion to object to his rule."

His Wisdom the Defender

It may be believed that Campbell did not eat much breakfast, especially when he was informed that a crowd of reporters were besieging the gate, determined to see him immediately, and would not take " no " for an answer. The situation was a critical one, and it was necessary to appear as cool and placid as possible. He went into his reception-hall and directed their admission. The red-headed man was in the front rank, but resigned his usual functions of spokesman to the *Times* man. Campbell noticed him with some surprise. He had expected to see a look of triumph on his rubicund visage, as much as to say, " Now, haven't I got you ?" But the only change in his usual smile was that it was tinged with a serious look, as if he had important business on hand. He had his note-book in hand, and seemed to have no other idea than that of reporting the proceedings of a meeting.

" Mr. Campbell, we have called to inquire about the article in the *Herald* this morning, which I suppose you have seen."

" Yes, I have seen the article, but I have not read it, and have not time to read it, so I don't know that I can tell you much about it. You know what it is, and I do not see why you come to me for information."

" We wish to know whether it is true. Everybody wants to know what you have to say on the subject. If it is not true, it is necessary for you to deny it."

" Here you place me in an embarrassing position.

A Feat of Journalism

You know I have already announced, as one of the rules of my organization, that no person in it is to deny any false report that may be set in circulation. Of course I must obey my own rules."

"But this is one of those extraordinary cases for which rules were never made."

"But let me remind you further that the rule does not prohibit the denial of a true report. Hence, as I have already told you, if I deny the report, it will imply that it is true. I am not prepared to admit the truth of the report. You must therefore excuse me from denying it."

"But it must be denied. The whole country is in a turmoil, greater than it was even on the morning after your motes were launched."

"But will it lessen the turmoil for me to say something leading to the inference that the report is true?"

"You surely can say something that people will believe and which will thus relieve the public tension."

Campbell pondered a moment. "Well, I will tell you one thing, which I trust you will all believe. If the report does prove to be true, I shall undoubtedly be an absolute monarch, shall I not?"

"That will depend on yourself. You will be what you choose."

"On the theory which you say was set forth in the *Herald* this morning, I could not be anything else. Then let me categorically inform you that if

His Wisdom the Defender

I do assume the position of ruling monarch of the world, my first official act will be to order the execution, by hanging, of the man who was guilty of the treasonable conduct of betraying my secret."

As he said this, he darted at the red-headed man a look which he intended to be very fierce. The victim winced for a moment. Then a smile spread over the faces of the assemblage, in which the red-headed man soon joined. They could not help smiling at the idea of the gentle little man before them ordering anybody to execution. His affected wrath was comical, and his threat seemed too ludicrous to be feared.

"Surely you can tell us something. Are the motes now practising in polar regions armed with machine-guns?"

"I don't see that anything I can say would be of the slightest use. If the theory set forth in the *Herald's* article is a correct one, of course I am not going to give my plans away by telling you about them. If it is false, no harm is done by my saying nothing, for the simple reason that no denial that I might make would be of any use. Of course, it might be necessary for me to deny it if it were true. When the proper time comes I shall speak; meanwhile, I propose to give you newspapers full swing to invent what you please."

"When will that proper time come?"

"I do not know exactly—possibly in a day or two, possibly not for a week. I had not intended to speak

A Feat of Journalism

for a month to come. I must ask you to excuse me from any further statement at present."

He left the room, only to be confronted by a messenger bearing a despatch of especial importance. It came from the British ambassador at Washington, and was couched in the following terms:

"His Britannic Majesty's ambassador at Washington desires the honor of an immediate interview with the Owner of the Motes. He is about to take a special train for Campbelltown with this end in view."

Campbell called his secretary and dictated the following reply:

"The Owner of the Motes will be very glad to receive the British ambassador. To facilitate his coming, a mote will be at once despatched to Washington to bring him hither."

He gave orders to have one of the smallest motes made ready immediately, and sent to Washington. Before it had time to leave, similar despatches came from the Russian, German, French, and Italian ambassadors.

Answers were sent to them that a mote would arrive at the State Department in about an hour to bring them to Campbelltown.

But before the answers were received, all were on the way to the railway station. The British ambassador arrived there first, and ordered a special car drawn by the best engine available, regardless of the wants of traffic. The other ambassadors arrived one

His Wisdom the Defender

by one before the engine was ready, and, easily guessing each other's errand, all came in the same car. It took two hours for the train to reach Campbelltown, and this gave Campbell time to think over what he was to say.

It was the most embarrassing situation in which he had ever been placed. The ambassadors, representing a good part of the civilized world, were not to be put off with any such light-hearted logic as that with which he had dismissed the reporters. Every direct refusal to answer their questions and every obvious evasion would increase the suspicion which the world now entertained as to his intentions. To say anything false or even misleading was not only too despicable to be thought of, but would seriously impair the universal confidence and respect which he hoped that his future course would command. Strictly construed, and considered as separate statements, the *Herald* article was a tissue of falsehoods which he could easily deny. He had no machine-guns. He did not intend to attack any army with deadly weapons, because he had no such weapons at command. He did not want to be a ruler of any sort. There was, therefore, no difficulty in denying in detail the assertions of the article.

The real cause of embarrassment was that the statements were untrue only when taken singly and verbally, and that the mind of the correspondent was cast in too small a mould to grasp the extent of his plans. The world, at first, would see little es-

A Feat of Journalism

sential difference between his actual plans, if he announced them, and those attributed to him. If he did not intend to become a ruler in name, he was determined, if possible, to perform the most important —we might almost say the sole—function of a ruler of the world—that of enforcing law and order in the intercourse of nations. If he was not going to sweep armies from the face of the earth, it was a part of his plan to abolish them. If he was not going to sink navies, he might haul them ashore. Of two plans so near alike, how was he to deny the one and not the other? The world in its present frame of mind would refuse to recognize any difference between the two. Persuasion or force was the only question the world had in mind, and this question he must evade.

The five ambassadors arrived in a body, and were, of course, immediately shown in. Their approach was marked with most perfect courtesy, and Campbell had collected his faculties sufficiently to receive them in a corresponding way. He invited them to be seated, expressed his pleasure at meeting them and his readiness to know to what he owed the distinguished honor of such a visit.

"Mr. Campbell, you have doubtless seen an article published in the New York *Herald* of this morning purporting to give an exposition of your policy and intentions."

"I have seen the article, and from the headings and some expressions scattered here and there I have a general idea of its contents. But I really have little time to read the newspapers, and have not attributed sufficient importance to the article to occupy my time in giving it serious attention. If you will state any points to which you wish particularly to refer, I will be glad to discuss them."

This indifference to so serious a subject disconcerted the visitors for a moment, but for a moment only.

"You will readily understand that the article in question is causing the greatest alarm to the people of every civilized country. We hope that you can make such a disavowal of the intentions accredited to you as will allay their anxiety."

"Do your Excellencies think that any statement I could now make would really have that effect? Either the assertions of the *Herald* are true or they are false. If they are false, then there is no occasion for alarm. If they are true, will any advantage be gained by my either admitting them or denying them? If I admit them, then the alarm will be well founded; but if I deny them, may it not be attributed to a desire to conceal my intentions? In a word, would a person speaking under such pressure command credence in any quarter? Might he not be expected to consider that prevarication would be excusable under circumstances so extraordinary?"

This frank presentation of the case, so different from what they had expected, puzzled the visitors, and it took them some time to frame a reply.

"However that may be, it is certain that a decli-

A Feat of Journalism

nation on your part to make a statement on the subject will be looked upon the world over as conceding the truth of the article to which we allude. The result will be an immediate decision by the authorities of the leading nations as to the course to be pursued under the circumstances. What this course will be it is not advisable, even were it possible, for us to say. A careful consideration of the emergency on your part will make the case as clear to you as it is possible for us to present it."

Campbell was annoyed that they were not more specific—that they did not ask questions instead of calling for statements.

"Granting the correctness of all that your Excellencies say, I do not see that the inutility of my making a specific answer to the allegations in question is thereby disproved. But I make no secret of the general objects and purposes which I have in view. Allow me to set them forth in an authoritative way.

"I am by nature and constitution an individualist. In my judgment, the whole history of modern progress shows that the highest development of men is reached when the individual has the largest liberty. Moreover, the sovereignty and independence of nations are of equal importance with individual liberty. It is this sovereignty and independence which will be in danger unless it is guaranteed that motes shall never be used by one nation in making war upon another. I desire so to strengthen my enterprise and my power that any such use of the motes shall be impossible. Whether I am able to do this, and, if I am able, the best way of bringing it about, are subjects on which I desire the wisest counsel that the world has to offer.

"At the same time I have reached certain conclusions on the subject which seem to me indisputable. These conclusions and a more complete statement of the principles governing my policy I desire to set forth at the earliest day when I can prepare a statement. If yourselves and other leading representatives of the governments and people of the world will do me the honor to listen, I shall gladly have you hear what I shall say on the subject."

"Are we then to understand that you decline to state specifically whether any of the assertions contained in the *Herald's* article are true or false?"

Campbell secretly rejoiced at this question. It gave him the opportunity to turn the inquiries of his visitors in the direction he wished them to take. He must, however, tempt them forward so gently as to make them feel they were advancing solely on their own volition.

"By no means, so far as any specific points are concerned. Your Excellencies have asked me to disavow intentions attributed to me by an irresponsible writer, in an article filling nearly two pages of a newspaper, which I have not even had time to read. I am sure the impossibility of my doing so will be evident on mature consideration, especially in view of the difficulty of my foreseeing what policy it is

A Feat of Journalism

best for me to pursue. But if you desire information as to the truth or falsity of any specific points mentioned in the article, I shall be glad to give it. I have nothing to conceal."

After a few whispers of consultation, the British representative, who was acting as spokesman, continued:

"We thank you, and ask that you will allow us to be as pointed in our questions as the situation calls for. First of all, we assume it to be true that you have, at some unknown point in the Arctic regions, a camp of instruction where several thousand men are practising aerial evolutions with several hundred motes."

"That I suppose to be true. It is certainly my intention." [Now we are getting on the right track. If only they don't touch the wrong thing while they are groping round in the dark.]

We put in brackets Campbell's unexpressed thoughts.

"It is stated in the article that this expedition is an armed one; that it is armed with machine-guns and perhaps other instruments of warfare. Have you any objections to telling us what truth, if any, there is in this statement?"

[Good!] "None whatever. The expedition has no machine-guns, no arms, or weapons of any sort" [I came very near saying "nothing that can properly be called arms or weapons"—what a lucky escape!] "unless they have been taken without either my or-

His Wisdom the Defender

ders or my knowledge." [That's a stunner.] "Stop! they have got fifty or a hundred rifles to shoot game and defend themselves against wild animals. I think that is all, unless some of the men carried knives or revolvers in their pockets."

"This statement of yours will, we are sure, be received with pleasure. With your permission, and without any intention of doubting your word, we shall make another inquiry. It is stated elsewhere in this same issue of the *Herald* that you purchased eight machine-guns from the American Arms Company. Is that true?"

[Lucky that I didn't let Gheen take those guns with him. I mustn't seem to remember them.] "I think—we—did—buy guns of some kind, including a cannon, about two years ago. We shall soon see." (Taps a bell.) "James, tell the property clerk to come here and bring his book of purchases with him.... I do not remember even opening the boxes containing the guns. If they have gone with the expedition, it is through some mistake. A great amount of material had to be packed up and sent off, and there is always a chance of things being taken by mistake."

The clerk entered with a big record book.

"Mr. Black, didn't we buy some guns a couple of years ago or so? If so, have you still got them, and where are they?"

The clerk laid the book on a desk and examined the index.

A Feat of Journalism

"If your Excellencies would like to see how my records of property are kept, I would be glad to have you look at the book."

The party went to the desk and looked over the clerk's shoulder. He found "Guns" indexed as on pages 247 and 350. Page 247 was found, and the following entry shown:

"Eight Gattling guns, 42 Sept. 7, Cellar A. 43 Nov. 13, Col. 41." "Yes, sir; they were first stored in Cellar A of the old building, and are now in room 41 of the Coliseum," said the clerk.

"Now, what's on page 350?"

"One three-inch cannon, in shed M. That's the signal gun that was fired for the launching."

"You are quite sure that Gheen did not take those things with the expedition?"

"If he did, it was without my knowledge," said the clerk. "But I can soon see if they are in their place."

"Do so, please, and let us know. If your Excellencies wish we can go with the clerk and satisfy ourselves that the guns are here."

"That is hardly necessary. We will take his word on the subject. But can you give the date of the purchase?"

By the property book they were received September 7, 1942.

"That is pretty close. The *Herald* gives the date of the bill as September 10, 1942."

[No need telling them that with those guns I in-

His Wisdom the Defender

tend to defend my works on the Island of Elba *à l'outrance.*]

" Then we are to understand you that the organization under Captain Gheen's command is in no sense a military one ?"

[Bad! but I must take the bull by the horns, and that boldly.] " I fail to see how a body of unarmed men can in any proper sense be called military. At the same time, I should be wanting in frankness did I not point out that the organization might as well be military. It must be quite evident to you that a body of men moving through the air in motes need only be supplied with arms to become a military force of the most formidable kind. These arms they can seize in almost any quarter and at any moment. The possibility of this is the great feature of the situation, the gravity of which I fear the world still fails to grasp, else your questions would, to-day, have taken a different turn."

The Property Clerk: " The guns are all there, sir. They are still boxed up. I do not think the boxes have been unscrewed since the inspection on arrival."

The ambassadors received this announcement with evident satisfaction.

" The frankness with which you have responded to our inquiries prompts us to offer a suggestion. It must be quite evident to you that the *Herald* article and the universal apprehension which it excites are due to your unexplained course in keeping this

A Feat of Journalism

expedition, a force which, as you say, may in a moment be transformed into a military one, out of sight of the world, making its doings and objects an impenetrable secret, and not allowing a word of intelligence to escape from it. If you should deem it proper to tell us why the expedition is kept where it is, and what it is doing, we are sure it would go far to relieve the apprehension which now prevails."

Campbell sprang to his feet.

"Gentlemen, I fear what you say is too true, so far as the apprehension and the method of relieving it are concerned. But this only shows—all the drift of your questioning shows—how lamentably men fail to grasp the situation. The great question between us this morning has been whether there is any danger of my using the motes in warfare. The question you should have asked me is how am I to prevent the motes being used in warfare? As long as the motes are controlled by one man, unless that man is lost to all sense of his responsibility, the world has nothing to fear. One man can have no object in ruling the world; and if he did want to rule it, what harm could he do so long as his rule was reasonably impartial? The real danger is from the love of conquest and dominion on the part of nations. International law still permits any nation to make war when it chooses, for any purpose it deems appropriate, and with the most effective appliances it can control. As long as that liberty is recognized, so long will the very existence of

His Wisdom the Defender

motes afford a just ground of dread to mankind at large.

"I have said more than I intended to say at present. Allow me to repeat that, in my next address, I expect to have the honor to make such further statements as may seem called for by the situation."

The ambassadors made no reply, and soon took their leave. Let us see what Campbell had to say on the subject in his journal:

"May, 1942.—This world of humanity is a queer compound of folly and wisdom. It worships most what it most abhors—force. If it sees a young man struggling against difficulties to carry on some great and useful work, it looks on with apathy or something worse, so long as he keeps strictly within the law. If he shows too much energy, it will enact laws to impede him. When he violates the law, every effort is made to crush him with its machinery. If he proves stronger than the law, more especially if his course is marked by such violence as to attract universal attention to his energy, if every effort to crush him proves futile, then the world proceeds to worship him and erects monuments to his memory; when, if he had done his work in a law-abiding way, he would have excited no notice from his contemporaries and been forgotten as soon as he was dead. Each of the six great manufacturing corporations of the country, which have proved instruments of such beneficence in making the necessaries of life cheap and plenty, were fought so bitterly at

A Feat of Journalism

every step that its managers had to get the upperhand of the public and rule it with a rod of iron. I except the seventh, my own, because I went about in such a way that men could find nothing to legislate about; so they could do nothing but spit gall and bitterness at me.

"Possibly my scruples against killing may be criminal weakness on my part. I cannot deny that the most certain and speedy way of inaugurating the golden age of universal peace and plenty would be to carry out the *Herald* programme—sweep armies off the face of the earth with murderous artillery, or drive their men into caves of refuge, inspire universal terror by my power, and say to the world, ' Behold your master; submit to his sway or see your cities destroyed and your works brought to naught!' There might be a few weeks of raging and gnashing of teeth. After that I should be worshipped by all but those malecontents whose principal trait is a state of congenital dissatisfaction with all that exists."

It is hardly necessary to say that the interview did not satisfy the *Herald*. It claimed that none of the really serious allegations made by its correspondent were denied, and that the most essential among them were admitted. Meantime guns could be put into the motes at any moment. No matter by what term he might call himself—King or Universal Judge—it was clearly the intention of the Owner of the Motes to exercise supreme authority over the nations of the world. The question whether they should submit to that authority was one for the nations themselves to decide.

Three days later an invitation to the following effect was addressed to the highest officers of the government and to all the foreign ambassadors and ministers:

" The Owner of the Motes requests the honor of your company on board the *Concordia,* in the city of Washington, on Tuesday next, the 12th instant. He will avail himself of the opportunity to make a public utterance on the subject of the political effects of the motes as bearing upon international law and the mutual relations of the governments of the world."

The invited party was more select than that which came together to witness the first running of the motes. It included only the President and his cabinet, the chairmen of the foreign affairs committees in the House and Senate, and the representatives of foreign nations. No invitations were extended to the press, except that the three press associations were each allowed to have a reporter present.

XII

Our Hero Makes a Clean Breast

THE position in which Campbell was placed by the *Herald* article was one of the greatest perplexity. Had it appeared a month later, when his preparations for action were complete, he would have cared but little. The real trouble was not that the article had revealed his plans—his interview with the ambassadors had gone far to relieve the public mind on that score—but that public attention had been pointedly called to what it was in his power to do if he chose.

History tells us that when horses were in use it was necessary to cover their eyes with pieces of leather known as "blinders," which kept them from seeing in any direction except straight ahead. The reason was that these animals were extremely timid, and liable to be frightened out of their senses by any unusual object in motion around them, and thus jump about in such a manner as to endanger both carriage and occupants. But if the driver could merely turn the horse's head so that the blinders would prevent his seeing the object, and could for-

His Wisdom the Defender

cibly keep him from looking at it, then the horse, although if he could be said to know anything must have known that the dreadful thing was still there, was immediately reassured. In fact, he feared only what he could see, not what he knew to exist out of his sight.

It was a good deal the same way with the world at this most critical moment in its history. What it could see was one man in possession of the power of doing almost anything he pleased to or with his fellow-men. This caused it universal concern, and so it wanted him deprived of his power. The world knew well that if this power was taken from him, and placed in the hands of any nation or of any combination of nations, the case would be yet worse, because, while an individual might lead a nation to conquest, he could not well engage in conquest himself without having a nation behind him. But this greater danger was not existent at the moment, and so was relegated to the background. The newspapers, with the *Herald* at their head, living on excitement, poured forth an unceasing stream of rumors, reports, and suggestions as to what Campbell intended to do or might do or had done, and added to the turmoil and uncertainty by contradicting each other, not to say themselves, as often as possible. Under these circumstances the *Herald* article had much the effect of the appearance of a wolf in the midst of a flock of sheep. But what was to be done?

At first nothing definite was proposed. But in

Our Hero Makes a Clean Breast

a couple of days the scattered thoughts of the frightened public began to take a common direction, and loud calls were made on the President to send a regiment of soldiers to Campbelltown and take possession of the entire place, its owner included. What good this would do when the owner could escape through the air with as many motes as he might choose to take, and, if his intentions were really those attributed to him, could do what he pleased to his assailants, no one stopped to inquire. Curiously enough, for some twenty-four hours a number of European journals joined in this cry. But it only took them one day to see that such a proceeding, if it were successful, would only result in placing the destiny of Europe in the hands of the most powerful and united country in the world, which, though noted for its justice and respect for international law, had for half a century been ambitious to rule. Then the cry changed to one for a union of European nations to offer an unbroken front to any invasion or attack that might hereafter be attempted either by the Owner of the Motes or the American government.

What increased Campbell's depression was that he stood alone, without, so far as he knew, either support or sympathy from any quarter whatsoever. Gheen was the only man completely acquainted with his plans; and he was only a trusted assistant—in no way a representative man.

Winthrop, on whom he expected most to rely, was

His Wisdom the Defender

absent on his European mission. He had visited London, Paris, Madrid, Rome, and Vienna, and was now in Berlin conferring with German publicists. In each capital visited he had selected a few of the most sagacious and enlightened professors of international law, one or two of whom were to be invited to the conference which Campbell had planned to hold. Four of these men, from England, France, and Italy, were with him as the nucleus of the proposed assemblage. His plan was to go from Berlin to St. Petersburg, and thence to China and Japan.

Campbell's idea was that, as the whole subject was thought over and talked over by these men, the absolute necessity of a universal disarmament and abandonment of war would be evident. Then the way in which this could be brought about would be discussed from day to day. The international rules which he had long been thinking over would be laid before them; and he was sure that the more these rules were examined and discussed, the more apparent would be their wisdom, feasibility, and justice, if only nations could be brought to accept them. A distinct goal being thus brought plainly in sight, the method of reaching it would be the next subject of study. When all other means had been shown impracticable or doubtful, then would Campbell for the first time propose his drastic plan of using force. Severe though this measure might be, it would only be directed towards the enforcement of written law.

Such being the case, he had not fully unfolded his

Our Hero Makes a Clean Breast

plans, even to Winthrop. And now the latter was away on his mission when his counsel was most wanted.

A change of programme was necessary. The *Herald* article had precipitated a crisis in which the well-considered and leisurely proceedings he had intended were impossible. He must either retire or go on as rapidly as possible at all hazards. The day after the visit of the ambassadors he telegraphed Winthrop to return immediately, bringing with him for consultation such of the publicists as were willing to come. The message was not unexpected by the recipient, and the second morning after the *Friede* was at Campbelltown, with Winthrop and the five European professors. The two leaders met in Campbell's private office. The first greetings were exchanged.

"Well! you have set the world in an uproar."

"I cannot deny the impeachment. The question is, what am I to do?"

"The situation seems to me a very difficult and perplexing one. I hope you have some way of getting out of it."

"My reason and my feelings are so much at variance that I find my resolution trembling in the balance. I have sent for you because I need sympathy as no man before ever needed it. I hope I may add support also, but I am not yet sure whether you are ready to support all my plans."

"I can speak better when I know them."

His Wisdom the Defender

"Let me repeat what I said to you the day of the launching. I told you my conviction that the more firm and aggressive my policy, so long as I keep within the bounds of law, the better for humanity. Under our system of international law, the first nation that can get possession of a fleet of motes will have power to make all other nations its vassals. Its right to do this if it can is recognized. To clarify our ideas, and not mislead you, let me say that this law was not altogether bad in the past, because the nation that could overcome in battle was the one that possessed in the highest degree those qualities of intellect, enterprise, courage, and patriotism which fitted it to rule weaker peoples for their good. But this is no longer the case when the conqueror is merely the first nation that chances to get a fleet of motes. We must, therefore, secure the independence of nations and peoples by law.

"Now, we cannot discuss the situation profitably unless we have some previously defined basis to start from. Allow me, therefore, to say that I have for years past—in fact, ever since I discovered that motes were possible—been perfecting a system of laws to govern the relations of nations. I want you to study them, and tell me what you think of them. I also want you to submit them to the counsellors you have brought from Europe, to be discussed and amended by them. Here they are; read them."

Winthrop read aloud:

Our Hero Makes a Clean Breast

"'Article 1.—There shall be no more war.'

"An excellent provision if you could enforce it. But how are you going to prevent nations from going to war? What are armies and navies for except to fight?"

"I am glad you put the question in that form, because that is just what I am asking myself. Now read on and see my answer."

"'Article 2.—There shall hereafter be no armies or navies except such as shall be necessary to the protection of life and property within the state to which they belong.'

"This is also very good, but how are you ever going to induce nations to give up armies and navies? One will always be waiting for another to disband first, even after they all agree to disband. Perhaps in a few hundred years they will do it, little by little, but in our time never!"

"First let me ask: will it be a good thing, under present circumstances, if war, armies, and navies be all abolished, and the relations of nations governed by law?"

"To that question there can be no two answers. My objection is not to the desirability, but to the possibility of the end."

"Very well; suppose I abolish the armies and navies of Europe by force?"

Winthrop looked at his companion in astonishment.

"Why, my dear friend, you nearly take my breath

His Wisdom the Defender

away. Is this really the object of keeping Gheen's expedition out of sight and hearing?"

"It is!"

"But you told the ambassadors it was not armed."

"It is not. I do not propose to use a weapon of any sort, except in self-defence. I have for a year been perfecting my plan in the minutest details. Nothing remains but to put it into execution, if I can."

"But what right have you, a private individual, to make war—for war it will be—on your own account?"

"So far as existing law goes, none whatever—no more than I have to batter down the door of a man's house and enter it by force to keep it from burning down. I hold that the might which God has placed in my hands makes right in such an emergency as the present one."

"But do you seriously believe that you have the physical force to disarm all Europe?"

"I cannot speak with entire confidence, but I think I have. If I cannot do more, I can at least demonstrate the uselessness of the existing armies, and thus pave the way for voluntary disbandment. I feel confident I can bring the nations of Europe to terms of some kind."

The speaker rose to his feet and continued his discourse with an energy that took his interlocutor quite by surprise.

"Let us rise above our petty surroundings and

Our Hero Makes a Clean Breast

look into the future. If I succeed in my efforts; if I induce or force the nations to accept the principle that all international differences are to be settled by impartial tribunals of statesmen and publicists; if I thus introduce an era of universal peace—what will the world of the future say? What will you say?"

Winthrop also arose, and paced the floor in meditation. Then he began to be imbued with some of the feelings of his companion.

"You will be the greatest benefactor of the human race that the modern world has seen!"

"That is enough. Now let me tell you what I want of you. I have long felt that if I should succeed in having my plans accepted by the world, I would want you as my leading official adviser, for a time at least, perhaps for good. Will you accept a position that I hope will be among the most brilliant the world can offer, if the time should come?"

"Is it necessary to decide in advance?"

"No, not absolutely. I only want to know your sentiments, because I want your help in the meantime. Let me explain. You know that to-morrow I am to meet the foreign representatives and the leading dignitaries of this country. I shall make what will be as good as a clean breast of my plans, omitting details. I want you to be present and receive as my representative. Immediately after my address I shall disappear. Remember, above all, that I do not want to involve you in any way. I shall tread

His Wisdom the Defender

the wine-press alone, and you can proclaim yourself as in no way responsible for me or my doings. I want you to stay here, or at Washington, as you deem best, and see people. But first of all I shall leave with you a number of printed copies of the proposed laws. I want you to lay them before our counsellors, and invite them to study and perfect them by amendments. Very likely they will decline, lest their own governments hold them guilty of high-treason. If so, let them return to their homes, and you can make the laws public as soon as you please. Before our own authorities you can disclaim all responsibility for my acts. You have neither aided nor abetted them in any way. You are simply one of my acquaintances—perhaps the one who has most influence with me. I do not know whether you can reach me by telegraph; when you can you may send me news, but I am not desirous of any word of discouragement."

"Allow me one word before we part," said Winthrop. "You are not sure of success; is there not something desperate in your resolve to risk everything in a single bold venture? What will become of you—what will become of your motes, what will become of all of us if you are driven to succumb? Is it not better, after all, to wait, watch the course of events, and make some arrangement with the world?"

"Here again you fail to grasp the logic of the situation. The world will come to no conclusion

Our Hero Makes a Clean Breast

until it knows by actual experience what the motes can do. If I fail, if I am forced to desist from my attempt, I can still say, 'Behold what a terrible power you see before you. What will you do to regulate it and insure that it shall be used only for the benefit of humanity?' Then, especially with my solution of the problem before it, the world will certainly be in a better position to reach a conclusion than it is now. I will explain this view in my address to-morrow. I do not see that we can profitably discuss the subject any further at present. Please return to the *Concordia* to-morrow at one o'clock and go with me to Washington. I shall see that our publicists are included in the invitation. Till then, adieu."

Just before the appointed hour the *Concordia* was seen hovering over the State Department, her motto, freshly gilt, shining in the sun. She came slowly and majestically to the ground in front of the building, and then threw out sumptuous steps, covered with velvet, on which the guests could mount into her. A crowd of policemen kept order in the precincts, and the attendants of the *Concordia,* in the white livery of the Owner's messengers, challenged all who came to the steps, admitting only the invitees. Arriving on the main deck the guests were ushered into a spacious room fitted up with a splendor which must have required many months of work.

Here they were received by Mr. Winthrop, who for the moment, represented the Owner of the Motes,

His Wisdom the Defender

with a ceremonious formality quite unlooked for. An usher inquired the official rank of each guest, and introduced him by his proper title.

First came his Excellency, the President of the United States. Then the Honorable Secretary of State of the United States. He was followed by the senior member of the diplomatic corps, his Excellency the Ambassador Extraordinary and Minister Plenipotentiary of his Majesty the Czar of all the Russias. And so on to the end.

The formality and the temporary absence of the principal figure caused some uneasiness among the foreign guests. If a *coup d'état*—the sudden assumption of a more than imperial authority over the affairs of the world—was really intended, a better opportunity could not have been found. All governments important enough to be in diplomatic communication with the leading country were represented here in the persons of their ambassadors. Could it be that the latter were entrapped into something in the nature of a coronation? Would they find the Owner of the Motes in the gorgeous robes of his self-assumed office? All that Winthrop could do to allay their apprehensions was to excuse the momentary absence of the Owner, who was in the adjoining saloon preparing his address.

Great, therefore, was the relief of all when the man they were looking for stepped in, as plainly clad as the rest. Even the red button of the Legion of Honor of France, which he habitually wore on cere-

Our Hero Makes a Clean Breast

monial occasions, was, with obvious propriety, replaced by a rose. Each guest was presented, then the whole party followed Campbell into the saloon. At the farther end stood a table, at which two secretaries were seated, one of whom had a pile of papers before him. Beyond the table was seen in artistically illuminated letters the lines:

"When the war-drum throbs no longer and the battle flag is furled,
In the Parliament of Man, the Federation of the world."

Campbell took his seat at the table, while the guests were being seated around the saloon. When all was still he arose, amid breathless silence, and began to read his address from the printed sheets, handed him by one of the secretaries, while the other took each sheet as its reading was completed.

He began with picturing the extraordinary crisis which the building of the motes was to make in the history of the world and the revolution which they would necessarily create in the relations of nations. The whole picture was drawn from the point of view of an impartial looker-on belonging to no one country, and not even bound to any one stage of civilization. Jew and Gentile, bond and free, European, African, and Asiatic were all considered as having equal rights. Then the results of using motes in warfare were touched upon. The world at large had already seen these results so clearly that there was no need of depicting them. One thing was evident—there could logically be only one more war.

His Wisdom the Defender

The outcome of the first war would be to make the conquering nation, whichever it might be, the master of the world. That nation would not be the strongest or the most civilized, but simply the one that should first get possession of a fleet of motes. The reasons why such a result was not to be tolerated were fully set forth.

Was it then possible to make any arrangements by which the practice of war should be continued, and yet the motes be neutralized by an international agreement that they should never be used in warfare? If such an agreement was made, would all implicitly rely on its performance?

Who could decide what "use in warfare" might mean? It would doubtless be easy to say that no troops will be transported in the motes under any circumstances, but how would it be with military supplies? How would it be with supplies necessary for defending a port? Would there not be something illogical in a people submitting to seeing its territory invaded, its fortifications bombarded, and its cities occupied by a foreign power, when it had a most efficient and certain means of defence within its reach, which, however, it had agreed not to use? Self-preservation is the first law of nature, for a nation as for an individual. "I ask you on your consciences, Excellencies and Gentlemen, whether any one of the nations which you represent would wage war upon another having in its hands the means to repel attack, with entire confidence that such

Our Hero Makes a Clean Breast

means would not be called into requisition? I am sure your answer would be in the negative; and this would be equivalent to admitting that war is no longer to be waged. If, then, we are to have no more war, are we still to have armies? These have no purpose except to fight. If a nation is resolved to fight no more, it has no use for an army. To maintain one would be making known to all other nations that it still had war in view. No obvious course seems open short of all nations coming together and agreeing each and all to absolutely abolish their military establishments?

"Such a course cannot for a moment be expected of them. No matter what agreement may be made, every one will wait for the others. It is impossible that all should keep step in full confidence that every other would accept the situation without reserve. No government would feel justified in going before its people with a proposition to disband all its armies unconditionally, until it has satisfied itself as to the means of defence it might then have against encroachments.

"What, then, is the situation? The world stands on a slumbering volcano, whose fires it has no means to quench, and from which it has no avenue of escape by its own act. Who brought it there? The man who has the honor to address you. What is the duty of one that has brought on such a crisis? To carry the world safely through it if he can. What can he do?

His Wisdom the Defender

"The answer is uncertain until he makes the attempt. It is still uncertain whether I possess the power to disarm and disband the armies of the world and to haul its navies ashore."

These words produced among those who heard them what might be described as a shock of silence. Every one started as if by an electric stroke, but uttered no word. The speaker continued:

"But if I should possess this power, then the question will arise whether the best interests of humanity do not demand its immediate exercise.

"If I should now proceed, without bloodshed, to disarm and disband the armies of the world, to haul its navies ashore, to assume for myself and my successors in office the title and functions of Defender of the Peace of the World; as such Defender to move all nations to the establishment of a central tribunal for the arbitration of all international questions, and for the exercise of supreme power over the system of international communication which I am now organizing—if I should thus put an end to war and assure to all nations and peoples the blessings of security and peace forever, then, whatever my contemporaries might think of my acts, would not all future generations call me blessed?

"Gentlemen, I am not here to conceal any thought from you. If you should ask me how I think and feel on this question, I would answer thus: When I reflect, on the one hand, how great the labor and how heavy the responsibility which I should assume

Our Hero Makes a Clean Breast

by the policy I have indicated; and, on the other, how easy it is to let events take their course and leave humanity to guard its own interests—I shrink from the task. But when I reflect that perhaps it is within my power so to guide the course of events that never again in human history shall father, son, or brother take leave of his loved ones to expose his person in battle; that never again shall a seaport fear the bombardment of a navy; that never again shall a city fear the attack of an army; that never again shall a people groan under a war tax; that never again shall a nation tremble for its independence—I feel moved to action by a power which I doubt my ability to resist."

These concluding words were spoken with a pathos which added to their force, and at the same time, if it were possible, calmed the feelings which they were fitted to excite. Printed copies of the address were circulated among the guests. The latter were so moved that they scarcely knew what to do first. As a matter of official duty it was necessary for the ambassadors to telegraph the address immediately to their respective governments. But they also wanted to confer together. To some it seemed necessary to give a word of warning to the Owner of the Motes as to the grave consequences of entering upon such a policy as he had indicated. A few hurried words were exchanged with the President and the Secretary of State. All the ambassadors had time to say was, "You had better not attempt it;

His Wisdom the Defender

count the cost. Mr. President, Mr. Secretary, the motes are under the control of a citizen of your country; give him due warning."

The President simply remarked, " I trust you will listen to what will be said on the subject. Let the Secretary of State speak."

" Mr. Campbell," said the Secretary, " when you were in my office a few days since I asked you as to your reason for maintaining in such secrecy, at some distant and unknown point, the expedition which you had sent out. Your answer to my question was evasive. Now an answer is no longer necessary. We conclude, and the world will conclude, that that expedition is an armed one, intended to attack countries with which the United States is at peace. You are a man of intelligence and learning, and are doubtless acquainted with the neutrality laws of your country. I feel it my duty to go outside the usual limits of my official position and ask you to reflect upon the consequences of such an act as you propose. You know what my painful duty will be should you enter upon it, and you cannot need any assurance from me that it will be performed, come what may. We must now leave you to your own reflections."

Again to Campbell's ear the voice, audible to none but him, repeated its maxim: " He who would wield the power of a god must bear the responsibility of a god."

In the excitement of the moment the visitors had overlooked a feature of their reception in which they

Our Hero Makes a Clean Breast

might have seen some significance. Among the two or three people who were in the room when they were presented to the Owner of the Motes was one of the leading artists of New York, who quietly remained in the background during the entire course of the proceedings. He was behind a screen at Campbell's right in the farther corner of the room. His head could be seen over the screen, behind which he was sketching the outlines of a picture. This was the origin of what is now one of the historic pictures of the world. The original is well known to every visitor who has called at the Defender's Palace in Uraniberg; a replica is one of the great attractions at the Metropolitan Museum in New York.

As soon as the last visitor had departed the *Concordia* sailed away for Campbelltown. There Campbell had everything ready for the instant departure of a second expedition under his personal command. No one was surprised when, shortly after dark, a hundred motes, most of which had been fitting out for several days, rose in the air and disappeared towards the north.

The departure was of course telegraphed immediately to all the journals of the world. The urgent inquiries made by correspondents and others of the superintendent left in charge at Campbelltown failed to reveal anything further as the intentions or projected movements of the Owner. Winthrop alone was in possession of the essential part of the secret, and he refused to say anything.

XIII

The Mysterious Expedition

WE now return to the fleet of motes, numbering more than two hundred, which so mysteriously disappeared from the channel in which they were moored more than a month before the date of the events recorded in the last chapter. The boats, as they were naturally called, were a mystery to all concerned, except their owner, Captain Gheen, and perhaps two or three of the leading Seraphs. As they floated they were arranged in rank and file; each was chained to the one in front, the one behind, and the one on each side of it, so that it was impossible for any one to escape from the serried mass. For several days the work of loading them had been going on. Not only every article which one could imagine to be required on any sort of an expedition, but countless mysterious boxes, some large, some small, some light, some heavy, were put aboard. That after being thus loaded all the motes seemed to float as lightly as swans, was only one of the many mysteries connected with this singular affair. For several nights the Seraphs and work-

The Mysterious Expedition

men selected for the expedition had been required to sleep on board in their respective stations, even when employed at their regular duties during the day. And yet, in the absence of any visible mode of propulsion, it could scarcely be believed that the expedition was really going to start soon.

Each boat had a captain, a lieutenant, and ten or twelve men. In each was a system of levers worked by an electric current, starting from the captain's mote in the centre of the fleet. To guard against any possible failure of the current to move these levers, it was explained to each captain that on a signal being given he was to see that the levers took their proper position. This was done so often without any effect occurring that captain and men looked upon the process with entire indifference. The sharp edge of curiosity as to the object of such eccentric proceedings had been worn away by custom until everybody went through his part with an approach to stolidity.

On the eventful night the men had nearly all retired to their respective bunks, while the captains, as usual, were watching the levers. A slight motion was given, when, to the surprise of the few who were awake and looking out, the whole fleet started down the stream, with about the swiftness of an average steamer. In an hour the mouth of the Potomac was reached, and the fleet was making its way into the Chesapeake. Gheen stood on the deck of his mote, peering round to see if any stray boat might be in sight to watch his movements. Seeing none, he gave the signal for setting the levers, and then touched the electric button which moved them. Those who were still awake felt so singular a motion that many jumped out of their bunks and mounted to the deck to ascertain the cause. To the astonishment of all, the water was no longer to be seen. The whole fleet seemed to be in a dark cloud. The astonishment among the lookers-out was such that they could not cry to their companions. Such exclamations, in a low voice, as, " Bedad, we're bewitched!" " Holy Mither, where are we?" " Virgin Mary, have mercy on us!" were all that one could have heard uttered.

One poor man jumped overboard in his fright, and of course was not again heard of. Very soon, however, the motion was so smooth that, swift though it was, the sleepers were not disturbed by it. Shortly the whole fleet was above the clouds, making its swift way to the north. It was extremely desirable that the journey should be made unseen from the earth.

The starting hour had been so arranged that it was hoped the northern limit of the Canadian border would be passed before sunrise. Fortunately the morning was cloudy in the region through which the motes ran, so that, being above the clouds, they passed on from below unperceived. In the afternoon the fleet was over Hudson's Bay and proceeded to follow the northern coast of Smith Strait, keeping a sharp lookout to avoid the possible eyes of men on

The Mysterious Expedition

board passing vessels. The problem was to get as far north as possible, so as to run the least danger of being discovered for at least a month, and to find a place which was not covered with snow. A map had been carefully prepared long before, showing the location of all the trading and fur posts in the region. A point was at length fixed upon which seemed to fulfil the necessary conditions as well as could be expected. The fleet, its motion guided by the adjusting levers, slowly and carefully came to the ground. Gheen called his captains together, and all joined in a prayer-offering of heartfelt thanks for having made their wonderful journey in safety.

"What does this mean?" was demanded of Gheen on all sides.

"It means," said he, "that we are the pioneers of a new dispensation; that we are to inaugurate a golden age; that, if we are true to each other, we shall soon be among the greatest men of the world. More than that I cannot now tell you. Unload the motes and pitch the tents."

On unloading, wood and iron for huts were brought forth, machinery of all sorts was taken out and put together, and comfortable beds were found and put into the huts. By nightfall, which, at that season and in that latitude, did not occur until ten o'clock, the encampment looked as if much of the wealth of a populous city had been suddenly poured down into the uninhabited place. As soon as possible all tried to sleep as best they could, either in the tents or in the motes. The men, nine-tenths of whom were natives of the Emerald Isle, had been so much fatigued that they slept soundly, regardless of the morrow. We doubt very much whether the same was true of the three hundred Seraphs. To them it was as if they had been suddenly transferred to some new world, where everything went by contraries. They puzzled their brains in vain to divine the object of their expedition. But all had pledged their honor to obey orders and ask no questions; so nothing could be done but await developments.

Next morning they had got sufficiently inured to their situation to at least recover their tranquillity. How long they were to remain, only Gheen and perhaps two or three others knew, but the pitching of the tents had shown that an immediate departure was not intended. After breakfast the work of unloading the motes was resumed. Within them were found the dissected parts of not less than two hundred daddies. All had been practised in putting these together, and in the course of a day the party had the satisfaction of seeing many of them ready for use, so far as externals went. But to all appearance they compared with those in the Coliseum only as dead men would compare with live ones. They lay prone on the ground with no apparent faculty of life or motion. The general idea was that they needed cords with which to be suspended, though of what use they could be even then no one could

The Mysterious Expedition

divine. Of the motes, about one-half were pierced with openings through which were to pass the linked arms, which, when in place, would turn them into the centipedes already described. Each centipede had its arms inside the mote which was to form its body. Taking them out and fitting them into place occupied the rest of the day. The party went to bed that night without seeing any more light on the problem what they were to do.

On the second morning a number of articles were unloaded which, if possible, were even more puzzling than those already brought out. They consisted of soft gunny-bags, about a foot in diameter and five feet long, each of which was stuffed with thin, empty bottles. Notwithstanding the delicacy of these bottles, they were made of very ordinary glass, like that of wine-bottles. Each was about four inches in diameter and a foot high, so that it would hold almost a gallon. A number of the men were employed in taking them out of the bags and filling them with water, corking them up and putting them back again in place. When properly arranged and tied up, each bag, stuffed as it was with bottles, could be stood erect.

While this was going on Gheen informed the Seraphs that their principal work while they remained at the station would be the practice of certain evolutions. The chains by which the motes had been fastened together had been removed in order to facilitate the unloading. Now, the captains were told,

His Wisdom the Defender

each mote would have to move on its own account, in obedience to orders from headquarters. They were warned in no case to go more than a mile from the central station, because the therm with which they were charged had been so nearly consumed by the journey that it might give out at any moment. When it did give out, it could be renewed by heat generated by the combustion of coal which had been brought along. Until this was done, it would be impossible for the motes to go any great distance.

Before operations could begin, it was necessary to charge the daddies so that they could be used. For this purpose a large supply of levers of the kind we saw in the workshop at Cambridge four years before were brought into requisition. Two pairs of these levers were placed in each daddie. A Seraph crawled into the hollow through the head and soon saw what was to be done from having practised in the Coliseum. As a precaution, each daddie was first tied down by a long rope to prevent the possibility of its flying off into space and never being seen again, through some blunder on the part of the man inside of it. The daddie first stood erect and then rose into the air, its long legs dangling below it. It was manœuvred by the man inside of it until it was certain that the method of managing it was fully understood. Then it came to the ground, the tether which fastened it was cast off, and in its place an electric wire was connected with a system of keys inside of it. The other end of this wire was carried

The Mysterious Expedition

to a centipede and then connected with a signal-board within it. In this way the man in the daddie could send such signals as he desired to the captain of the centipede, who was to stand at the switchboard. Inside the daddie the electric wire was wound round a roll, so that it could be drawn in or pulled out at pleasure, thus permitting of the daddie being either close down to the mote or at a height of several hundred yards in the air.

To communicate orders from headquarters, a number of electric syrens had been provided. The largest of these were on board of Gheen's mote. They emitted a musical note, the tone of which could be changed at pleasure, so as to play any required tune. The volume of sound emitted by them was such that they could be heard at a distance of from one to two miles. Twenty of the daddies were supplied with smaller syrens, by which any signals received from the great ones could be repeated. A system of numbers was devised, so that every man in charge of a daddie or a mote should know for whom an order was intended.

When everything was ready, evolutions were begun. The commanding mote took its position half a mile in the air. Practice was first begun with a single centipede. When the latter was in operation each of its dozen legs was worked by a man inside the body of the mote, and therefore invisible. The twelve men sat in two rows, six on each side. Alongside of each opening through which an arm went was

His Wisdom the Defender

a small round hole, about an inch in diameter, in which was fitted a peculiar binocular telescope, especially designed for the purpose in view. By putting his eye to this telescope, the man who was managing the arm could see round and below him on the outside. At the word of command the mote rose and fell, described a circle in one direction or another, or rested on the ground while the arms worked in the air. Everything being understood, the gunny-bags, with their strange contents, were stood up in a row, about four feet apart. Every one was then informed that a centipede was to approach these bags, seize them gently in its tentacles, lift them into the air, and stand them on the deck of the mote without breaking any of the bottles. This took a good deal of practice, and so many bottles were broken in the beginning that new bags had to be several times filled. Then similar practice was had in putting the bags, not on the deck of the centipede itself, but on the deck of another mote. The first attempts of this sort were so destructive to the bottles that, instead of practising the remaining centipedes on them, a dozen wooden logs, which had been brought along for the purpose, were stood up to take the place of the gunny-bags.

The first practice of this sort was witnessed by the assembled crowd in order to familiarize it with what was to be done. Then one mote after another was gradually landed and put through the motions, until the whole fleet was manœuvring simultaneously

The Mysterious Expedition

over a space extending a quarter of a mile on all sides of the camp. Sometimes orders were given directly to the mote and sometimes to the daddie. As a general rule, the captain of the mote kept his position in the daddie, that he might see what was going on.

It would take too much time to enumerate all the evolutions that were performed. Besides those already mentioned, practice was had in the management of powerful hooks attached to about a dozen of the daddies, much larger and more powerful than the others. There was nothing in the region that we should call trees, only some low shrubbery showing itself here and there above the moss-covered ground. The hooks in question were employed in tearing these up by the roots, in digging in the ground for stones, in rolling logs, and in pulling things to pieces generally. The other daddies were practised in the use of their hands and feet, so that they could pick up almost anything, large or small, and handle it at pleasure. To give interest to the exercises, games were devised which could be played sometimes by the centipedes or the daddies by themselves, and sometimes by both combined. In one game the centipedes were on one side and the daddies on the other.

When great facility in manœuvring the tentacles of the centipedes and the hands of the daddies was attained, a different kind of practice was begun. Several hundred of the men would be arranged in

His Wisdom the Defender

ranks, like a company of soldiers, with sticks in their hands to serve as arms. The daddies and the centipedes were to go up to them, pull these sticks out of their hands, and deposit them in the motes, without endangering the men. The latter were to fight against this by brandishing their sticks and pushing off the daddies, if possible. Very soon the metallic finger of the crooked beings acquired such dexterity that the stick could be instantly seized in spite of everything which the holder could do to prevent it.

This exercise seemed to throw light on a possible object of the whole affair. What that light was our readers can judge as well as we can tell them. When an army used to suffer, for a period of several weeks, the ennui of camp life, the soldiers felt ready for any adventure, regardless of consequences. It was not at all wonderful that the members of this isolated community, after a month of labor in a position where they were completely cut off from all contact with the rest of the world, got into a state of mind not altogether different. They were not exactly desirous of a fight, for, so far as had yet appeared, no fight was in view. But they did get very anxious to try their newly acquired skill on a large scale, and a feeling of recklessness as to the way in which their skill should be used gradually took possession of them.

The directions given to Gheen were that, after his men had gotten into thorough practice, the whole expedition was to move over to Iceland and camp on

The Mysterious Expedition

the peninsula in its northern portion. There the exercises were to be renewed, and thither supplies of everything necessary would be sent him.

At the end of a month Gheen received the message we have already mentioned, directing him to be in readiness as soon as possible. He lost no time in packing up and moving the whole encampment over to Iceland. Here everything was again unpacked and put into working order, evolutions recommenced, and further orders were awaited. Before a week had been passed at the new station, one of the men caught sight of an approaching fleet of motes in the air. It was the supplementary fleet with which the Owner himself had started from Campbelltown on the evening before. The new-comers were welcomed with their supply of several weeks' news from the outer world, besides fresh provisions and a number of miscellaneous articles conducive to human comfort. They learned for the first time of the great unveiling and the universal excitement thereby caused. As a matter of prudence, Campbell had not allowed any papers containing the discussions of the past weeks as to his objects and purposes to be brought along. But letters from families and friends were brought in sufficient number to compensate for the absence of the latest general intelligence.

As every hour's delay in commencing active operations would enable the authorities of Europe to prepare against possible attack, he took Gheen's word that everything was in readiness, and ordered the

His Wisdom the Defender

expedition to start. He waited only to call the Seraphs together and make a short speech on the importance of their enterprise. "If you are true to one another," he said, "and if you falter not, you will make more and better history during the next six months than all the kings and rulers of the world have made in a thousand years. You will be among the greatest benefactors of the human race that have ever appeared on the earth. Your children's children will remember your title with pride; the insignia of your order will be a source of greater honor than the stars of any order in Europe."

Campbell and Gheen had long before decided that their first attempt should be made on the German armies. Minute information respecting encampments, arsenals, factories, stores, and everything else pertaining to the German military organization had been collected. So towards Berlin the fleet took its way, arriving just before sunset. After making a survey of the city and the surrounding country, a point in an unfrequented locality, about twenty miles north of Berlin, was selected in which to pass the night. In order to relieve the captains of the necessity of keeping the motes afloat, the repose of night was sought with the motes resting on the ground. Of course the point was chosen as far as possible from railways and telegraphs, so that there should be no danger of an attack before morning. Meanwhile, a messenger was sent with a letter to the German Emperor, to the following effect:

The Mysterious Expedition

"*To His Majesty, the German Emperor:*
 "May it please your Majesty—
 "Deeming it of the greatest importance to the human race that the question whether I possess the power to disarm and disband the armies of Europe should be decisively settled, at the earliest possible moment, I beg leave to inform your Majesty that I propose to learn by actual experiment whether I possess the power to disarm and disband your Majesty's armies. Should the result be in the affirmative, I shall consider myself bound to protect the German territory from any attack by another power, if only your Majesty's government shall enter into some arrangement for abolishing the practice of war. It is also my intention to compensate the treasury of your Majesty for all property that may be destroyed by my operations."
 "Your Majesty's obedient servant,
  "ARCHIBALD CAMPBELL."

The problem how to get this letter into the hands of the Emperor was no easy one. It was first sent direct to the royal palace, but the messenger returned with the statement that the sentry stationed at the door had refused to receive it. The plan was therefore adopted of sending it to the nearest post-office. The messenger who carried it was conveyed in a small but swift mote, from which he descended out of the sky almost in a moment, as it were.

His Wisdom the Defender

The rules did not permit the postmaster to transmit the letter unless assured of its legitimate character. But, in the present case, telegraphic communication with the central postal authorities resulted in the letter being speedily forwarded. What its result was Campbell could only guess.

XIV

The Attack on the German Armies

WE now return to the world at large and review its history during the days following the address of Campbell to the assembled dignitaries. The excitement caused by this message exceeded even that which had followed the previous developments of these eventful weeks. The calmest view of the case was taken by the New York *Evening Post* in the following terms:

" Never in history have words been spoken of such import to mankind as those which are found in our present issue. Almost before the end of the address was reached, every telegraph line in the world was carrying the message under the ocean and through the air to all the nations and peoples of the globe. In the most distant parts of China men are telling the news to their neighbors; on the plains of Tibet the assembled tribes are hearing it from their leaders; in Australia men are running to and fro asking each other what is to be done. Round every camp-fire in Africa sable crowds are gathered, listening to the reading. Every crowned head and every prime-min-

His Wisdom the Defender

ister in Europe is absorbed by the questions which it raises. Men everywhere have abandoned their usual occupations and are eagerly awaiting the blow that is to be struck. For the first time in the history of the world only one subject is being discussed by the learned and the ignorant, by savage and sage, by the rulers and the masses." . . . .

By some telephatic process, perhaps, a general impression was spread abroad that, if Campbell really entered upon his daring attempt, the German armies would be his first object of attack. How the attack would be made, by what means he could possibly expect to disarm a hundred thousand men, and that without bloodshed, even with the advantages offered by the motes, no one could anticipate. The German Emperor spent most of the day in council with his generals as to the proper disposition of the troops in order that they might defend themselves to the best advantage.

Two views were held by members of the council—the one prudent, the other bold. The counsel of the more prudent leaders was to order all the troops into their barracks, or quarter them everywhere in houses, so that it would be as difficult as possible to get at them, and to keep them there until the plan of attack was discovered. This party urged the imprudence of massing men in the open field against an aerial enemy that might be armed with machine-guns. Who knew but that, after all, the statements of the New York *Herald* might not be literally true? Grant-

The Attack on the German Armies

ing that Campbell had no purchased machine-guns with him, he might have made any number in the secret recesses of his vast establishment, which no visitor had ever been allowed to see. His denial that his force was not armed with these or any other weapons could not be trusted. If he lied outright, what resource was left against him? He would claim that the end justified the means, and all ethical argument with him would be useless. If he had sent guns, an army in the field would, as the *Herald* had said, melt away like snow under a tropical sun, unless the lives of its soldiers were saved by an unconditional surrender.

It was urged, on the other side, that soldiers hidden away in barracks and houses would be like chickens in a coop. They might be captured or killed, but could not fight. For all practical purposes an army of such soldiers was already disbanded. The whole country would be at the mercy of the enemy, who, if he had guns and ammunition, could riddle the barracks with shot and burn down the houses in which the men were quartered. An enemy which would attack a body of helpless men with murderous weapons would devastate the country and burn and destroy property without limit.

The Emperor spoke. " I am in favor of the more active course. Armies are organized to fight. The day their men are scattered in houses where they can not fight they cease to be armies."

A middle course was at length decided on. Of

His Wisdom the Defender

the army practising the autumn manœuvres, 100,000 should be massed in the field where they now were, and the remainder should be sent to their barracks until it was seen how the others fared, or, at least, how they were to be attacked.

"A system of defence must next be devised," said the Emperor. "To do this we must have some idea of the probable mode of attack. Can any one of the generals make a suggestion on this subject?"

"The matter presents itself to me in this way," said General Steinitz. "Notwithstanding all that has been said as to what schemes our enemy may have in mind, I am disposed to attach credence to his utterances. He has absolutely denied having deadly weapons in the possession of his forces. Both in his address and in his letter to your Majesty he has spoken only of disarming, not of fighting. To attack with missiles of any sort would not be to disarm. He cannot disarm without sending his forces to grapple hand to hand with our troops. Now let us take this point of view, as to the possibility of doing this. He knows, or at least may well think, that, if he can once get into the midst of a regiment with his motes, he can act with impunity, because he cannot be attacked by guns of any kind without our own men being killed. While he is in the air he can bid defiance to artillery; it is impossible to point a gun at a flying object. As for musketry, we may assume that all the motes he intends to attack us in are built with the toughened alloy, and are therefore

The Attack on the German Armies

bullet-proof, as we have already found by experiment. At any rate, if they are not proof, our task will be a very simple one. Troops firing in the air can all fire at once and incessantly without breaking their ranks or moving from their places. Motes not bullet-proof would therefore be riddled before one of them could reach our army. The enemy must know this, and have guarded against it. Thus the problem is how our troops can defend themselves from an enemy in their midst without danger to themselves?"

"How heavy a shot is required to pierce the toughened alloy?" asked the Emperor. "I have not the results of the trials in detail in my mind."

"We found that to really pierce a plate of the metal one centimetre thick required a steel shot of the weight of three ounces. A lighter steel shot, or a leaden shot of that weight, would indent the plate but would not pierce it. The weight of metal required was proportioned to the thickness of the plate."

"In all likelihood the sides of the motes are at least a centimetre thick," said the Emperor; "it is clearly useless to attack with anything lighter than the Nordhoff repeating-guns."

"If our men should throw themselves flat on the ground, could not the Nordhoffs be fired at the motes over their heads?"

"We should hit more of our men than of the enemy," replied the Emperor, "and I do not want it said that our men merely killed each other."

His Wisdom the Defender

"Suppose we instructed our troops to break ranks, and run from the mote in each direction the moment one landed in their midst. This would leave the enemy alone for at least a few seconds, and then the gun could put in its work."

"We are talking as if the enemy had no eyes," said General Müller. "If we had Nordhoff guns or any other artillery in the field, he would make for them first and carry them off in a jiffy."

"We can conceal them," replied the other, after a pause. "We can put them under small tents or even sheets of canvas, leaving a hole to fire through. Let them be trained so as to enfilade our ranks; then, when our ranks scatter, they can be trained on any mote near the line of fire in an instant."

This plan soon received unanimous approval, though the Emperor was somewhat fearful that the gunners might lose their heads in the turmoil and fire while their own men were in line. "Select the coolest gunners in the army for this work," said he to the chief of artillery. "I leave the details to the several generals. The chief of cavalry is to have all the cavalry within reach drawn up to help the infantry if possible."

The question of this arm had not even been considered in council, and the generals doubted the wisdom of calling on it. But the case was not clear enough to warrant the raising of any objection to the imperial will.

"Now," said the Emperor, "I want the result

The Attack on the German Armies

to be decisive if possible. The men who shall attack us to-morrow have no standing in the eye of the law. They will be outlaws, pure and simple, from the moment that they strike a blow. The Adjutant-General will therefore issue a general order to the army in the terms which I am now going to dictate:

"It is expected that you will be attacked by bandits from the air, either to-morrow morning or at some very early day. Defend yourselves to the utmost. Fire at the armies in the air as you would fire upon armies on the ground. Capture the enemy and his ships, if possible. Show no quarter to any, but put every man you find in the motes immediately to death, with bullet and bayonet."

There were no late sleepers next morning in northern Germany. Every one well enough to move was up at daylight, and, if near enough to Potsdam, was on his way to see what should happen. The troops were marshalled on the proposed place at break of day.

Let us now return to the attacking party. The leaders were as much in the dark trying to guess the policy of the Germans as the latter were to guess the mode of attack. Would the Emperor show fight, or would he surrender to superior force with all the protestations necessary to save his honor? Could an army be induced to fight vigorously against a foe in the clouds, or would hereditary superstition so

His Wisdom the Defender

demoralize them that they would lay down their arms at the first blow? If determined to defend themselves to the bitter end, what would be their tactics?

These questions could be answered only by trial. The whole plan of attack was in Gheen's hands. He had been somewhat uneasy as to this, but his solicitude on this point was set at rest by the declaration of his chief:

"Heretofore we have consulted at every step. We have now reached a stage where, for the time being, vigorous and united action is the watchword. From this moment you are sole commander of our forces, and I am only a spectator, except when some question of policy arises which I am to decide. So give your orders and change your plan of battle from moment to moment as you deem best, consulting me only in case you are in such trouble that I must decide upon the course to be pursued. We both need a sound night's sleep to prepare us for the morrow. So try to sleep as if you had nothing on your mind. They say that a condemned man always sleeps well the night before he is to be hanged, and that an army does the same when it expects to be awakened by the rattling of musketry. Perhaps the rule will apply to our case."

It did. Both men were surprised when informed by the sentries that it was nearly sunrise. Gheen wanted to start early, because he did not know where or in what condition he might find the enemy.

The Attack on the German Armies

As he was getting ready he was surprised by one of the captains of the centipedes asking to have a confidential interview with him. The captain reported that suspicions existed among several of the Seraphim as to the loyalty of one of their number. The suspected person was in charge of daddie 79. He had made several remarks to his fellow-men expressing deep concern as to the legality of the undertaking in which they were engaged, and a keen appreciation of the advantages that would accrue to any one who should succeed in putting his instrument into the possession of the Germans. Gheen thought it best to take no action in the matter, but simply to keep a look-out on the suspected daddie.

Naturally the first place to look for the army was on the field of manœuvres, where he hoped it might be bivouacked. He was therefore agreeably surprised to see the enemy drawn up in the very array he would have chosen had he been allowed to direct its formation. What he had most feared was being under the necessity of chasing scattered squads here and there over the country, a proceeding which might have worn him out, enticed him into ambushes, and led to the capture of some of his motes. In serried ranks the enemy had no chance of escape, unless by some device he had not foreseen.

At six o'clock the fleet of 350 motes was over the field, a mile high, looking like so many huge vultures about to pounce upon their prey. Lowest of all were the plain motes, about two hundred in number.

His Wisdom the Defender

They were followed by 150 centipedes. Above and around them was a cloud of daddies. Still higher up were Gheen's headquarters on board the captain's mote. Above all, looking on but taking no active part in the struggle, was the *Concordia,* with the Owner on board.

As the motes approached, a perfect hailstorm of bullets was poured upon them from the army, but the aim was mostly too low; and the few that struck did no harm, because, as our readers know, the material of which they were made was bullet-proof, even if vulnerable to heavy shot. It was different with the centipedes, for, although they were made of the same material, there were joints and openings through which the bullets might enter and disable either the men or the delicate machinery. They were therefore ordered to stop and rise above the motes, out of the range of musketry.

While this was going on, Gheen surveyed the field. No heavy artillery, machine-guns, or ammunition wagons were in sight. Evidently the soldiers had no ammunition except what was in their pouches, and it would not take long to exhaust the supply if such a fire were kept up. He therefore directed the motes to sway back and forth, up and down, approaching the army and receding again, so as to tempt it to keep up the fire.

He thought the arrangement of the tents on each flank looked unusual, and, fearing a trap, ordered some daddies to pull a few of them up. Nothing un-

The Attack on the German Armies

usual being found under any of those removed, his suspicions were allayed. Still, he thought it prudent to begin his attack with a small force.

The work began without apparent loss of life or even serious injury to the infantry, as Campbell had hoped; but there was one tragic, if rather ludicrous incident. We have said that the Emperor, determined to use all his forces, had called out the cavalry as well as the other arms of the service, though it was difficult to see of what use it could have been. The unaccustomed sight of an armed force approaching in the air so frightened the horses that they became unmanageable, and ran away in a compact body, falling down and rolling over each other in their vain struggles with the bits of their riders. The result was that many of the latter suffered severe injuries, which proved fatal in not a few cases. The destruction among the horses was, of course, yet greater. That squadron of cavalry was most effectually disbanded.

When the fire began to slacken three or four centipedes came down side by side, swayed almost upon the ground alongside the front ranks of the soldiers, and proceeded to seize the arms from their hands and throw them on board, with a dexterity gained by long practice. The soldiers retreated slowly at first, closely followed by the centipedes. Then they suddenly turned and ran. At the same instant a machine-gun, concealed in a tent, opened fire. The shot was so heavy that the few which took effect com-

His Wisdom the Defender

pletely pierced the nearest mote. Not only were two men seriously wounded by the flying missiles, but the great tube, containing the etherine, which gave buoyancy to the vehicle, was pierced. The daddie immediately above the mote, grasping the situation, pounced upon the tent before more than three or four rounds could be fired, and carried the gun off with the greatest ease, throwing it after the retreating men as it had formerly thrown the gigantic tennis-balls in the Coliseum. The injured mote undertook to rise, but soon fell to the ground, fluttering like a wounded bird. It was first blood for the Germans.

The device was now obvious, and no difficulty was found in discovering the other guns concealed in the same way. All the tents along the flanks were demolished, and whatever guns were found in them were thrown to the ground in a moment. Then the great mass of motes came down upon the ranks of the army. In the main, the method of attack was to have a centipede settle on one side of a rank of soldiers and a plain mote on the other. As neither touched the ground, it was very easy in this way to follow the men as they tried to retreat. The centipede took the arms out of the mens' hands and put them on top of its own deck, and then took the men up and put them on the upper deck of the mote. Here, unarmed as they were, they were quite helpless, and obeyed the order to go below till the two lower decks were crowded. When a mote had as

The Attack on the German Armies

many of the disarmed men as could find a place on the decks, the men were asked to what part of the country they belonged. Usually all, or nearly all, on any one mote were from the same town or region. The mote was despatched to take them home, and on reaching their destination they were turned loose in the streets.

Campbell and Gheen had planned a scheme for requiring the men to put off their uniforms and dress in plain clothes, to be supplied them, but this was one of the arrangements which had fallen through in consequence of the necessity for a premature execution of the plan. The soldiers were therefore allowed to go home in their uniforms, thus leaving it possible to identify them as soldiers and collect them again if the opportunity offered. But it was hoped that the opportunity would not be offered.

The few mounted officers who had brought their horses into the field suffered as the cavalry had done, and were glad to dismount and let their horses run away. The men were in such good discipline that the confusion thus caused in the ranks was soon repaired, but the officers were on foot, like the men, and were sent off with them, a course quite different from that which had been intended.

"What does that mean?" said Gheen's signal officer, just at the height of the turmoil. Both men looked at a manœuvre not in the day's programme.

Daddie 79 was flying high above the main body of the force and making its way with all speed tow-

His Wisdom the Defender

ards Berlin. "Tell centipedes *King* and *Paul* to follow it and bring it back," said Gheen.

The centipedes were, of course, much swifter than a daddie; but the latter was lighter and could be moved about more readily. When the centipedes overtook and sought to seize it, it had no difficulty in evading them by an upward, downward, or lateral movement, without slackening its onward course. It kept on in this way, reached Berlin, and landed on the Unter den Linden immediately in front of the royal palace, before which a company of the Imperial Guards was stationed. The Seraph in charge of it opened its port and sprang to the ground. He was immediately pierced by a volley of balls from the soldiers, who naturally supposed that an attack on the palace, or on the person of the Emperor, was intended. A moment later the two centipedes followed. A volley was discharged against them, but, being shot-proof, no harm was done them. The foremost had no difficulty in seizing the daddie when the latter was on the ground, and in carrying it off. The only result of the incident was the death of the traitor by the hands of the enemy.

It is needless to say that a deep impression was made on the attacking army by this tragic result. It showed that, as a mere matter of safety, loyalty was the best policy.

When it became evident that the success of the plan was possible, a new and strange sight greeted the eyes of both armies. It was an immense banner, a

The Attack on the German Armies

hundred feet long and sixty feet in breadth, floating in the air between two motes, and bearing the words *—

> STRECKET GEWEHR
>
> DANN FRIEDE UND FREUDE
>
> EUCH KINDERN UND
>
> VATERLANDE

Many of the troops were quite ready to obey this request when it was seen that resistance was no longer possible. By nightfall three-quarters of the army assembled on the field were disarmed and sent to their homes, while the remainder, in a dazed and frightened condition, had thrown away their weapons and taken refuge in the barracks, thereby demoralizing their companions, or were wandering aimlessly over the country. Desirable though it was to lose no time in the pursuit, nothing could be done in the darkness; besides which, the men of the attacking party, though mostly working in two relays, were thoroughly exhausted. The fleet was therefore recalled at sunset, and a camping-place for the night was selected.

Up to this moment Campbell and Gheen had heard nothing from the world since the former had made

---

* Lay down your arms, then peace and joy for yourselves, children, and fatherland.

His Wisdom the Defender

his address and left his home to join forces with Gheen. Although he had deliberately reached the conclusion that the less he knew of what men thought of his doings, the better he could carry out his work, his curiosity had now got the upper-hand. He called three messenger motes and directed their conductors to sweep over the streets of Berlin, look for newspapers, and bring him a copy of each separate paper they could find. They were notified that the three must keep together, so that, in case anything happened to one of them, the two others could come to its rescue. Copies of several Berlin daily papers were thus secured, which the two leaders eagerly scanned.

What Campbell most feared was some concerted action by the leading nations to checkmate him by a common resistance to the bitter end. But the numerous telegrams from all quarters told of little but wild excitement, unreasoning comment, and proposals and suggestions of every degree of sanity and unsanity. So far as any thread of consistency could be traced in the mass, the feeling was in favor of waiting to see what the motes could or would do before taking decided action.

"But," said Campbell, studying the army news in the evening paper, "here is something we have got to look into."

"Well, what is it?"

Campbell read the Emperor's general order and looked at his companion.

The Attack on the German Armies

"I am rather glad our men did not know of that," said Gheen. "It might have enraged them or frightened them, and I don't know which would have been the worse."

"As they did not know it, I can't say that I am altogether sorry the Emperor has taken such ground. We want to know whether the old *régime* is to stand or give way to the new. The more desperate the fight it makes, the more decisive will be its defeat, if defeat it is, and the more readily men will welcome the victor. For this reason I am disposed to meet the Emperor's order with action as aggressive as his words. Would there be any difficulty in capturing him if he shows himself in the field to-morrow as he did to-day?"

"Not the slightest; but I don't believe he will show himself again. We should likely find it necessary to hunt him up in the council-chamber of the Schloss. He must have learned prudence from the day's experience."

"I am hardly prepared to go so far as to drag him from his council-chamber just at present. If he is seen out of doors, have him captured at once and brought on board the *Concordia*. If he keeps under cover—well—we will think the matter over."

"I should capture him wherever found on the very grounds you have taken. But there is no hurry, and perhaps we shall find him."

The Emperor's general order proved innocuous, as the troops had not found it possible to make any pris-

His Wisdom the Defender

oners or to seize a single mote except the disabled one, which was of no use to any one, and was therefore left on the field. When the worst of the fight was over a daddie was sent to blow it to pieces with dynamite.

The Emperor again spent the evening in council with his generals. Of the great army, 100,000 strong, which in the morning had been drawn up on the plains of Potsdam, hardly a vestige could be found. Telegrams from various towns in the provinces of Brandenburg and Mecklenburg showed that a large part of the men who had formed it were at their several homes, without arms, and that it was doubtful if they could be again brought together without a complete re-enlistment. The remainder had taken refuge in tents, barracks, or private houses, wherever they could find shelter, or were wandering aimlessly through the streets or over the fields. Decidedly the party which sustained the waiting policy was vindicated.

Only one course seemed feasible. All the troops in the neighborhood of Berlin, still numbering more than 100,000, must be gotten into their barracks or into the casemates of the fortifications before the attack was renewed in the morning. As the tents afforded no protection, those who were quartered in them might remain there for the night, but must join their comrades in the barracks by daylight. The weapons and artillery were to be stored out of sight so far as possible.

The Attack on the German Armies

When the aerial fleet returned to the attack in the morning not a vestige of an army could be seen. All the arms which had been taken from the soldiers the day previous had been left in piles on or around the field, and there they still lay. Every preparation for disposing of them had been made long before. In the imperial park at Potsdam was an artificial lake, about four acres in extent, in the midst of which a fountain played on gala days. A squadron of fifty centipedes was directed to pick up the arms, carry them to Potsdam, and throw them pell-mell into the centre of the pond. When the top of the pile got above the water, the muskets were to be piled up on top of those already there, so as to form a huge pyramid. When the pile was complete, several carboys of sulphuric acid were poured over the top of it, which would be carried through the whole mass by the first shower of rain.

While this was going on the main body of the fleet scoured the region for its prey. Even without the maps which Gheen had with him there would have been little difficulty in finding the barracks in which the garrison was ordinarily lodged. Those at Teltow were first reached. They comprised ten immense buildings, each capable of lodging 2500 men with their officers. Of course, the motes could not enter by the doors or windows, and it is quite possible that, for this reason, the military authorities hoped to foil their enemy. But if they did, their mistake was soon evident. A half-dozen dad-

His Wisdom the Defender

dies mounted, or rather settled, on the roof of each building, and, with their sharp and well-practised claws, proceeded to tear off the tiles and sheathing as a flock of hens might scratch up a flower-bed. The rafters followed, leaving the upper story entirely exposed. The soldiers who occupied it, as soon as they found the roof doomed to destruction, ran downstairs and joined their companions on the floor below. The tops of the brick walls were then attacked in like manner, but the well-hardened cement proved too strong even for the powerful claws of the daddies. A few of the centipede motes were supplied with crow-bars for seizing and pulling down walls, and these speedily reduced the buildings to a mass of ruins. As the work progressed the unfortunate inmates rushed down from floor to floor, and at length out into the parade-ground, only to find themselves so completely surrounded by the enemy that nothing but surrender was possible.

XV

A Captive Emperor

I STRONGLY suspect that, had Campbell better understood the spirit in which the German Emperor fought his battle, he would have been disposed to deal more gently with him, and condone his murderous order as something he was right in executing if he could. But neither of the antagonists knew how like was the spirit of their fight. The one saw that the old *régime* could not be claimed to have passed away forever unless it made the most desperate fight in its power to sustain itself. If it did not fight to the death; if it begged for a compromise, or even a truce, and succeeded in obtaining either, none could foresee how much vitality it might have left, or how long it might rule the nations by the right of the strongest. Hence his desire to carry his work to the end without giving any power the chance to propose a truce, and without exposing himself to the temptation to compromise, which a knowledge of what was going on below might have held out. If, after all, he could not overcome the passive resistance of united Europe, then he could

His Wisdom the Defender

say to the world, "Behold my power; what do you want me to do with it? Make known your wishes to my headquarters in Elba."

The Emperor, on his side of the contest, viewed the situation in much the same spirit. The honor of his house, vigorously upheld through all the generations from Barbarossa to himself, was dearer to him than life. That honor was associated with the old *régime;* and it required that he should uphold that *régime* to the bitter end. He could make no terms with the low-born person who was now seeking to establish a new order of things. What he might be forced to do if finally vanquished, he did not allow himself even to consider. He would cross that bridge when he came to it.

On the second morning of the contest he was at work from daylight discussing the reports of the disaster of the day previous, and trying to invent some new way of meeting his foe. He sent for Prince Waldeck, his Minister of Foreign Affairs, with whom he drew up a despatch to the German ambassador at Washington, directing him to make a vigorous representation of the case to the American government, and to ask for the immediate enforcement of its neutrality laws. The official despatch was accompanied by private instructions to urge on Secretary Bayne the immediate seizure of the works at Campbelltown by such force, military or civil, as could securely hold them and prevent any help being sent to their owner. Then he sent personal messages to the

A Captive Emperor

heads of the principal European states inviting them to take concerted measures for the common defence; if possible, indeed, to come to Berlin, or send a special representative to observe the proceedings and discuss the situation. On his cousin of England, and his friend the President of the French Republic, he urged the seizure of the loomotes *Hesperus* and *Cynthia,* which were already making regular trips between New York, Paris, and London. He asked the President of the Italian Republic to take immediate military possession of the works at Elba, and prevent their being used as a base of operations.

Of course no ruler could leave his kingdom at so critical a juncture, but the request to send envoys to Berlin to observe and report on the situation was gladly complied with. The question of seizing the motes and the works at Elba and Campbelltown was a more delicate one. How it was dealt with we shall see later.

About ten o'clock, just as he had finished his despatches, he received word of the attack on the barracks at Teltow, the destruction of the roofs of the buildings, and the difficulties which the attacking party was meeting in trying to tear down the walls. He immediately arose and expressed his intention of proceeding at once on a tour of inspection, going, indeed, as far as Teltow if necessary. General Müller was present and heard the announcement.

"Will your Majesty allow me to make a suggestion?"

His Wisdom the Defender

"What is it?"

"I suggest the question whether it is prudent, in so critical a situation, that your Majesty should expose his person to a possible assault by the enemy."

"But I surveyed all the operations yesterday without any attack on me or my staff. Besides, what good would it do him to attack my person? What could he do with me? Cast not the fashion of uncertain evils."

"There are occasions when we should act in direct opposition to this maxim, guarding ourselves most carefully against uncertain evils, and this is one of them. If there ever was a juncture at which Germany could not spare the head of her State, this is one."

"Never shall I allow Germany to feel that, at the most critical moment in her history, her Emperor heard counsels of prudence when the interests of his empire were at stake. Germany can dispense with her Emperor better than he can say a word or perform an act unworthy of his house or of his exalted position. He cannot stay concealed in his palace while his soldiers are being carried into captivity. And, if he should, could not the enemy find him there as easily as in the field?"

"If such is your Majesty's view, I shall gladly accompany him to the field. In that case, as the body-guard would be of no service for defence, it might be well that we went alone. We should attract less attention without the guard."

A Captive Emperor

"I do not want it said that the German Emperor escaped the fate of his army by a subterfuge of any sort, such as going without his usual guard would be. Telephone Steinitz and such other generals, as are within reach, to meet me at Schöneberg in three-quarters of an hour from now."

A ride of half an hour brought the Emperor and Müller to the appointed place, where several other generals joined them, one by one, and made their reports. From Teltow the news was bad. Most of the buildings were already razed to the ground, and the soldiers were being carried off as they were the day before. If the remainder of the army was to be saved, it must be concealed in the casemates of the fortifications, or in houses where their presence might not be suspected by the enemy.

As these alternatives were being discussed, a fleet of motes, accompanied by a flock of daddies, were seen in the air. The latter pounced upon the party like fish-hawks diving for their prey. The Emperor felt himself lifted out of his saddle as if by a pair of powerful arms. In a moment he was seated on something, he knew not what, gently enough, yet held firmly as in a vice. Then he saw the ground receding below him, and felt the blast as of a heavy wind from being carried through the air. The daddie had him seated on its knees while it was holding him in its hands to keep him from falling, much like a child going through

"Ride a cock-horse to Banbury Cross."

His Wisdom the Defender

The experience would have unnerved an ordinary man; but he was not such. Dazed at first, he recovered his mental equilibrium in a few minutes and calmly awaited his fate. In less than ten minutes he saw the *Concordia* before him. A door opened in her side, through which he was lifted, he hardly knew how. Placed upon the deck, he soon recovered from the bewilderment of his wild flight. He was received with the greatest deference by an usher clad in white, who showed him to a room. As he passed along he glanced with some interest at the motto.

Campbell, suspecting the Emperor's feelings, considered that there was no occasion for requesting a personal interview. In fact, it was not at all likely that such an interview would be productive of any good result. He therefore directed that the Emperor be taken by the usher into one of the cabins and asked to occupy it for the time being. The usher returned and reported his duty performed. Campbell then dictated the following, which was written in a plain hand on the most sumptuous kind of paper:

"Should his Majesty, the German Emperor, be graciously pleased to annul and revoke his general order directing that no quarter be shown to the forces who are endeavoring to disband his armies, an opportunity is now afforded him to do so."

The usher was sent back with the paper and with writing materials. The latter were placed on a table in front of the Emperor, the former was placed in his hands. He glanced listlessly at it for a moment,

A Captive Emperor

and then laid it on the table without saying a word. The usher, in doubt whether he had really read it or not, returned to report to his master.

The Emperor remained in gloomy silence for half an hour, determined that the first question or the first proposal should come from the other party, who was expected to feel that he, as Emperor, was not going to enter into any arrangements whatever. At the end of the half-hour, the usher paid the Emperor a second visit, doing so by Campbell's direction in the most courteous and ceremonious manner.

" I am directed to say to your Majesty that if you have any communication, written or verbal, to make either to the Owner of the Motes or to your own army or government, the Owner of the Motes will be very happy to consider or communicate it."

The Emperor replied not a word, still maintaining a dignified and gloomy silence. He might have been a blind deaf-mute. The usher returned and reported no progress.

" How does he look ?" asked the Owner.

" I cannot say that he looks at all. When I first showed him into the cabin he took his seat by the table, with one hand resting upon it, and his face turned towards the door. When I went in again he was still in the same position. He might be a statue for all the notice he takes."

An uneasy thought entered the Owner's mind.

" Is he wearing his sword ?"

" Yes—that is, he has on what seems a sword."

His Wisdom the Defender

Campbell mused. "It would be a terrible thing if he should kill himself. If he did, would I have the nerve to go on with my work? I think not. If he wanted to speak to me he could surely have said something to the usher. I think I can divine what he is thinking. Whatever I do he wants to boast that he never deigned to address me a word or notice my presence, even when he was my prisoner."

This divination was quite correct. The Emperor was thinking thus: "I have yielded to a brute force which has taken possession of my person. The man who wields that force can do with my person what he pleases. But he shall not have the satisfaction of knowing that a Hohenzollern proposed terms to him or even honored him with a word or a look. He may do his worst."

The question of the sword perplexed Campbell extremely. He was several times on the point of sending the usher to ask that it be surrendered. But what if it was refused? To attempt to take it by force might precipitate what he wanted to avoid. He finally hoped that the same pride which led the Emperor to take the stand he did would prevent his doing anything so vulgar as killing himself. So he drew up the following paper:

"Mote 'Concordia,' *May, 1946.*

"Whereas, his Majesty, the German Emperor, has been pleased to issue a general order to his army

A Captive Emperor

that no quarter be shown to the forces of the Owner of the Motes, who are endeavoring to disband that army, which order is couched in the following terms: (Here follows the order as we have given it.) Now, therefore, protesting against this my act being ever taken as a precedent, or being justified by any law, but desiring that it shall ever be regarded as called forth only by the exigency of the present situation, it is hereby ordered:

"That the said Friedrich Wilhelm, German Emperor, be kept in close confinement in such place as the Owner of the Motes may from time to time direct, until the said order shall be revoked or annulled by such regency or other authority as may wield supreme power during the absence of the Emperor, and, furthermore, until his Majesty shall have indicated his concurrence in the said annulment.

"CAMPBELL,
"Owner of the Motes."

The usher carried this order to the Emperor. The latter refused even to look at it, sitting at the table unmoved. The usher could do nothing but return to his chief and report.

"Did he not read the order?" asked the latter.

"Not while I was there. I offered it to him, but he took no notice of my movement. So I laid it on the table by his side."

"I suspect that he looked at it after you left. But even if he did not, it will make no difference."

His Wisdom the Defender

The question now was where to keep the prisoner. It would be very disturbing to the Owner to have him on the *Concordia*. Campbelltown was too far away, and, even if it had been nearer, to send him thither would involve complications with the American government. There was only one spot in Europe over which Campbell had complete control, and that was Elba. The principal danger in sending him thither was that the Italian government might attempt his release. But plans were all made to protect the island—an easy task, because it could be invaded only by water, and the motes could command the sea even better than the land. So Elba was chosen.

The works at Elba had been placed in charge of one of the most trusted officers of the Order of the Seraphim, under the title of "Commander," with whom, however, Campbell had had no communication since he commenced his great movement. The latter could now be left entirely in Gheen's hands, and it was imperative that he himself should take personal charge of affairs at his only base of operations. Gheen was notified to go on with the work in hand according to his best judgment, and to detail fifty daddies and twenty centipedes to accompany the Owner to Elba. A small mote was also detailed for the transportation of the Emperor. This was one of a few *motes de luxe* which had been fitted up and brought along for the transportation of distinguished personages with whom the Owner might

A Captive Emperor

want to confer, or to whom he might tender a compliment. It was placed alongside the *Concordia* and fastened to her in such a way that a person could step from one into the other with entire security. Its captain and lieutenant were summoned to the Owner's room to receive their instructions.

Campbell now began to be uneasy lest he had failed to treat the Emperor with due courtesy. Under ordinary circumstances he ought to have received him in person on his first arrival, as the master of a house receives a distinguished guest. Perhaps it was owing to this neglect of the amenities that the Emperor had demeaned himself so haughtily. So when everything was ready for the Emperor's departure the usher again presented himself.

"I am directed by the Owner of the Motes to inquire whether it will be agreeable to your Majesty to allow him to pay his respects in person before your Majesty's departure. If it will be agreeable he will do so immediately."

During the two hours of the Emperor's enforced leisure he had enjoyed a better opportunity for reflection than had ever before been afforded him. As a result of this reflection certain facts which, though he had known them from infancy, had modestly kept themselves in the background, now obtruded themselves on his thoughts in a very disagreeable way. One of these facts was that Nature had made emperors on the same general plan that she had made peasants and philosophers, subjecting them

His Wisdom the Defender

all alike to the common limitations of humanity. One of her inexorable laws was that the man who ate nothing in the morning but a biscuit should get very hungry before noon. It was now noon. A principle of international law that he had long ago been taught also insisted on presenting itself in a new light. It was that accomplished facts were to be accepted, how unpleasant soever they might be. Two accomplished facts stared him in the face. He was a prisoner and he was hungry. Not being aware of the excellent culinary arrangements in mote 92, on which he was soon to embark, he began to reflect seriously on the possible consequences to his stomach of a continued policy of absolute silence.

As to receiving Campbell, his feelings were mixed. He did not want to see him. And yet he was incensed at the slight shown his royal person by Campbell's not receiving him. An interview would have been disagreeable to both parties, and yet it could not be avoided without discourtesy on one side or the other. But he must relax a little.

"I am a prisoner," he at length replied, "and have nothing to say on the subject of my visitors."

"Will your Majesty allow me to explain the situation more exactly?"

"I will listen to anything you may have to say."

"I then beg leave to say, on behalf of the Owner of the Motes, that he has refrained from trespassing on your Majesty's privacy from a fear that a personal interview might not be agreeable to you, and a

A Captive Emperor

feeling that no good result would flow from it. As you are about to leave the *Concordia*, he desired me to make this explanation, and to ascertain whether he was wrong in this impression. Will your Majesty be pleased to favor me with a more precise statement of his wishes on the subject of receiving the Owner of the Motes?"

"I have no wishes on the subject. If the gentleman presents himself, I shall of course receive him. That is all I can say."

"I fear the Owner of the Motes will be embarrassed by his lack of certain knowledge what course on his part will be most agreeable to your Majesty. My duty will end with reporting what you have said."

A few minutes later the usher returned, accompanied by the captain of mote 92.

"I am directed by the Owner of the Motes to say that, acting on his own judgment, he reaches the conclusion that a personal interview will not be agreeable to your Majesty. He therefore presents his apologies, accompanied by his earnest hope for your Majesty's speedy return to his empire. I now have the honor to present the captain of the mote, who has been detailed to take you from the *Concordia*."

"If you would like some lunch, sir—I mean, your Majesty—we have it nearly prepared on my mote, if you—your Majesty will come along with me."

The captain stood back, waiting for his distinguished prisoner to move. The latter was perplexed.

His Wisdom the Defender

He had, of course, read the order for his imprisonment, but had no idea how or where it would be carried out, and could not ask. He suspected that the present move was to his prison, and so would rather have stood where he was. But to what new humiliation might he not subject himself by refusing to stir? Moved by this consideration, he allowed himself to be ushered to the door of the mote.

He winced a little on stepping into the other mote, half a mile in the air, but soon recovered his balance. He asked not a question as to where he was going or what was to be done with him. The mote cast loose immediately and started for Elba, preceded by the *Concordia,* which, being faster, arrived there first. This gave the Owner time to make arrangements for the reception of his prisoner-guest, and ascertain whether any hostile attempt had been made by the Italian government. The *Concordia* landed late in the afternoon, and was at once visited by the commander and his two lieutenants, Johnson and Miles.

"Well, I am glad to see you and find things here undisturbed. Has anything happened? Have the Italians shown any sign of hostility?"

"You cannot be gladder to see us than we are to see you. Are you not getting us all into a dreadful scrape? The Leghorn papers tell us of your attack on the German army; and only half an hour ago Benson wired me that you had carried off the Emperor, no one knew where."

A Captive Emperor

"We'll talk about that later. I want to know whether we are to be attacked here. Have you any news as to that?"

"Only what is in the morning papers. Have you seen them?"

"No, what do they say?"

"The German government has proposed to all the powers that their Mediterranean fleets combine and seize this place, bombarding it if necessary. Austria and England have partly consented; Italy is so far non-committal, and France has not yet been heard from. The Italian police have been very inquisitive, but I have not heard of any hostile movement on their part."

"If that's their move, I hope to be ready for them by this time to-morrow. Meanwhile, we have a little business to attend to for the Emperor. He will arrive in No. 92 in about an hour, and I propose to keep him in my house, under close guard, I remaining here. Let Miles make the arrangements at once. He is to be treated with all the deference due to his rank, but not allowed to leave the house. James will go with you, and assist in receiving his Majesty with all the honors. Trust him for that. He did it royally this morning!"

The Emperor had not deigned to speak one word during the entire journey except to the waiter who served his lunch. He preserved the same silence when he was received by the officers and shown to his lodgings. The limits within which he was to be

His Wisdom the Defender

confined, including a parlor, bedroom, and dressing-room, were shown to him, and he was left to himself. Then, for the first time, human nature asserted itself, and he expressed a wish. It was that his valet might be brought to him.

XVI

The Naval Attack on Elba

IT took three days to prepare for the naval attack on Elba. Let us take advantage of the lull to view the storm which was raging over Europe, and learn how the little island came to be chosen as the site of Uraniberg—the seat of empire.

The latter can be told in a few words. Campbell wanted an island for his seat, because an island could be more readily defended against attack or invasion, and would be more easily commanded, than a region with purely artificial boundaries. He wanted to place his seat in Europe rather than his own country, because the latter with its traditional policy of peace and good-will would require less of his attention than the war-ridden countries of Europe. He wanted a seat favored by its climate, and so preferred the Mediterranean to the Baltic. He would have preferred a situation farther west—one of the Balearic Islands, for example. But the rugged surface of these mountain ranges, rising above the water, could not be made the site for a great city, such as he contemplated. So Elba was chosen. These reasons

His Wisdom the Defender

seem good enough to do away with the suspicion frequently expressed, that it was Tiana who really fixed the site of Uraniberg. Yet, we must admit that she made the founder better satisfied with the circumstances that dictated his choice.

It goes without saying that Campbell had all along taken every measure that his foresight could suggest to guard his base of operations against a naval attack. The commander of the place was, next to Gheen, the most trusted officer of the Angelic Order; and as soon as the details of construction of the daddie had been perfected a number of these instruments were made expressly for use in dealing with armed ships. Now that an attack was imminent, it was not prudent to remain in ignorance of what the world might be about to do. So the Italian journals were sent for and eagerly scanned.

If he had not felt himself across the Rubicon, with his bridges all burned behind him, their contents might well have appalled him. From every quarter only one story came—that of unbridled denunciation and fierce resistance. The London *Times,* ever mindful of its dignity, approached the nearest to moderation and reasonableness in its comments. But even it had no word of apology:

" Never was so great an opportunity placed within the grasp of a human hand, and never did the possessor of an opportunity waste it as Campbell has done. Wielding the power he did, all the world would have listened with respectful attention to any

The Naval Attack on Elba

proposals he might have made to insure that his enterprise should be productive of nothing but that good to mankind which he declared to be his supreme object. The powers were ready to deliberate on the subject and devise from time to time the measures best adapted to meet the emergency. They would naturally have looked to the United States to take the lead in executing their plans. He would thus, with the concurrence of the leading nations of the world, have earned for himself imperishable fame. All this he has thrown away with a recklessness to which no parallel can be found in history. He has become not only a criminal, but an outlaw. Whatever power succeeds in capturing him may deal with him at its own will. That his forces must soon be exhausted, no reasonable person can doubt. All that is to be feared is a general attempt on the part of some one nation to seize the remnants of his power. This can easily be guarded against by a concurrent agreement, which we believe can be reached without even waiting for the final downfall of the man who has pitted his strength against that of the world."

These denunciations, universal though they were, formed only one of the clouds in the horizon. Yet blacker ones were that men everywhere lost their heads. At the exchanges and bourses stocks and bonds of every kind were being sacrificed in so mad a rush that these institutions were closed through the voluntary act of the brokers themselves. Universal bankruptcy seemed to stare the commercial

His Wisdom the Defender

world in the face. Laborers were everywhere thrown out of employment, because all demand had ceased, and employers did not know what was to come next. People were going insane with excitement in such numbers that the asylums would not contain the crowds that were brought to their doors for treatment. Mobs were everywhere rampant, especially in Germany. Sometimes the police could control them and sometimes not. They were destroying life and property in every direction. The requisition of the German government on that of the United States to prosecute Campbell for violation of the laws of neutrality had been promptly answered with the assurance that every measure in the power of the government would be taken to execute the law. Warrants had accordingly been issued, and whenever Campbell should return to his own country he would at once become a prisoner at the bar of justice.

But what was the world to do? We might almost say that no two men were agreed except on a single point. The offender must be resisted to the bitter end. Every journal declaimed in its own way and proposed plans from day to day, only to have them shown impracticable the day following.

One idea was to seize all the motes that could be found and send them over to fight the insurgent owner. The proposal of the Emperor that the Secretary of State and the English and French governments cause the seizure of the *Cynthia* and *Hesperus* met with general approval. But what could

The Naval Attack on Elba

have been done with them after they were seized? To look for Gheen, as he was flying from place to place, would have been useless. He encamped every night on a different spot, and no one knew beforehand where that spot would be. No one knew how to make a centipede or a daddie, or how to construct any of the apparatus that Campbell was employing. And if men did learn, weeks of practice would still be required to use the machines. The British and French governments had agreed that the neutrality of the motes should be respected. The terms of this agreement we have already stated. Campbell had been extremely cautious that no excuse for violating it should be offered, and nothing to be used by him was transported in these vehicles.

The seizure of the German Emperor added new fuel to the flame. If it did not increase it, it was only because any increase was impossible. The same might be said of the suicide of the Czar of Russia, which occurred the moment it was discovered that the annihilation of the Russian military power was to be as complete as that of the German. Messages looking to a conference of the heads of the European states were sent to and fro, but none of these heads felt justified in leaving his kingdom in such an emergency.

The proposed joint attack of the navies upon Elba looked so feasible that it was received with universal approval. A new impetus was given the proposal when it became known that the seat of the Owner of

His Wisdom the Defender

the Motes had been chosen for the German Emperor's prison. It was felt that such an indignity to the head of the leading State in Europe was not to be tolerated, and the only question was how to release him.

As he was imprisoned on Italian territory, the government of Italy was looked to to take the lead. But this government showed great lukewarmness in the premises. The fact was that, under arrangements which Campbell had begun to make with it, Italy was to be the first European beneficiary of his enterprise. And when called upon to seize its own island of Elba by military force, it had a more valid excuse than this. It was impossible to send an army over from the mainland without its being speedily destroyed by the forces which Campbell had placed there for its defence. It was not for a moment to be supposed that the position destined to become his main base of operations had been left in an undefended condition; it was well known that after having intrusted the disarmament of the Russian armies to Gheen, he had remained at Elba, making every preparation for its defence. A cloud of daddies which appeared from time to time over his headquarters showed that he was preparing for an emergency.

But a naval attack looked more hopeful. It is true that Campbell had spoken of hauling the navies of the world ashore as a part of his programme. But no way of doing this was apparent, and, in any case,

The Naval Attack on Elba

if all the navies together could not fight the Owner of the Motes, the sooner they were sold for old iron the better for all concerned. It was agreed that the combined fleets should be under command of the ranking officer, who proved to be the British admiral. The port of Bastia, on the east coast of Corsica, about forty miles from Elba, was chosen as the rendezvous, where preparations for the attack should be made. The English, German, Italian, and Austrian fleets all reached this point four days after the capture of the Emperor.

The French fleet failed to come. Its non-appearance and the general attitude of the French government caused great uneasiness. It began to make conditions as to the command and the movements of the combined fleets of so dilatory a character as led to the suspicion of an *arrière-pensée* of some sort. But there was no time for dilly-dallying, and the other four powers ordered their fleets to proceed without regard to France.

Campbell's determination and courage rose to the height of the crisis. He began to suspect that there was something illogical in the idea of forcibly putting an end to war without even a battle, and began to feel like accepting a challenge. Still he felt some concern lest his motives might be misconstrued if he made an attack on the fleets before they attacked him, especially if, as was inevitable, loss of life should result. So to satisfy his own conscience, if for nothing else, he decided to make public his in-

His Wisdom the Defender

tention to defend his position at every hazard. The best medium of communication seemed to be the London *Times,* to which he telegraphed the following communication as soon as he heard of the proposed movement:

" I understand that the powers contemplate a combined naval attack on my station at Elba. As such a course will lead to a speedy solution of the important question whether I possess the power to destroy the navies of Europe as well as to disband its armies, and as such a solution may be desirable in the general interests of humanity, I cannot disapprove of the proposed attack. At the same time, I must express the fear that the conflict which will thus be precipitated will be attended with loss of life, as my preparations for dealing with armed ships are far from being as complete as those for disarming land forces. I have to add that I shall regard any entrance of war-ships into the Ligurian Sea as being made with hostile intent, and shall take such measures for their destruction as I may have at command.

" Campbell,
" Owner of the Motes."

In issuing this challenge our hero builded far better than he knew. It was characteristic of the system of fatalism that, when the victim was warned of his fate, and, in consequence, took every measure he

The Naval Attack on Elba

could to guard against it, these very measures proved to be instruments in executing the decree. It was so in the present case. The naval authorities, thus forewarned, determined to elude their adversary by a change of plan. The post of rendezvous was changed from Bastia to San Florenza, on the west shore of Corsica; and the fleet was to sail from this point for its destination by night, so as to reach the harbor of Porto Ferrajo by daybreak, and begin bombarding the place, or landing sailors, before their presence was known to the defenders.

As fate would have it, the latter could not have wished for any better policy than this. Looking back, it does seem curious that the military powers should have supposed that their adversary, who had been planning everything for years, would have failed to be on his guard against a night attack, and, with all the contrivances he had at hand, would not be more at home by night than by day. But perhaps we should have done no better than our grandfathers in such an emergency.

The fleets gathered according to orders. A study of the problem by the admirals and captains in council led to a plan by which it might be possible for the ships to defend themselves mutually against any attack by motes. Machine-guns throwing shot of a weight sufficient to penetrate either a mote or a daddie could without difficulty be mounted in the tops of the men-of-war. To reach any one of these guns without encountering its fire, the attacking party

His Wisdom the Defender

would have to come towards it from above. The search-lights could be turned upon the descending motes; then all the ships around could fire at them as they were coming down without endangering each other.

The combined fleet was sixty strong in ships, and the crews numbered nearly forty thousand. The plan of attack and defence, of which these were the main features, was matured on the evening of June 26. The whole of the next day was spent in mounting machine-guns so that they could be fired in the air, and practising the men in handling them. Before nightfall all was ready, and sunset was awaited with the greatest anxiety, for then the combined fleets were to leave their moorings.

But the sun had not set before the officers were astonished, and the men filled with superstitious fear, by the appearance of a score of motes—" aerial ships " they were then called—at a great height in the blue sky. Scarcely one, even of the officers, had yet seen a mote. Half an hour after the aerial fleet was first sighted, it was in the zenith, and there seemed to come to anchor, so immovable was its position. This very stillness added to Jack's discomfort. He was always a superstitious fellow, and the calmness with which the demoniac power looked down upon him suggested the placid certainty with which a gigantic vulture might watch its prey. As minutes, which seemed hours, passed away, and the enemy remained as if nailed to the sky, the feeling extended

The Naval Attack on Elba

from sailors to lieutenants, from them to captains, perhaps even from the captains to the admirals.

"There's somethin' fallin' from one of them things, sir."

The officer addressed looked up. It was not from one thing alone that something was falling, but from all. A few moments later a crash was heard and a violent shock felt.

"What is that?" said the captain, as he ran amidship.

"What is it?" asked all the officers, as they gathered round a hole in the deck large enough for a man to pass through. "Dynamite?"

"No, the sound was not that of an explosion."

"See, there's a hole in the main deck, too!"

"Go below and see what's to pay."

Before this last order could be executed a report as to what was to pay became no longer necessary. The sound of rushing water in the boiler space was heard by all. Men ran up from below reporting that the ship was filling.

"Lower the boats! Carpenter, take soundings!"

Within the space of five minutes experiences such as these were suffered on twenty of the sixty ships. Twenty others had heard or seen something drop in the water alongside of them, but did not know what it was. Signals of distress arose from the first twenty, and boats were lowered from all to aid their sinking companions or save their own men. Twelve thousand of the latter were landed; the remainder were

His Wisdom the Defender

missing or were added to the complement of the remaining ships. The number of ships afloat was reduced to forty. The enemy was seen sailing slowly away in the sky, as if satisfied with what had been done.

The British flag-ship was among the forty left afloat, and her admiral was the coolest and most resolute of men, a worthy successor of Nelson. The fleet of boats had not done picking up the men struggling in the water or clinging to the spars of the sunken ships when he signalled requesting a conference with the other admirals. They all gathered in his cabin.

" It is now sunset, the hour for sailing. Were my own fleet the only one concerned, I should immediately order it to proceed to the attack, but, in view of the deplorable accidents to so many of our ships, I deem it courteous to ask you whether you are ready before giving sailing orders. If you are, we sail at once for Ferrajo, as agreed upon."

The Austrian and Italian admirals protested against so imprudent a course. The German was silent. He thought of his imprisoned monarch, and could not lag behind when an Englishman proposed to rescue him, whatever he might think of the prudence or practicability of the attempt.

" I think we should be encouraged by what has happened," said Admiral Collins. " The enemy has spent his force, and will pass the night in fancied security, feeling sure that he has disabled us. These

The Naval Attack on Elba

are the very conditions under which he should be attacked, without an hour's delay."

"We should at least await further orders from our governments," said the Austrian.

"That will involve a day's delay and give the enemy so much more time to prepare himself. I have my orders and mean to act on them."

The result was that the English and German fleets, numbering twenty-five ships, sailed to the attack, the other two fleets awaiting orders. While the former are on their way, let us take a glance at Elba.

We have already intimated that Campbell had not been able to contrive any quite satisfactory method of attacking and rendering harmless a fleet of warships. The problem was to sink the ships or haul them ashore without killing or drowning the sailors, and without exposing his own men to danger from their fire. One plan was to drop battering-rams from a height of several thousand feet, of such size and weight as to go through a ship from top to bottom. But he foresaw the difficulty, perhaps impossibility, of adjusting the position of the mote and the moment of dropping the ram with such precision that the latter would strike the ship in its fall, especially if the ship were in motion. Still, he determined to try the experiment, and had fifty such rams constructed. Each was a steel-pointed cylinder, a foot or more in diameter, and twelve feet long, filled in the interior with lead, and weighing some five tons. We have seen what measure of success was gained

His Wisdom the Defender

by this contrivance. If he had foreseen how well it would work, he might have sunk the whole of the combined fleets with the greatest ease, as he had actually sunk one-third of their ships.

But there was no time to cry over lost opportunities. The war-ships were steaming ahead. They were rounding Cape Corso when search-lights more powerful than their own shone on them from above and around. No doubt could remain that their movements were as well known at Elba as if they had been made by day. The fleet reached Porto Ferrajo at dawn without any other incident. Admiral Collins inwardly felicitated himself on his foresight. The boats were lowered and men began to jump into them. Before they could push off, the admiral began to lose his self-complacence at the sight of thirty daddies rising up from the town to the height of a thousand feet. Telescopes showed that a cord was suspended from each. Tracing these cords downwards something that looked like an enormous shell was seen at the end of each. The way in which the machine-guns were to be evaded was now plain. If these objects were torpedoes, the daddies could explode them alongside a ship and yet remain a thousand feet in the air. At this height it was very doubtful whether the machine-guns of the fleet could be pointed at them. They were soon suspended over the fleet. Then one after another they slowly descended in such a way that each torpedo should gently dip into the water immediately

The Naval Attack on Elba

alongside a ship. The torpedoes were so constructed that a pressure of ten feet of water upon an air-bag attached to each would explode the weapon, which contained two tons of nitrogelatine.

As the daddies descended, the machine-guns from the ships directed a rather wild fire into the air. Accurate aim was impossible, because no idea of the range could be formed; but a better defence was made than had been made by any of the armies which had been attacked. As the torpedoes approached the water, the daddies from which they were hung had to move with great deliberation so as to get their charges into the right position. This gave the gunners their opportunity. As the charges began to explode here and there among the fleet, several daddies, one after the other, were struck by shot. The men inside two of them were killed, and three or four others were so damaged that they dropped into the water. The remainder reached the shore in safety after exploding their torpedoes. The result at this stage of the contest was that four men out of sixty on Campbell's side were lost, while all but a half-dozen of the ships were sunk or sinking.

Although the self-complacency of the admiral had evaporated, his resolution was as firm as ever. It was to be determined, once for all, whether one of the most powerful naval forces ever collected could or could not successfully cope with the new machinery of war; and the decision of this question justified the most heroic measures. If the sinking ships had to

His Wisdom the Defender

be abandoned, the men should take to the boats with their arms in their hands and row to the shore.

Never before had men escaped from drowning in order to form an attacking force. Whether to save their lives or to storm the place, there was but one thing to be done. The boats must land their men as rapidly as possible and then return to take off those who might be left. The water where the ships had come to anchor was so shallow that the upper works of the sunken ones were mostly above its surface, and to these clung such of the crews as could not at first be taken in the boats.

Besides the daddies which had attacked the ships, there were a number held in reserve. These attacked the boats with their claws. But an annoying musketry fire was kept up from the boats, which, although it did not penetrate the walls of the aerial machines, served to distract the men who were in them. The boats were too heavy to be lifted out of the water, and when the effort was made to upset them they were merely pulled to one side through the yielding fluid in which they floated. Only about a dozen were successfully upset. The men in these threw down their arms and swam to the shore. The other boats succeeded in effecting a landing, and their crews formed for a march upon the factories, while the boats returned to the ships. But before they could even form in marching order, they were thrown into confusion by an attack of centipedes. The arms were pulled out of the hands of the sail-

The Naval Attack on Elba

ors just as they had been pulled out of those of the German soldiers, and, being so damaged by the pressure of the iron claw as to render them useless, were thrown away. In this way, not only was the number of effective men every minute diminished, but those who kept their arms were so busy defending themselves that they became oblivious of their main object. Their officers tried to rally them, and actually succeeded in getting a force about a thousand strong, half English and half German, to run up towards the factories. But the centipedes captured the officers with the greatest ease, depositing them upon their upper decks, and leaving the men with no clear idea what to do. At the end of an hour what was left of the naval force consisted of some 6000 unarmed men scattered along the shore in a dazed and demoralized condition, and the few ships still afloat, having on board of them the remnants of their own crews and of those of the sunken vessels.

What was now feared on the land was a bombardment by these ships. As there were no defensive works, this mode of attack would not have been in accord with the customs of war; but one could not feel sure what desperate measures might not be taken by men in such an emergency. It was therefore imperative that a truce should be agreed upon or that the remaining ships should be sunk by the only mode of attack available—the torpedo. No time was lost in preparing for either course of action.

A daddie bearing a flag of truce carried to the Brit-

His Wisdom the Defender

ish flag-ship a letter in one of its claws, and deposited it on the quarter-deck. It was picked up and handed to the admiral, who was sufficiently alive to the situation to open and read it. It contained a statement that if the fleet were willing to surrender, no further attempt would be made to sink the remaining ships. The alternative was made evident by the sight of twenty daddies hanging over the shore awaiting the order to attack. The admiral had to consult with his German coadjutor, a proceeding which took some time.

Before reaching a conclusion the situation was summed up. Of the combined fleet of sixty ships, perhaps the most powerful, if not the most numerous, that had ever been assembled, only a half-dozen remained. The approaching fate of the latter was read in the metallic visages of the curious beings hanging over the shore, each with a cord much longer than had been used in the first attack. If a new force were landed, nothing could save it from the centipedes which, having already disarmed the force on shore, awaited its arrival. Any attempt to continue the attack would result only in a useless destruction of life and property.

The flag of truce returned with the answer of the two admirals. They agreed to surrender, but requested facilities for communicating with their respective governments as to the disposal of the ships' crews, whether on board or on the shore. An interview was requested to arrange details.

The Naval Attack on Elba

Campbell replied, acceding to the interview, and offering every facility for the communication desired. He would send a messenger mote to Piombino, the nearest town on the Italian shore, with any despatches which the admirals wished to send. If no further hostilities were intended, it would be easy to send the sailors to Piombino or Fonnolica on the remaining ships. Time would be given to transport the sailors from the shore to the ships. If the latter did not then sail away, he reserved the right on two hours' notice to sink them if he could. Next morning the sailors were all put on board the ships by centipede motes, and orders from the governments were awaited. After much telegraphing the powers decided to give up the attack for the time being and recall their fleets.

XVII

The French Attempt on the *Cynthia*

ON the day that the remnant of the combined fleets sailed away from Elba with their human freight an event occurred which filled Campbell with deeper emotion than any he had experienced since commencing his movement. We have already alluded to the fact that, through all his attacks upon the German armies, he had allowed the two great loomotes, the *Hesperus* and the *Cynthia,* to continue their regular trips —the *Hesperus* between New York and London, the *Cynthia* between New York and Paris. Few passengers had, however, been carried, because men were naturally timorous in undertaking a journey across the ocean by such a method until experience had demonstrated its safety. Moreover, few were disposed to choose a period of such universal turmoil to make a journey. Great surprise was therefore felt at the continued running of these motes, because it seemed to be placing within reach of the British and French governments a means of attack and defence which might result in their owner's de-

The French Attempt on the *Cynthia*

feat. If they chose to seize these vessels, fill them with armed men, and send them to Elba, what was to hinder them from inflicting a crushing defeat upon their owner? It was supposed that the latter disregarded this danger, because he had entire confidence in the British and French governments carrying out their agreement guaranteeing the motes from seizure.

To understand the event now to be narrated, we must begin by a brief description of these first loomotes, of which the construction differed in some points from that with which we are familiar. The central portion being cylindrical in form and sixty feet in diameter, it was sixty feet from the bottom to the top of the motes. They had three decks. The lower deck was twenty feet above the bottom at its lowest point. This space formed the main hold. Owing to the curvature of the bottom, the height of the hold diminished continually towards each side. The rear half of it was occupied by the great furnaces which were necessary to keep the etherine thermalized, and which burned a hundred tons of coal on each trip. The remainder of the space was taken up with the mail-rooms and store-rooms for passengers' baggage.

The space between the next two decks was entirely filled by the state-rooms. On the deck above them were immense dining-halls and sitting-rooms. Above this deck the great arched roof formed by the upper part of the cylinder rose twenty-four feet at its centre. It was built of aluminium arches, the narrow spaces between which, only about one foot in width, were filled with thick, strong glass. This glass vault was in the daytime almost as bright as the sky outside, and, being airy, was the general place of resort for the passengers. At the usual running height of 15,000 feet above the ocean, it was necessary to the comfort of the passengers that the air pressure around them should be higher than it was outside. This was brought about by having the prow of the mote terminate in a circular opening six feet in diameter. The rapid motion of 350 feet a second would have caused a violent rush of air through this opening had there been one equally large at the other end for its escape. At the stern, however, the opening was made comparatively small, so that the air which actually entered at the front was just sufficient to give good ventilation and feed the fires below. The result was that the advancing mote exerted a pressure upon the air in the front opening, the reaction of which kept the barometer inside the mote some four inches higher than it was outside. To prevent the force thus generated from bursting the roof, the latter was made strong enough to bear the pressure of an entire atmosphere.

As we have said, there was a free space of twenty-four feet between the deck and the roof. This was partly filled by a promenade deck twelve feet in breadth, extending through the forward two hundred feet of the mote, about eight feet above the main deck.

The French Attempt on the *Cynthia*

A strong metallic cylinder, eight feet in diameter, passed vertically through all the decks, as well as the vault above, at a distance of fifty feet behind the prow. The upper part of this cylinder formed the pilot-house, which projected about three feet above the top of the mote. Here were stationed the captain and pilots. From our description it will be seen that the latter, when in such a position that they could look around, would stand with their feet some twelve feet above the promenade deck, but, being enclosed within the metallic cylinder which we have described, were entirely invisible.

It was noticed by the passengers that neither captain nor pilot was ever seen. Walking to the front of the promenade deck, one could pass round the cylinder below the pilot-house, and examine it on all sides. There was nothing about it to excite notice except what looked like a door with an ordinary handle to open it, and a key-hole. Although it seemed plain enough that this door was the entrance to the pilot-house, it was noticed that no one was ever known to come through it. This was attributed to prudence, which required that the conductors of the mote should, during the voyage, not be allowed to leave their posts or engage in conversation with the passengers.

The fact was that this supposed door was a sham. The real entrance to the cylinder was a secret one, through what looked like a room devoted to rubbish in the hold of the mote. The whole interior of the

His Wisdom the Defender

cylinder was taken up with elevating machinery, and with the rods and levers which passed from the pilot-house downward and worked the elevating arms by which the etherine was made more or less buoyant, as might be required, or impelled in the direction the mote was to take. There was also an elevator by which the conductors and pilots could be lifted most of the way through the sixty feet they had to mount to reach the pilot-house. The secret door at the bottom, by which an entrance to the cylinder was gained, closed perfectly air-tight. About ten feet below the pilot-house there was a horizontal floor or diaphragm, with an opening for passage up or down, which could be made air-tight. In case of an emergency, the captain and pilots could pass below this diaphragm and close the opening above them so as to be enclosed in the air-tight part of the cylinder. Here they would find a duplicate set of apparatus for guiding and running the mote, including compass and barometer. On the inside of this part of the cylinder were tanks filled with oxygen at high pressure. It was thus possible in an emergency for a mote to be run from this lower part instead of from the pilot-house, and for the men to remain there for an hour or more without suffocation. These arrangements were known only to the captains, who were sworn to the most absolute secrecy. What other instructions they received in order that they might meet an emergency will appear subsequently.

The French Attempt on the *Cynthia*

The pilots reached the pilot-house from the outside by a ladder passing over the roof of the mote and thence to the ground. The object of this singular proceeding, when to all appearance there was a door inside for them to ascend by, no one suspected, not even themselves.

In addition to the captain and pilots, some of whom were always on watch in the pilot-house, a watchman was kept continually on the roof outside the pilot-house while the mote was at its station either in Paris or London. The instructions to these watchmen were to keep a constant lookout for any attempt by a possible body of men, who were not passengers, to enter the mote in a threatening way. In case of such an attempt, an electric alarm was to be touched, which would set in motion two rows of gongs. On sounding these gongs the watchman was instructed to jump into the pilot-house and go below with the captain and pilots. There was no secrecy about this danger signal. The printed instructions for passengers notified them that in case of any catastrophe being threatened while the mote was in port a danger signal was to be sounded, on hearing which all the passengers were to leave as soon as possible. Similar directions were given to all the workmen within, who were to abandon their work and leave whenever the great gongs were sounded.

At noon, on June 15th, the *Cynthia* gently settled into her station on the Champs de Mars, as usual. No one noticed that on the last two voyages several

His Wisdom the Defender

passengers went from Paris to New York and came back on the return trip. Had this been observed, suspicion might have been aroused as to the motives which inspired so rapid a double journey. Equally unnoticed was the curiosity shown by these passengers in examining every part of the mote to which they were allowed access, such a sentiment being almost universal. Nor did any one observe the proceedings of one of these Frenchmen who, on the preceding voyage, had occupied himself in making wax impressions of the sham key-hole in the door leading up to the pilot-house. This false door was in front of the great cylinder we have described, and, being near the end of the promenade deck, was concealed from the great body of passengers thereon. It thus happened that the little space in front of it was frequently empty, and then the locksmith could carry on his work without being seen.

The *Cynthia,* as we have said, settled quietly into her resting-place. The doors were opened on the side for the exit of passengers, those on the other side, intended only for entrance, being kept closed until all the arriving passengers with their baggage had left the mote. During the two hours required for the landing it was quite common for departing passengers to wait outside the entrance gates before they were opened for admission. Thus the curiosity shown by certain persons who were peering through the iron bars excited no remark. Everything went on as usual until the baggage was nearly all landed.

The French Attempt on the *Cynthia*

Then something happened so unexpected that the lookers-on were for a moment quite dazed.

A crowd of men in citizens' clothes, but armed with muskets, bayonets, sledge-hammers, and chisels, came suddenly running to the exit gate of the enclosure. They knocked down the two watchmen on guard and rushed through the crowd of panic-stricken passengers to the mote. The guards could offer no resistance, and had no time to close the great aluminium doors. The watchman on top was so taken by surprise that the head of the column had nearly reached the mote before he sounded the gong. The porters and firemen within had not time, after hearing the alarm, to get out before their exit was barred by the inrush of men; so they ran to the entrance side, hastily opened a door, and jumped to the ground.

As soon as the watchman had sounded the alarm, he jumped into the pilot-house, while the captain and pilots ran below into the air-tight space we have described, the watchman following. The captain was for a moment in doubt what to do. His orders in such an emergency were to fly as high as possible immediately and bring the mote to Uraniburg. He ventured to hesitate so far as to run up to the pilot-house himself, in order to be sure of the necessity of this heroic measure.

There could no longer be any doubt. The armed men were rushing through the open doors in two columns. He turned the lever which caused the

His Wisdom the Defender

mote to rise, and again jumped into the compartment below and closed the air-tight trap-door over the heads of himself and the other two occupants. Now, as we have said, the mote could be navigated for a considerable distance without seeing outside the cylinder. An electric light permitted the reading of the barometer, which showed the air pressure both without and within, as well as the compass. There was no difficulty in going on a voyage so long as life and activity could be maintained by the stream of oxygen which could be turned on from the holders below.

About fifty of the assailants had succeeded in getting into the mote, when she slowly began to rise. The last dozen who had entered, alarmed at this, retraced their steps and jumped out. The remainder were obliged to stay whether they wished to or not. They lost no time in trying to gain possession. The leader, followed by his men, climbed as fast as possible, with the cry "*En avant!*" to the upper deck, mounted the narrow promenade, and then ran forward to the base of the pilot-house. Taking out a key which had been carefully filed to fit the sham lock of the door, he inserted it. To his surprise, it turned round loosely without unlocking anything or producing any effect. He vainly tried to make it catch hold of a bolt.

By the time he had satisfied himself that he could not unbolt the door, a roar was heard, both above and below. Below, it was the rush of the air

The French Attempt on the *Cynthia*

out of the mote through the open doors as that outside grew rarer with the ascent. Above, it was the low roar always produced by the rapid motion of the mote upwards and onwards.

"Try your bayonets," said the leader, when he saw that the door could not be unlocked.

The bayonets were inserted in the false crack between the door and the cylinder, with a view to prying it open, while the leader took a small dynamite torpedo from his pocket and put it into the keyhole to blow the lock to pieces. Of course both attempts were vain. The bayonets simply bent in the crack, and the torpedo did no damage except to blow off some of the metal round the lock.

Then they began to beat the supposed door with the sledge-hammers and the butts of their muskets, crying to those inside to open. And every moment they felt themselves flying higher and the air getting rarer.

Finding that the door resisted every attack, yet more violent measures were attempted. There was a narrow, horizontal opening in the cylinder just below the roof of the mote. This was closed by glass, forming a sort of window through which an indistinct view of the now empty interior of the pilot-house could be obtained.

"Fire through the window!"

The volley of musketry, fired at a venture with the view of alarming the supposed inmates, produced no effect except to destroy the window. All within was as silent as the grave. Every minute the roar

His Wisdom the Defender

of the air increased and the situation grew more desperate.

"Mount and climb into the window!"

Some of the most agile of the men undertook to obey the order by climbing up to the roof of the guards round the promenade, in order to enter the pilot-house through the broken glass. One managed to get his head through the window and was dumfounded to find the place quite empty. He had to drop immediately, as he found himself without breath for such exertion.

The programme of the attacking party had been very simple. By guile or force, with key, chisels, or hammers, as might be required, they were first of all to get possession of the pilot-house, while the mote lay in her bed, and shoot the inmates if they offered any resistance. If they did not resist they were to be compelled to show the victors how the mote was navigated. This, however, was not important, because, once in possession of the wheels and levers of the navigating power, it would only take a few hours to find out how they were worked. The idea that the mote might run away with them before they could get possession had scarcely entered their minds. When they found it doing so, they were at first so intent upon executing their plan that they failed to think of anything else.

Now, frustrated in the attempt to enter the pilot-house, they had time to think, and soon realized the terrible situation. The mote was carrying them

The French Attempt on the *Cynthia*

higher and higher, and the continued rarefaction of the air would soon cause suffocation. Only one resource was within reach.

"Run below and close the doors of the mote!"

As the men who tried to do so approached the first door, the outrush blew the three foremost of them out like feathers. Those behind them on each side were obliged to grasp the rails of the stairway in order to avoid meeting the same fate, and made their way back against the air-storm with the greatest difficulty. Arriving again at the upper deck, exhausted and out of breath, they could only report the fate of their fellows and their inability to do anything.

Every minute the air grew rarer. Every minute exertion became more difficult. A dozen hammers and as many muskets beat loudly upon the outside of the pilot-house, but no sound came back. "Open! open! for God's sake, open! We are your prisoners! We surrender!"

But there was no response. Were those within dead, or had they escaped by some secret passage? Minute snowflakes began to form in the air; the fingers of the men were soon chilled with the cold of a winter day.

"We must get into the pilot-house! Try again!"

A desperate attempt was made to carry out this order by the men climbing on each other. A dozen of them got on their knees and let a half-dozen mount on their shoulders, while several more climbed up by the guards as before. The first set stood up, lifting the second with them, while the third stepped on the shoulders of the latter. But they no sooner had got so far than the whole body fell to the deck with weakness and suffocation.

"Load and fire once more!"

The muskets were reloaded, and again a volley was fired into the pilot-house and against the cylinder, with no better effect than before. Cries of entreaty and despair that were intended to be loud and piercing were sent forth by the doomed men, calling upon those within for mercy. But the loudest were now as faint as the wail of an infant a hundred feet away, and fell like whispers against the deaf, metallic wall.

Blood began to pour from their noses and run upon the snow-covered deck. Looking round once more in their despair for an avenue of escape or a source of help, each saw in the livid faces of his companions the reflection of his own. A last desperate cry was attempted, but it was only a gasp; the tongue could no longer make an articulate sound. It protruded from each mouth and could not be drawn back into place. They felt the air within their breasts pressing to burst them, as if some demoniac power was pumping it into them. Their bodies swelled. The increasing stream of blood from their noses was followed by one from each of their blinded eyes; their livid faces grew cold; one after another the unhappy men fell into the pool of their own blood, which was now running from the promenade to the deck below.

The French Attempt on the *Cynthia*

The world faded from their eyes, and they all became unconscious in the embrace of death.

In a few minutes the report of the attempted seizure of the mote, and its unexpected escape, had spread through Paris. An hour later the mangled remains of three men, apparently fallen from the sky, were found in the park at Vincennes. All Paris was impressed with the feeling that some mysterious calamity had happened, and anxiously awaited further intelligence. But none was forthcoming. The authorities professed ignorance of the affair, and for some time it was not even known to the public who or what the attacking party was.

About five o'clock sentinels at Uraniburg, always on the lookout, were surprised to see a great loomote approaching from the west. A telescope was levelled upon her, and a few minutes sufficed to ascertain that she was the *Cynthia*. What could have happened? Campbell's first impression was that she had been captured by the enemy and was sent out, perhaps filled with armed men and explosives, to attack his headquarters. His small available force was called together as rapidly as possible to await events and make the best defence possible. But the accuracy of her movements soon relieved his mind. She must at least be directed by his own captain and pilots, for it would be impossible for any other set of men to manage her as she was being managed without weeks of instruction and patience. True, his own men might

His Wisdom the Defender

have been forced to conduct her under threat of their lives. But even in this case they would still, to a certain extent, have the captors at their mercy. It was impossible that she should make any successful attack unless her conductors managed her accordingly. The fears of all were allayed as she approached nearer and slowly and skilfully was brought to the ground.

The first one to emerge was the watchman, who gave a hurried account of what had happened. True to discipline, the captain and pilot remained at their posts. Campbell and a dozen of his followers ran in and mounted the stairways. As they reached the upper main deck, pools of blood met their eyes. Mounting the promenade, an appalling sight was disclosed. The bodies of thirty-five men were heaped in a pool of gore round the base of the pilot-house. The captain and pilot looked out from the window below.

"What has happened to these men? For God's sake, how were they so mangled?"

"They were not mangled at all, sir, so far as we know. The mote was attacked, and we simply obeyed your orders. We mounted upward until the pressure on the outside was reduced to five inches, and the air within, notwithstanding the supply of oxygen, grew so close that we could scarcely breathe it. Then, taking our course towards this point, we descended as rapidly as possible. By the time the air barometer outside rose to twenty inches, we were ourselves nearly suffocated, and were obliged to open

The French Attempt on the *Cynthia*

the trap. While the mote was rising we heard a great pounding against the side of the pilot-house. Of course we took no notice of this. It ceased about the time we reached the highest level. When we were able to look out we could see what had happened, but we were powerless to do any good, so we continued our journey here, according to orders."

Campbell was almost overcome by the catastrophe. With all his philosophy, with all the consciousness that a million of lives were as nothing compared with the human interests intrusted to him, he could not view such a horror without feeling as if he were himself a murderer. What bore most heavily upon him was the consciousness that the tragic result was one that he had himself planned. He had arranged to defend the motes from capture by having them, in case of attack, fly many miles above the earth, carrying their captors with them, if they remained on board. Intellectually speaking, he knew that this course would lead to their speedy destruction. And yet he had never pictured to himself the possibilities of his plan being carried out with such terrible success. He could not help trying to think, now that it was too late, how the safety of the mote might have been secured by some proceeding less destructive to life. Every such thought only added to his depression. He tried in vain to sleep that night. Whenever he closed his eyes there floated before his vision the livid faces of ghastly cadavers, each lying in a pool of its own blood.

His Wisdom the Defender

It is said by the most advanced students of evolution that our nightly visions are inspired by the thoughts and sentiments of savage or brute ancestors, which take advantage of the relaxation of sleep to assert themselves in us. But in the present case it was the conscience of the civilized man rather than that of the brute which dominated.

Next morning his incessant attention was demanded by the events which he was to guide. It was absolutely necessary to cast off the thought of what he had seen and to devote himself wholly to the work in hand. The contest he was waging against the world was not alone a physical one. Had such been the case there would have been little doubt of his ability to carry it through, especially if he cast aside his scruples against taking human life. What made it trying was its being waged against the feelings and opinions of the race. The soldier goes to his death because he is inspired by the feeling that his countrymen are looking upon him and approving his acts. Ability to defy the good opinion of mankind is the principal mark of a criminal. To one of sensibilities so highly educated the contest would have been an unequal one had he not felt that he was backed against the humanity of the present by the humanity of the near future. Under these circumstances, a visitor who could entertain the slightest personal sympathy with him was doubly welcome, even had he come to be his executioner. Such a visitor he was soon to receive.

XVIII

Austria Threatens Checkmate

WE left Gheen demolishing the barracks around Berlin, carrying off generals, and disarming all the soldiers he could find. From Feltow he went to the barracks at Zehlendorf and demolished them in like manner. But the third barracks which he attacked were nearly empty—only a corporal's guard was in them. From the men he learned that all the soldiers who were left around Berlin had taken refuge in the casemates of the fortifications. It was evident that the task of reaching them in such a retreat would be one of great difficulty and possible danger. He was amply equipped for tearing down the strongest buildings and capturing any armed force in the field. But the masses of earth, stone, and iron by which the capital was defended were practically unattackable by his machinery. The steel doors of the casemates would resist, he knew not how long, all the force he could bring against them. There was no doubt that by taking time enough, and perhaps bringing new modes of attack to bear, he could ultimately succeed even

His Wisdom the Defender

against this strong defence. But to do this would take much time, involving something like a regular siege. Such an undertaking might well be postponed in view of the fact that an army driven into its defences like a flock of sheep would be too much demoralized to become an important factor in the affairs of the world. The last instructions he had received before leaving were not to spend time on the German armies if they succeeded in making an effective resistance; but, in this case, to carry out the rest of the programme and then disband the armies of Russia and Austria, leaving those of Germany to be disposed of in the future. All the details had been left in his hands, and, unless he received orders to the contrary from his chief, he was to go on doing all the harm he could to the military power of the leading nations, regardless of consequences.

He spent the next three days in a general sweep over all the military posts of northern Germany, cutting the telegraph wires so that the local authorities could receive no immediate instructions from Berlin. All the soldiers that could be found were sought out, disarmed, and sent home in the same way as before. To guard against any attempt at collecting the scattered fragments into a new force, all the field officers that could be captured were sent in a body to the island of Rügen, in the Baltic. The railway connecting this island with the mainland was destroyed.

Austria Threatens Checkmate

When this was done, the Germans were yet more surprised by a sudden attack upon the arsenals and manufactories of arms in the empire. Both the centipedes and daddies were effectively used for this purpose. The former, with their powerful claws, tore off the roofs from the buildings, while the daddies helped to demolish the walls. The machinery for the manufacture of arms was torn to pieces, and all the plans, models, moulds, and drawings that could be found by the most careful search were broken or torn up and heaped into a pile. Sulphuric acid was poured over the mass as it had been on the arms taken from the soldiers, in order that it might not be possible, in the near future, even to fit up a new factory. All the arms that were stored in the arsenals were treated in the same way.

The outcome of the week's work may be briefly stated: The German military power was practically annihilated, except for the remnants of the army hidden in casemates and the garrisons of the posts on the French frontier. Not only had Germany no army for active operations, but, in order to organize one, work would have to be begun at the bottom. There would have been no arms for the infantry, no guns for the artillery, and no machinery to make either arms or guns. The whole empire was for the moment helpless against any attack from its neighbors, unless it should receive aid from the same power which had destroyed its means of defence.

The smallness of the loss suffered by the attacking

His Wisdom the Defender

force can be accounted for only by reflecting that two men, one of them a military expert, had spent two years in elaborating the most careful preparations for the work, and this without their intention having ever been suspected until they were nearly ready to act. The only mishap had been that arising from the attention of the world having been temporarily called to the possibilities of the case by the correspondent of the New York *Herald*. Fortunately the preparations were so well advanced that this did little harm beyond necessitating more prompt and decisive action.

The result of all this foresight was that out of the three hundred and fifty motes which made up the attacking fleet, only one had been totally destroyed, none had been captured until after they had been made useless, and only a dozen had suffered damage which could not be speedily repaired. Only three men had lost their lives—one through treachery to his own cause, and the others through what was almost equivalent to an inadvertence. About twenty had been disabled by injuries more or less serious. For all practical purposes the attacking force was therefore as effective as ever. The coal and petroleum necessary for running the motes, and the provisions and other supplies necessary for the commissariat, could be seized wherever they were to be found. No defence of person or property against an army flying through the air where it chose, and pouncing down on any place at any moment, was possible.

Austria Threatens Checkmate

There was nothing to prevent the military forces of other nations being dealt with in the same manner as those of Germany, unless some new mode of defence should be devised. Gheen felt it necessary to forestall this possibility by disorganizing, without loss of time, the other great armies. For this purpose it was essential that as little as possible should be known of the policy by which the Germans had temporarily evaded the attacking force. So the telegraph wires were everywhere ruthlessly cut, and every railway train that attempted to run anywhere in eastern Germany was pulled off the track. The tracks themselves were torn up and many bridges destroyed. The result was that the military authorities at St. Petersburg and Vienna had, for the moment, no detailed information as to events in Berlin. They knew of the capture of the Emperor, and had heard rumors of the German troops being obliged to take shelter wherever they could find it, but they had not received any authentic announcement of the date at which their own armies might be attacked, and, indeed, did not know that they were to be molested at all.

On June 29th, Gheen, with his whole force, arrived at St. Petersburg and proceeded to search out and disband the Russian armies in the same way that they had the German. The Russian soldiers, owing to their inferior intelligence, were even less able to offer effective resistance than their neighbors had been. The Czar, like his friend the Emperor,

His Wisdom the Defender

had attempted to take command of his forces. Finding resistance in vain, he adopted the course of one of his ancestors of the nineteenth century, and committed suicide, though not in the same way. He swallowed prussic acid. On July 1st the force proceeded from St. Petersburg to Warsaw without waiting for the complete disarmament of the armies around St. Petersburg.

The main feature of our hero's policy, from the beginning, had been to demonstrate his power by every means that did not involve injury to the beneficent institutions of civilization. As we have already seen, he well knew that the old *régime* would yield to nothing but force. Physical force alone might, in the end, have conquered. But in a project which must, in a not distant future, involve serious changes in political institutions, he felt it essential that, if possible, he should also show that he possessed political power. There was one region of Europe in which such a power could be exerted in entire conformity to the political principles which he intended should control the relations of nations under his new *régime*. This region was that which had formerly been occupied by the kingdom of Poland.

The history of the re-establishment of this kingdom under the personal guidance of the Defender is too well known to find a place here. So we shall follow the operations of his army.

The entire force under Gheen's command, coming from Warsaw, passed one night in a field

Austria Threatens Checkmate

near Ernstbrunn, a village about twenty miles north of Vienna, as far from railway and telegraph as it was convenient to get. Next morning the aerial army gathered over Vienna and made the circuit of the fortifications in search of the Austrian troops. It was quite an agreeable surprise to see more than fifty thousand soldiers stationed in front of a long line of works waiting to receive the attack. The space occupied by this army extended a mile along the line, and was from a quarter to half a mile in depth. The tops of the fortifications were armed with an extraordinary number of field batteries, evidently stationed there for the occasion. In addition to this, a number of rapid-fire guns had been taken from naval vessels and were also mounted on the fortifications, ready for such use as might be required.

Heretofore, Gheen had attacked the troops with confidence under the line of fire of batteries, because it was impossible for the artillery to open fire upon him without destruction to its own men. But these preparations made it look as if, in the present case, the Austrians were ready to sacrifice their own troops for the purpose of destroying his forces once and for all. In order to disarm the troops, the centipedes must come down among them, and then, if the artillery chose, it could fire upon them with destructive effect to both sides. A few thousand Austrians might be killed, but his own force would be permanently disabled.

His Wisdom the Defender

Gheen and his adjutant, also a West Point man, who kept at his elbow, surveyed the scene.

"What do you suppose they are after?" said the chief.

"I think if we attack as we did at Potsdam the rapid-fire guns will open upon us, regardless of their own men."

"That would be so contrary to every sentiment and tradition of civilized warfare, I can hardly believe it possible."

"But," replied the adjutant, "the men stand as if they expected death. See how they have been drilled. Every battalion and every company keeps its place, and the soldiers stand at attention, their rifles on the ground, without the slightest movement. They really seem to await their doom from their own artillery, in order to bring about our destruction."

"Any way," said Gheen, "the rapid-fire guns can be aimed at our motes while they are descending, and several shots might be fired from each before the motes could get among the soldiers on the ground."

The conclusion was that it would not be prudent to sweep down like a hawk upon its prey, as had been done with the Germans and Russians, and a reconnaissance was decided upon. A line of six plain motes, each manned only by the three men necessary to manage it, was ordered to form and approach the ground, not among the soldiers, but at a distance of half a mile on the right flank, at a point where the rapid-fire guns could not play upon them. Then they

Austria Threatens Checkmate

were to make a dash for the armed troops, keeping as near the ground as possible, flying directly through the lines at a rapid rate, and then rising and returning on the other side. If the artillery seriously intended to destroy the attacking party, at all hazards, regardless of their own men, they might try to fire upon these swiftly flying motes, but would not be likely to hit any of them. If fired upon, the motes were to suddenly change their course and return without passing through the lines.

Gheen from his eyrie watched the six motes dash in single file through the Austrian ranks. Not a soldier budged, not a weapon was moved in self-defence. Such stolid immobility seemed superhuman. Suddenly a deadly fire was opened upon the advancing motes from hundreds of guns, the Austrians mowing down their own men without mercy. The state of the case was seen by the captains of the motes and grasped by Gheen almost at the same moment. The supposed army which held out so inviting a temptation to come and disarm it was made up of dummies—men literally of straw—in the uniforms of soldiers, with their arms resting on the ground. It was fortunate, indeed, that the whole force had not, in its enthusiasm, flown to the attack. Two of the motes were disabled, the others effected their escape. The former succeeded in rising a short distance and then fell to the ground. The men on board of them jumped out and made signs of surrender.

The Austrians were too anxious to secure posses-

His Wisdom the Defender

sion of the curious vessels to destroy them by a continued fire. The real troops ran out, took the six men prisoners, and eagerly climbed upon the motes. The latter were of course immovable, and would be of little real use to their captors except as objects of curiosity. The only hopeful result in getting possession of them would be the discovery of the secret by which they were managed. As each weighed many tons, it would be impossible to remove them without machinery and appliances which it would require several days to get into operation. But the great cylinders running through nearly their whole length, and containing the etherine which gave them buoyancy, had been pierced by the shot. The etherine itself was escaping and running like an oily fluid into the bottom of the mote. As much as possible of it was collected and carried off for scientific examination and chemical analysis.

Leaving the fortifications, Gheen proceeded to attack the barracks round the city in which the troops were supposed to be quartered; but none were found except a few soldiers necessary to guard them. The Austrian authorities had followed the German example of hiding their troops in the casemates of the fortifications or quartering them in houses throughout the city. There would be no difficulty in effecting their capture by a thorough search of the city and by blowing up the casemates, one after another, with dynamite. But to reduce every fortified city in Germany and Austria in this way would be a long

Austria Threatens Checkmate

and tedious job. A messenger was therefore despatched to Elba for instructions as to the course to pursue. A complete statement of the situation was sent to Campbell. The despatch arrived the day after the attempt on the *Cynthia,* and it elicited the following instructions:

"Keep your force together and do as much harm to the military equipment as you can without causing great destruction of private property. Do not operate on two successive days at the same place unless some decided advantage will result. So far as possible move from place to place in the night, and let your men encamp in the daytime whenever they are fatigued. If, after attacking the Austrian troops one day, you should appear at Berlin next morning, you would probably find that the army had come out of its hiding-place, so that it could be again reached."

Gheen proceeded to carry out this programme, with even more success, moral as well as physical, than he could have anticipated. While he is thus spreading alarm, let us return to headquarters.

XIX

The Dawn

IT was every hour becoming plainer to all but the most obstinate men that some other policy than that of defiance of the new power must be adopted. As a first step towards a change of front, it must be ascertained what terms of peace Campbell was disposed to demand, or what arrangement could be made with him. Not only men, but even countries, must sacrifice their dignity, at least to the extent of trying to bring some inducement to bear upon him to cease his mad career. The first step in this direction was taken by Lord Worcester, the English Premier. Knowing in what intimate relations Winthrop stood to Campbell, he addressed him through Secretary Bayne, asking if he could not immediately visit London in the *Friede,* which had been left at his disposal, to confer with representatives of the British government. After an assurance that no attempt would be made to interfere with the *Friede,* the request was complied with. Winthrop landed in Hyde Park the next day. It was soon agreed that he should be one member of a delegation, of which Lord

The Dawn

Churchill would be the other, to interview the Owner of the Motes in the interests of peace.

Before starting Winthrop explained the very delicate position in which he was placed. Not only was he the friend and adviser of Campbell, but he entirely sympathized with his objects. All he could do was to facilitate their being carried out by negotiations. With this understanding he and Churchill proceeded in the *Friede* to Elba.

"Let me see him first," said Winthrop, "and explain our coming to him. Then I will introduce you, and you can say what you please."

I need not describe the greeting of the two friends under such circumstances. For a few minutes Campbell was quite overcome. Then Winthrop proceeded to business.

"I have come to you simply as the bearer of a message. They want you to stop."

"How can I stop? What shall I do with my force? Surrender it? If so, to whom? The power to which I surrender it will be master of the world. Can you name any power which the world is willing to accept as master? My constant prayer is that I may look beyond the sea of troubles that now rages around me to the haven of rest that lies beyond."

"I cannot gainsay a word you utter," was the reply. "I do not want you to stop until your end is gained. But now I think the road is open and that you can make your own terms."

"You save my life when you say that. I am so

His Wisdom the Defender

worn that I doubt whether I can stand this strain for another week and live. But reason makes it plain as day that I must go on and finish my work.

The man who for years had been planning his ends with infinite resolution, who had driven the armies of Europe into caves and dens to hide from his power, was overcome. He sprang to his companion, embraced him, and, laying his head on his shoulder, burst into tears. Having thus relieved his mind, he was ready to talk with the other.

Lord Churchill presented the state of Europe in strong colors. In Germany anarchy reigned triumphant. Mobs of half-starved workmen were marching round, and no power could suppress their violence. Half the city of Giessen had been burned before the frightened inhabitants could defend themselves against the attack. Buildings in smaller towns were almost everywhere in flames. In all the bourses stocks were practically worthless. Business of every kind was at a standstill. " Can you not stop?"

Campbell felt that this was the real crisis of his career. The appeal struck what he knew was his weakest point. He had always been an implacable fighter as long as his enemy kept up the contest. But on the first signs of weakening his disposition had been to go more than half-way and surrender almost everything. Happily, being conscious of this weakness, he had gone through a course of self-reproof and self-discipline, with a view of guarding against it.

The Dawn

"How can I stop? Is Europe ready to disarm voluntarily? Is your government ready to abolish its military establishment and sell its navy to me for old iron? If England is ready, are France and Austria ready? Will all the nations enact a law that there shall be no more war, and abide by it? When they do this, then I am ready to stop, and not before."

To these questions Churchill could give no satisfactory reply. He was not, in fact, authorized to offer any terms or propositions whatever. All he could do was to beg Campbell to stop long enough to receive such communications as the combined governments of Europe might choose to make.

"I cannot stop," said Campbell, "until I have an assurance that not only her Majesty's government, but that of France, is willing to acknowledge my authority as Defender of the peace of the World."

"I will convey your answer to my government. While it is considering it, can we not have at least a truce?"

"I fail to see how anything that could properly be called a truce is possible. The very term implies a combat the continuance of which is harmful to one or both the opposing parties, and the cessation of which will facilitate peace. No such combat is going on. You have placed in a very strong light the deplorable conditions that exist throughout Europe. Would any truce that I could enter into better those

His Wisdom the Defender

conditions? What good would it do if I should now bring my forces to Elba and cease active operations?"

"It would at least help to calm the public mind," said Churchill, "prepare it to weigh the situation in all its aspects, and reach a conclusion as to the best course to pursue under the circumstances."

"But my force would be as much of a menace then as now. Allow me to repeat what I have so often tried to say, but have never seemed to succeed in impressing on men's minds. What the world really wants is not merely a cessation of my operations, but an assurance that motes shall never be used in warfare under any circumstances. When the world is ready to accept what I think the only solution of the difficulty—one leading to this assurance—I am ready to confer on the subject."

"Will you kindly tell me more exactly what course you think will lead to the end you deem so desirable?"

"I have already pointed out what I deem the only available course. I am deliberating on the details of my plan, and will make them public as soon as they are matured."

"All Europe will, I am sure, be glad to know that you have a definite plan. So far as I can see, nothing remains but to report your attitude to the authorities at whose request I am here."

The two men shook hands and parted, Churchill returning to London alone.

The Dawn

Winthrop had another commission—that of trying to secure the release of the Emperor.

The regency that acted during the absence of the latter was so far from being animated by his unyielding spirit that it was ready to sacrifice a little dignity to the exigencies of the situation. An appeal had therefore been made to Winthrop to secure his aid. To accomplish this, the regency had formally annulled the order that no quarter should be shown to the attacking forces. To fulfil the conditions of release, it only remained that the Emperor should approve of this action. Campbell was glad to accede to the desire of the regency, and requested Winthrop to go to the Emperor, inform him of the action of the regency, and ask him to approve of it.

The Emperor was notified by his attendant that a representative of the Owner of the Motes desired an audience on a matter seriously affecting his Majesty's interests. After some hesitation Winthrop was admitted.

"I am here on behalf of the Owner of the Motes to advise your Majesty that the regency, acting in your Majesty's absence, has annulled the proclamation which you were pleased to issue, ordering your army to show no quarter to any of the forces of the Owner of the Motes that might be captured. Should your Majesty be pleased to acquiesce in this action, it has been ordered that you be returned to your capital."

His Wisdom the Defender

The Emperor received the announcement in sullen silence.

"Writing materials are here at your Majesty's disposal. At what hour shall I return to receive your reply?"

This question was as unsuccessful as the previous statement. Imperial dignity maintained itself in silence.

"If your Majesty has no reply to make, I will bid you adieu."

The single word "adieu" was uttered in reply.

A calmer and more self-possessed man than Winthrop never existed, but he had a hard struggle with himself as he returned and reported the ill-success of his mission.

"What would you do with such a man?" inquired Campbell.

"I would pour a bucket of cold water over his head, morning and night, until he yielded. Meanwhile, he should be kept in solitary confinement and not allowed to see even his attendant."

"And, just to think, I had intended to send him home in the finest mote I could spare—perhaps the *Cynthia* itself—with his imperial standard floating upon it, in order that the German people might see that I not only bore him no ill-will, but was disposed to show their monarch every honor. But let us look at the situation calmly. We have a more serious problem before us than that of punishing the most obstinate of men. We expect the Germans to

The Dawn

come under our system, and the only question is, how we can best bring it about."

"Perhaps it is better that we should be governed entirely by reason and show no irritation at all, but it goes very hard on the flesh to do so. It is too late to act to-night; let us see how we shall feel on the subject to-morrow morning."

Next morning it was decided to send the Emperor home, and there release him, but to dispense with the unnecessary exhibition of the imperial standard over his mote.

"Is it necessary that either of us should communicate our decision to him?"

"No," said Winthrop, "I certainly want to have nothing more to do with him, and I am sure you agree with me. Just send a messenger mote after him, and let the messenger inform the attendant what he has come for. The slowest of your motes can easily reach Berlin before nightfall."

A messenger was sent for and ordered to get his mote in readiness for conveying the Emperor to Berlin. He was then to go to the house where he was imprisoned, inform the attendant of his mission, and signify to the Emperor his readiness to execute the mission with which he had been charged.

The attendant, overjoyed at the news, conveyed the message to his royal master.

"Was will Majestät?" he inquired, with that respectful familiarity which marks the intercourse of a valet with his king.

His Wisdom the Defender

The Emperor hesitated long before replying. When Winthrop had called upon him the night before, as the representative of the Owner of the Motes, he felt that it was a slur upon his imperial dignity that the Owner had not called in person. After his return he put this forward as the reason of his discourteous reception of Winthrop.

"I should have been glad to call on his Majesty in person," said Campbell, when, long afterward, this sentiment of the Emperor was made known to him, "but, do you suppose he would have treated me in any way different from what he treated Winthrop? I do not believe that he would, and this is the reason that I did not go in person."

Now the Emperor felt that, partly through his own proceedings, a yet greater indignity was done him. Neither his captor nor a representative was sent to inform him that he would be set at liberty, but, instead of this, he had to receive the information through an underling. But for the demands of the situation he would have adhered to his policy of grim silence and refused to move; but he felt that this would be almost suicidal. The interests of his empire imperatively demanded his presence at his capital, and he had gone as far as was prudent in his defiance of the power which held him in captivity. His conscience told him that he had brought this new humiliation upon himself, and that he had better make the best of his situation. So he told the attendant that they would pack up their

The Dawn

few belongings and leave in the proffered conveyance.

During the rapid passage northward through the clouds, the first sentiment of the Emperor was naturally that of nervous fear. Then, as their frail conveyance seemed as secure as a boat floating on a river, his curiosity got the better even of his imperial dignity, and he eagerly questioned the messenger, not only as to the system on which the motes were run, but as to what he could tell him of the course of events during his captivity.

The telegraph had conveyed the news in advance of the mote, but had given no information as to where the landing might be effected. It was thought prudent to leave this matter to the judgment of the conductor. Had the place of landing been announced in advance, there was no telling but that the German authorities might have availed themselves of the opportunity to seize the mote and every one in it. To guard against this the conductor landed them in the centre of the Thiergarten, before any one saw them coming. The Emperor was told that he was at liberty. His few belongings were rapidly thrown out, and the mote returned to its station.

XX

The Proclamation

THE fire which had been raging for more than a month, threatening to destroy civilization itself, seemed at last to be burning itself out. The weak-minded people had all gone crazy, leaving only those who could keep their heads to look after the world's affairs. The mobs, exhausted by their efforts, had begun to take a rest, and were being fed by a concerted plan to give them work whenever it could be found. Merchants and brokers were taking account of stock, and waiting for something to turn up. The news that the aerial force had encamped, now here and now there, or had caught some unwary regiment venturing out for exercise, was almost getting to be monotonous. Statesmen actually began to think over the situation and consult on plans. The only men who kept their faculties at the highest tension were the journalists, who found that their presses no longer had to run all day and all night to supply the public demand, and tried to keep this demand from falling off too rapidly.

Two of the world's great powers stood unchanged

The Proclamation

in their attitude because they had never been carried off their feet by the storm. They were Secretary Bayne and the London *Times*. The former took the ground that he had nothing to do in the case but perform his duty and execute the laws. So he had made a formal requisition on the Italian government for the extradition of one Alexander Campbell, a fugitive from justice in the United States, who had fled to Italian territory, and he now awaited an answer to this demand. The *Times* adhered to its position that the men who were disturbing the peace should be treated as outlaws, and condemned the course of the government in allowing Churchill to hold negotiations with their leader.

But the world began to change its point of view. In spite of all the *Times* could say, Churchill's interview and the restoration of the German Emperor to his throne were both looked upon as auspicious events. From the former it was learned that a proposition looking to peace might soon be expected from the great disturber. The past and the present were almost forgotten in the eager cry, What will it be? Men had not long to wait.

The question was answered by a proclamation such as they had never before heard. It appeared in all the journals of the world; messengers flew with it to every capital; all mankind read it, for to them it was addressed.

His Wisdom the Defender

"THE DEFENDER OF THE PEACE OF THE WORLD TO ALL MANKIND

"*GREETING:*

"The fulness of time being come when war should cease and all mankind dwell together in amity;

"And I, being vested by Almighty God with power to prevent the movements of armies, the sailing of navies, and the prosecution of war by any agency;

"And believing that this power can best be exercised under an official name and title;

"Now, THEREFORE, know all men that I have created and assumed, and do by these presents create, and for myself and my successors assume, the office, title, and functions of

"DEFENDER OF THE PEACE OF THE WORLD.

"And to the end that the office of Defender may be so executed as to secure the independence of all nations, the liberty of individuals, and the general welfare of humanity, I do enact and publish the statutes hereto appended, to be obeyed and enforced by the Defender as the supreme law of the world until they shall be amended or repealed in the manner therein set forth.

"GIVEN UNDER MY HAND AND SEAL this four-

The Proclamation

teenth day of July, 1946, at my seat at Uraniburg, in the island of Elba.

"Campbell,

"Defender."

The accompanying statutes were promulgated under five titles. The first consisted of definitions showing the exact sense in which various expressions occurring in the statutes should be construed; the second related to the political functions of the Defender; the third to his control over the motes; the fourth to the administration of his revenues, and the fifth to miscellaneous matters pertaining to future conferences among nations, his council, and the modes of amending the statutes.

In Title I. confederate nations were defined as those who should, by the act of their highest legislative bodies, adopt the statutes as their supreme law, and who should, in pursuance of this act, have abolished their military and naval establishments. An army was defined as any organized body of men armed with deadly weapons to be used on the bodies of their fellow-men. To guard against too wide a construction of the term "deadly weapon," this again was defined as a weapon specially designed to inflict mortal wounds, thus excluding all appliances suitable only for a police force.

We give the statutes of Title II. in full:

"Article I.

"There shall be no more war.

His Wisdom the Defender

"ARTICLE II.

"There shall hereafter be no armies or navies except those which the Defender shall adjudge to be necessary to the protection of life and property.

"ARTICLE III.

"The Defender shall ever recognize and never abridge those rights which peoples enjoy under the law of nature and of nations. The basic principle of this law shall be: The earth belongs to the people who inhabit it, and every part of the earth belongs to the people who inhabit that part, subject to such restrictions as imperfect civilization, the development of customs and institutions, and the necessity of promoting the general welfare may render necessary. In pursuance of this law, the following rights of nations and peoples shall forever be recognized:

"The right on the part of each independent nation to continue its ancestral form of government under its chosen or accepted rulers from generation to generation forever;

"The right by peaceable measures to change this form of government from time to time when its people, in their wisdom, shall deem such change conducive to their welfare;

"The right to manage its own internal affairs in its own way, and to regulate its dealings with the rest of the world according to its own judgment, subject to such treaties as it may for good reason and

The Proclamation

valuable consideration have voluntarily entered into, and to such general regulations as may be established to promote the general welfare.

"The corresponding rights of dependent peoples shall be:

"To be humanely governed in accordance with their laws and traditions;

"To become a sovereign and independent nation when they shall so desire, and when it shall be shown to the Defender that their welfare may thus be promoted.

"ARTICLE IV.

"The Defender shall not take part in enforcing the laws of any nation or state, nor shall he act as a ruler of men outside the limits of his seat, unless temporarily, to arrest or cure a condition of anarchy; but notwithstanding these and other restrictions he may protect life and property against unlawful destruction whenever required by the interests of humanity.

"ARTICLE V.

"The Defender shall, whenever requested by the parties in dispute, arbitrate any question at issue between nations or peoples. In pronouncing his award he shall state the facts and expound the law on which his conclusions are based; but he shall never award exemplary damages nor impose humiliating conditions.

His Wisdom the Defender

"ARTICLE VI.

"Whenever it shall appear to the constituted authorities of a confederate nation that any policy or proceeding of the Defender, contemplated or actual, is injurious to the interests of said nation, or not in accord with equity; or if it shall appear that the Defender can adopt any policy or perform any act that will promote the interests of such nation without injury to any other nation, then, in every such case, the said authorities shall have the right to make to the Defender such representations on the subject as shall to them seem meet. To all such representations the Defender shall give respectful attention, and, if he is unable to comply with any wishes which may be thus expressed, he shall set forth the reasons for such noncompliance.

"ARTICLE VII.

"The Defender shall have the right to choose and appropriate to his own use such place, places, region, or regions, as he shall deem suitable for his seat; but not more than two hundred thousand square miles shall be taken for this purpose from the territory of any nation without the consent of said nation.

"ARTICLE VIII.

"The Defender shall have sovereign and plenary power to govern his seat, and shall enjoy the right of eminent domain over its territory.

The Proclamation

"ARTICLE IX.

"The Defender shall not use his power in the propagation of any form of religious belief, worship, or observance.

"ARTICLE X.

"The Defender shall not enter into any secret treaty or arrangement with any nation or power whatever; nor shall he take any measures which might injuriously affect the interests of any nation without giving due notice of his intentions.

"ARTICLE XI.

"Neither the Defender nor any of his officers of state shall accept any present or mark of distinction from any political personage or power."

The mutation of public opinion during the next week is so well reflected in the comments of the London *Times* that it will be sufficient to give an extract from its editorial columns for each day of the week following the issue:

Wednesday, July 15.—"If this aspirant for a more than royal eminence supposes that any official notice will be taken of his utterance, he has less sagacity than has been supposed. It is difficult to see what object he had in view in issuing this paper. He is and must remain an outlaw. How soon the guardians of order in Europe and America shall

His Wisdom the Defender

get possession of his motes and execute their laws upon his person is merely a question of time."

Thursday, July 16.—" Those who read the statutes which the so-called Owner of the Motes issues with his proclamation will view his mad proceedings with even greater regret when they notice that the imagined laws really have some features worthy of consideration. That a man capable of framing a law of any sort should have entered upon such a reckless course is one of the wonders of the situation."

Friday, July 17.—" One cannot study these alleged statutes without being surprised at the restrictions which their framer has thrown around his own power. Seen by the side of his mad and reckless proceedings, the contrast is most striking. It seems quite likely that if referred to an international convention, many features of these laws might be accepted with advantage."

Saturday, July 18.—" The destruction of the military power of at least Germany and Russia and the reduction of that of Austria to bodies of half-armed soldiers hiding from the enemy wherever they can get shelter are accomplished facts which we shall be wise to recognize. The question what we should do to promote the national interests is one to be calmly studied with a view to the future rather than the past."

Monday, July 20.—" The interview of Lord Cardigan with the self-styled Defender must be regarded

The Proclamation

as in every way gratifying. Nothing could be more admirable than the utterance of philanthropic sentiments and expressions of regard for law by a man who, from our point of view, has violated all law. If Campbell adheres to the construction he puts upon his proposed statutes, neither the political nor commercial interests of Great Britain in any part of the world will be endangered. Under the proposed law the inhabitants of British India are regarded as a dependent people, and no restriction is placed upon England's methods of governing them which is not in strict accord with England's practice. His Majesty's Indian Empire cannot be erected into an independent government under these laws, except on the condition of a desire for such independence on the part of the Indian people, and a demonstration that their welfare will thus be promoted. It is difficult to anticipate the time when both of these conditions will be fulfilled; but, if it should come, Great Britain will no longer insist on her sway."

Tuesday, July 21.—" The policy of his Majesty's government in meeting the new conditions will meet with the approval of all sensible men. An unequalled opportunity is offered us to assume that leading position which every loyal British subject must desire. By promptly accepting the situation as it is, British commerce will be extended into the very centre of Asia and Africa, and a new impetus will be given to the enterprise of our people."

Wednesday, July 22.—" The bill introduced by

His Wisdom the Defender

the government into Parliament last evening recognizing the functions of the Defender of the Peace of the World, accepting his statutes, and providing for the abolition of his Majesty's military and naval establishments, is one which will commend itself to general approval.

"The prompt action of the United States government in the same direction shows a wise appreciation of the new conditions. The Defender's propositions were accepted and embodied into law by the almost unanimous vote of both Houses of Congress. Among those in power, the only dissenting voice was that of Mr. Secretary Bayne, who vigorously adhered to the position he had taken—that the government could not recognize one of its own citizens, especially a fugitive from justice, in the position assumed by the Defender. The wisdom of Congress in refusing to accept this view is shown by the rumored proceedings of the Defender in constituting a council, of which one of America's most eminent citizens, President Winthrop, is to be the head.

"It is rumored from Berlin that the German government is seriously considering the question of accepting the new system. The first nation to adopt this measure will not only set an excellent example to the rest of the world, but will naturally be the leading nation for many years to come. Prompt action by Parliament is therefore of the utmost importance. A multitude of details will have to be settled, but these can well be left to the future."

The Proclamation

The German government was moved in the same direction by a motive yet more urgent than any that could be felt in England. It is true that the Emperor was still smarting under the indignity of having been seized and imprisoned. But a situation stared him in the face which called for action. France had never ceased to deplore the loss of Alsace and Lorraine. The statue of Strasburg in the Place de la Concorde at Paris still wore the weeds of mourning in which it had been draped more than seventy years before. The ineffectual attempt to recover the provinces which had been made in the meantime had served to keep alive the national feeling of France on the subject. Now all that was wanted to gain the object was the consent of a single man. If Campbell chose, he could in a single day disarm the German troops in the two provinces and turn them over to France. He could say to France, Take them for yourself; I will not interfere. The armies already being mobilized in the eastern departments were sufficient to overcome the feeble and demoralized German garrisons. There was no course left open but to accept the situation and make the best of it. A bill to this effect was introduced into the Reichstag, and was passed by an almost unanimous vote.

XXI

Rah! Rah! Rah! the Defender!

THE man for whom there had been erstwhile nothing but execration was now the hero who had guaranteed peace and liberty to all the world by a system of laws that nothing could subvert.

All nations were hurrying into the fold as fast as their methods of legislative procedure would admit. As they did so, each received a formal invitation to send delegates to a world's congress, which should be charged to revise and amplify the Defender's statutes as might be necessary. The council of the Defender met daily to consider the multifarious questions raised by the new order of things.

Among the questions under discussion at one of these meetings was that of the title by which the Defender should be addressed. The invention of a suitable one was no easy task. "Your Majesty" was clearly inappropriate, because it belonged to a ruler of men—a function which the great actor had from the beginning been entirely sincere in repudi-

Rah! Rah! Rah! the Defender!

ating, and of which he had forbidden the exercise in his statutes. "Highness" and "Excellency" were too common and would not mean anything, even if adjectives without end were added. Some one suggested "Greatness."

"That suggests too strongly the idea of a little man stuck-up," said Campbell. "My inclination would be to dispense with any title whatever. I have always felt that expressions implying superiority on the one side and inferiority on the other were not appropriate in the Golden Age which we are now inaugurating. At the same time, I recognize the fact that human nature and the habits of thought and expression which have come down to us from our ancestors cannot be speedily altered. Assuming, then, that a title must be found, the matter presents itself to my mind in this way: The most appropriate title is one expressive of the qualities which we suppose the person addressed ought to possess. Why is a king called 'His Majesty'? Because the quality implied by that word is the one which a monarch should show in the eyes of his people. Nothing is more appropriate to the head of a state than 'Majesty.' Why do we call the Pope 'His Holiness'? Because holiness is the quality which is implied in his position.

"What attribute, then, is the most appropriate to the position which I have assumed? It seems to me that there can be but one answer to this question. What I need more than anything else, and

His Wisdom the Defender

what I pray God to imbue me with, is wisdom. Why should not the Defender be called 'His Wisdom'?"

The suggestion was received with enthusiasm. The council arose as one man, the members went forward and grasped the hands of their leader.

"We congratulate 'Your Wisdom' on the position he has assumed, and on the brilliant prospect which is before him. May he long adorn his exalted position and enjoy unbroken success in the administration of his office."

As soon as the crowd without heard the news, it took up the cry of "Long life to His Wisdom the Defender!" The cry spread through the length of the island as fast as sound could carry it. "God bless his Wisdom the Defender!" As the news flew over the electric wires by land and sea, every point which it reached resounded with the cry of "All Hail His Wisdom the Defender!" The students assembled in the grounds of Harvard shouted with their clarion voices, "Rah! Rah! Rah! the Defender!" As the sun went its round the cry rose from every continent and from all the islands of the great ocean in every language spoken by man.

A yet more human interest in the great character was stirred up when it became known that it had been responsive to the gentler sentiments of our humanity, and that the world's most beautiful palace was to be presided over by one of the most lovely of her sex. How did it come about? This is the

Rah! Rah! Rah! the Defender!

one great secret of Uraniburg which has never been divulged, and which men were too much occupied with passing events to pry into. Hardly a month after the cry we have described, another rose with equal volume — " All Hail Her Wisdom the Defendress!"

Why should we go on with a history known to every school-child? Not an intelligent youth in this land but can tell something of the great world's congress and its work; how the principle that every people — the weak as well as the strong — should enjoy liberty and independence was established and accepted by all; how the strongest nations found their interests and the welfare of their people promoted by the submission of all disputes to a common arbitrator; how the fact that a nation could extend its trade to every land without the use of force was proved by experience, until men came to wonder that any other policy had ever been pursued.

And one need not even go to school to learn what the Defendress did for suffering humanity — how, commanding the great wealth of the Anita Company, she became such a Sister of Mercy to the afflicted of the world that as long as she lived, and after her death, she was called in every language of the world " Tiana the Blessed."

THE END

SCIENCE FICTION

An Arno Press Collection

FICTION

About, Edmond. **The Man with the Broken Ear.** 1872

Allen, Grant. **The British Barbarians:** A Hill-Top Novel. 1895

Arnold, Edwin L. **Lieut. Gullivar Jones:** His Vacation. 1905

Ash, Fenton. **A Trip to Mars.** 1909

Aubrey, Frank. **A Queen of Atlantis.** 1899

Bargone, Charles (Claude Farrere, pseud.). **Useless Hands.** [1926]

Beale, Charles Willing. **The Secret of the Earth.** 1899

Bell, Eric Temple (John Taine, pseud.). **Before the Dawn.** 1934

Benson, Robert Hugh. **Lord of the World.** 1908

Beresford, J. D. **The Hampdenshire Wonder.** 1911

Bradshaw, William R. **The Goddess of Atvatabar.** 1892

Capek, Karel. **Krakatit.** 1925

Chambers, Robert W. **The Gay Rebellion.** 1913

Colomb, P. et al. **The Great War of 189—.** 1893

Cook, William Wallace. **Adrift in the Unknown.** n.d.

Cummings, Ray. **The Man Who Mastered Time.** 1929

[DeMille, James]. **A Strange Manuscript Found in a Copper Cylinder.** 1888

Dixon, Thomas. **The Fall of a Nation:** A Sequel to the Birth of a Nation. 1916

England, George Allan. **The Golden Blight.** 1916

Fawcett, E. Douglas. **Hartmann the Anarchist.** 1893

Flammarion, Camille. **Omega:** The Last Days of the World. 1894

Grant, Robert et al. **The King's Men:** A Tale of To-Morrow. 1884

Grautoff, Ferdinand Heinrich (Parabellum, pseud.). **Banzai!** 1909

Graves, C. L. and E. V. Lucas. **The War of the Wenuses.** 1898

Greer, Tom. **A Modern Daedalus.** [1887]

Griffith, George. **A Honeymoon in Space.** 1901

Grousset, Paschal (A. Laurie, pseud.). **The Conquest of the Moon.** 1894

Haggard, H. Rider. **When the World Shook.** 1919

Hernaman-Johnson, F. **The Polyphemes.** 1906

Hyne, C. J. Cutcliffe. **Empire of the World.** [1910]

In The Future. [1875]

Jane, Fred T. **The Violet Flame.** 1899

Jefferies, Richard. **After London; Or, Wild England.** 1885

Le Queux, William. **The Great White Queen.** [1896]

London, Jack. **The Scarlet Plague.** 1915

Mitchell, John Ames. **Drowsy.** 1917

Morris, Ralph. **The Life and Astonishing Adventures of John Daniel.** 1751

Newcomb, Simon. **His Wisdom The Defender:** A Story. 1900

Paine, Albert Bigelow. **The Great White Way.** 1901

Pendray, Edward (Gawain Edwards, pseud.). **The Earth-Tube.** 1929

Reginald, R. and Douglas Menville. **Ancestral Voices:** An Anthology of Early Science Fiction. 1974

Russell, W. Clark. **The Frozen Pirate.** 2 vols. in 1. 1887

Shiel, M. P. **The Lord of the Sea.** 1901

Symmes, John Cleaves (Captain Adam Seaborn, pseud.). **Symzonia.** 1820

Train, Arthur and Robert W. Wood. **The Man Who Rocked the Earth.** 1915

Waterloo, Stanley. **The Story of Ab:** A Tale of the Time of the Cave Man. 1903

White, Stewart E. and Samuel H. Adams. **The Mystery.** 1907

Wicks, Mark. **To Mars Via the Moon.** 1911

Wright, Sydney Fowler. **Deluge: A Romance** and **Dawn.** 2 vols. in 1. 1928/1929

SCIENCE FICTION

NON-FICTION
Including Bibliographies,
Checklists and Literary Criticism

Aldiss, Brian and Harry Harrison. **SF Horizons.** 2 vols. in 1. 1964/1965

Amis, Kingsley. **New Maps of Hell.** 1960

Barnes, Myra. **Linguistics and Languages in Science Fiction-Fantasy.** 1974

Cockcroft, T. G. L. **Index to the Weird Fiction Magazines.** 2 vols. in 1 1962/1964

Cole, W. R. **A Checklist of Science-Fiction Anthologies.** 1964

Crawford, Joseph H. et al. **"333": A Bibliography of the Science-Fantasy Novel.** 1953

Day, Bradford M. **The Checklist of Fantastic Literature in Paperbound Books.** 1965

Day, Bradford M. **The Supplemental Checklist of Fantastic Literature.** 1963

Gove, Philip Babcock. **The Imaginary Voyage in Prose Fiction.** 1941

Green, Roger Lancelyn. **Into Other Worlds:** Space-Flight in Fiction, From Lucian to Lewis. 1958

Menville, Douglas. **A Historical and Critical Survey of the Science Fiction Film.** 1974

Reginald, R. **Contemporary Science Fiction Authors,** First Edition. 1970

Samuelson, David. **Visions of Tomorow:** Six Journeys from Outer to Inner Space. 1974